Christmas Stories for the Young & Old

CONTENTS PAGE

A Christmas Dream, and How It Came to Be True

By Louisa May Alcott

"I'm so tired of Christmas I wish there never would be another one!" exclaimed a discontented-looking little girl, as she sat idly watching her mother arrange a pile of gifts two days before they were to be given.

"Why, Effie, what a dreadful thing to say! You are as bad as old Scrooge; and I'm afraid something will happen to you, as it did to him, if you don't care for dear Christmas," answered mamma, almost dropping the silver horn she was filling with delicious candies.

"Who was Scrooge? What happened to him?" asked Effie, with a glimmer of interest in her listless face, as she picked out the sourest lemon-drop she could find; for nothing sweet suited her just then.

"He was one of Dickens's best people, and you can read the charming story some day. He hated Christmas until a strange dream showed him how dear and beautiful it was, and made a better man of him."

"I shall read it; for I like dreams, and have a great many curious ones myself. But they don't keep me from being tired of Christmas," said Effie, poking discontentedly among the sweeties for something worth eating.

"Why are you tired of what should be the happiest time of all the year?" asked mamma, anxiously.

"Perhaps I shouldn't be if I had something new. But it is always the same, and there isn't any more surprise about it. I always find heaps of goodies in my stocking. Don't like some of them, and soon get tired of those I do like. We always have a great dinner, and I eat too much, and feel ill next day. Then there is a Christmas tree somewhere, with a doll on top, or a stupid old Santa Claus, and children dancing and screaming over bonbons and toys that break, and shiny things that are of no use.

7

Really, mamma, I've had so many Christmases all alike that I don't think I can bear another one." And Effie laid herself flat on the sofa, as if the mere idea was too much for her.

Her mother laughed at her despair, but was sorry to see her little girl so discontented, when she had everything to make her happy, and had known but ten Christmas days.

"Suppose we don't give you any presents at all,--how would that suit you?" asked mamma, anxious to please her spoiled child.

"I should like one large and splendid one, and one dear little one, to remember some very nice person by," said Effie, who was a fanciful little body, full of odd whims and notions, which her friends loved to gratify, regardless of time, trouble, or money; for she was the last of three little girls, and very dear to all the family.

"Well, my darling, I will see what I can do to please you, and not say a word until all is ready. If I could only get a new idea to start with!" And mamma went on tying up her pretty bundles with a thoughtful face, while Effie strolled to the window to watch the rain that kept her in-doors and made her dismal.

"Seems to me poor children have better times than rich ones. I can't go out, and there is a girl about my age splashing along, without any maid to fuss about rubbers and cloaks and umbrellas and colds. I wish I was a beggar-girl."

"Would you like to be hungry, cold, and ragged, to beg all day, and sleep on an ash-heap at night?" asked mamma, wondering what would come next.

"Cinderella did, and had a nice time in the end. This girl out here has a basket of scraps on her arm, and a big old shawl all round her, and doesn't seem to care a bit, though the water runs out of the toes of her boots. She goes paddling along, laughing at the rain, and eating a cold potato as if it tasted nicer than the chicken and ice-cream I had for

8

dinner. Yes, I do think poor children are happier than rich ones."

So do I, sometimes. At the Orphan Asylum today I saw two dozen merry little souls who have no parents, no home, and no hope of Christmas beyond a stick of candy or a cake. I wish you had been there to see how happy they were, playing with the old toys some richer children had sent them."

"You may give them all mine; I'm so tired of them I never want to see them again," said Effie, turning from the window to the pretty baby-house full of everything a child's heart could desire.

"I will, and let you begin again with something you will not tire of, if I can only find it." And mamma knit her brows trying to discover some grand surprise for this child who didn't care for Christmas.

Nothing more was said then; and wandering off to the library, Effie found "A Christmas Carol," and curling herself up in the sofa corner, read it all before tea. Some of it she did not understand; but she laughed and cried over many parts of the charming story, and felt better without knowing why.

All the evening she thought of poor Tiny Tim, Mrs. Cratchit with the pudding, and the stout old gentleman who danced so gayly that "his legs twinkled in the air." Presently bedtime arrived.

"Come, now, and toast your feet," said Effie's nurse, "while I do your pretty hair and tell stories." "I'll have a fairy tale to-night, a very interesting one," commanded Effie, as she put on her blue silk wrapper and little fur-lined slippers to sit before the fire and have her long curls brushed.

So Nursey told her best tales; and when at last the child lay down under her lace curtains, her head was full of a curious jumble of Christmas elves, poor children, snow-storms, sugarplums, and surprises. So it is no wonder that she dreamed all night; and this was the dream, which she never quite forgot.

9

She found herself sitting on a stone, in the middle of a great field, all alone. The snow was falling fast, a bitter wind whistled by, and night was coming on. She felt hungry, cold, and tired, and did not know where to go nor what to do.

"I wanted to be a beggar-girl, and now I am one; but I don't like it, and wish somebody would come and take care of me. I don't know who I am, and I think I must be lost," thought Effie, with the curious interest one takes in one's self in dreams. But the more she thought about it, the more bewildered she felt. Faster fell the snow, colder blew the wind, darker grew the night; and poor Effie made up her mind that she was quite forgotten and left to freeze alone. The tears were chilled on her cheeks, her feet felt like icicles, and her heart died within her, so hungry, frightened, and forlorn was she. Laying her head on her knees, she gave herself up for lost, and sat there with the great flakes fast turning her to a little white mound, when suddenly the sound of music reached her, and starting up, she looked and listened with all her eyes and ears.

Far away a dim light shone, and a voice was heard singing. She tried to run toward the welcome glimmer, but could not stir, and stood like a small statue of expectation while the light drew nearer, and the sweet words of the song grew clearer.

From our happy home
  Through the world we roam
 One week in all the year,
  Making winter spring
  With the joy we bring,
 For Christmas-tide is here.
  Now the eastern star
  Shines from afar
 To light the poorest home;
  Hearts warmer grow,
  Gifts freely flow,
 For Christmas-tide has come.
  Now gay trees rise

Before young eyes,
  Abloom with tempting cheer;
    Blithe voices sing,
    And blithe bells ring,
  For Christmas-tide is here.
    Oh, happy chime,
    Oh, blessed time,
  That draws us all so near!
    "Welcome, dear day,"
    All creatures say,
  For Christmas-tide is here.

A child's voice sang, a child's hand carried the little candle; and in the circle of soft light it shed, Effie saw a pretty child coming to her through the night and snow. A rosy, smiling creature, wrapped in white fur, with a wreath of green and scarlet holly on its shining hair, the magic candle in one hand, and the other outstretched as if to shower gifts and warmly press all other hands.

Effie forgot to speak as this bright vision came nearer, leaving no trace of footsteps in the snow, only lighting the way with its little candle, and filling the air with the music of its song.

"Dear child, you are lost, and I have come to find you," said the stranger, taking Effie's cold hands in his, with a smile like sunshine, while every holly berry glowed like a little fire.

"Do you know me?" asked Effie, feeling no fear, but a great gladness, at his coming.

"I know all children, and go to find them; for this is my holiday, and I gather them from all parts of the world to be merry with me once a year."

"Are you an angel?" asked Effie, looking for the wings.

"No; I am a Christmas spirit, and live with my mates in a pleasant place, getting ready for our holiday, when we are let out to roam about the world, helping make this a happy time for all who will let us in. Will you come and see how we work?" "I will go anywhere with you. Don't leave me again," cried Effie, gladly.

"First I will make you comfortable. That is what we love to do. You are cold, and you shall be warm, hungry, and I will feed you; sorrowful, and I will make you gay."

With a wave of his candle all three miracles were wrought,--for the snow- flakes turned to a white fur cloak and hood on Effie's head and shoulders, a bowl of hot soup came sailing to her lips, and vanished when she had eagerly drunk the last drop; and suddenly the dismal field changed to a new world so full of wonders that all her troubles were forgotten in a minute. Bells were ringing so merrily that it was hard to keep from dancing. Green garlands hung on the walls, and every tree was a Christmas tree full of toys, and blazing with candles that never went out.

In one place many little spirits sewed like mad on warm clothes, turning off work faster than any sewing-machine ever invented, and great piles were made ready to be sent to poor people. Other busy creatures packed money into purses, and wrote checks which they sent flying away on the wind,--a lovely kind of snow-storm to fall into a world below full of poverty. Older and graver spirits were looking over piles of little books, in which the records of the past year were kept, telling how different people had spent it, and what sort of gifts they deserved. Some got peace, some disappointment, some remorse and sorrow, some great joy and hope. The rich had generous thoughts sent them; the poor, gratitude and contentment. Children had more love and duty to parents; and parents renewed patience, wisdom, and satisfaction for and in their children. No one was forgotten.

"Please tell me what splendid place this is?" asked Effie, as soon as she could collect her wits after the first look at all these astonishing things.

"This is the Christmas world; and here we work all the year round, never tired of getting ready for the happy day. See, these are the saints just setting off; for some have far to go, and the children must not be disappointed."

As he spoke the spirit pointed to four gates, out of which four great sleighs were just driving, laden with toys, while a jolly old Santa Claus sat in the middle of each, drawing on his mittens and tucking up his wraps for a long cold drive. "Why, I thought there was only one Santa Claus, and even he was a humbug," cried Effie, astonished at the sight. "Never give up your faith in the sweet old stones, even after you come to see that they are only the pleasant shadow of a lovely truth."

Just then the sleighs went off with a great jingling of bells and pattering of reindeer hoofs, while all the spirits gave a cheer that was heard in the lower world, where people said, "Hear the stars sing."

"I never will say there isn't any Santa Claus again. Now, show me more."

"You will like to see this place, I think, and may learn something here perhaps."

The spirit smiled as he led the way to a little door, through which Effie peeped into a world of dolls. Baby-houses were in full blast, with dolls of all sorts going on like live people. Waxen ladies sat in their parlors elegantly dressed; black dolls cooked in the kitchens; nurses walked out with the bits of dollies; and the streets were full of tin soldiers marching, wooden horses prancing, express wagons rumbling, and little men hurrying to and fro. Shops were there, and tiny people buying legs of mutton, pounds of tea, mites of clothes, and everything dolls use or wear or want.

But presently she saw that in some ways the dolls improved upon

13

the manners and customs of human beings, and she watched eagerly to learn why they did these things. A fine Paris doll driving in her carriage took up a black worsted Dinah who was hobbling along with a basket of clean clothes, and carried her to her journey's end, as if it were the proper thing to do. Another interesting china lady took off her comfortable red cloak and put it round a poor wooden creature done up in a paper shift, and so badly painted that its face would have sent some babies into fits.

"Seems to me I once knew a rich girl who didn't give her things to poor girls. I wish I could remember who she was, and tell her to be as kind as that china doll," said Effie, much touched at the sweet way the pretty creature wrapped up the poor fright, and then ran off in her little gray gown to buy a shiny fowl stuck on a wooden platter for her invalid mother's dinner.

"We recall these things to people's minds by dreams. I think the girl you speak of won't forget this one." And the spirit smiled, as if he enjoyed some joke which she did not see.

A little bell rang as she looked, and away scampered the children into the red-and-green school-house with the roof that lifted up, so one could see how nicely they sat at their desks with mites of books, or drew on the inch-square blackboards with crumbs of chalk.

"They know their lessons very well, and are as still as mice. We make a great racket at our school, and get bad marks every day. I shall tell the girls they had better mind what they do, or their dolls will be better scholars than they are," said Effie, much impressed, as she peeped in and saw no rod in the hand of the little mistress, who looked up and shook her head at the intruder, as if begging her to go away before the order of the school was disturbed.

Effie retired at once, but could not resist one look in at the window of a fine mansion, where the family were at dinner, the children behaved so well at table, and never grumbled a bit when their mamma said they could not have any more fruit. "Now, show me something else," she said, as they came again to the low door that led out of Doll-land. "You have seen how we prepare for Christmas; let me show you where we love best to send our good and happy gifts," answered the spirit, giving her his hand again.

"I know. I've seen ever so many," began Effie, thinking of her own Christmases.

"No, you have never seen what I will show you. Come away, and remember what you see to-night."

Like a flash that bright world vanished, and Effie found herself in a part of the city she had never seen before. It was far away from the gayer places, where every store was brilliant with lights and full of pretty things, and every house wore a festival air, while people hurried to and fro with merry greetings. It was down among the dingy streets where the poor lived, and where there was no making ready for Christmas.

Hungry women looked in at the shabby shops, longing to buy meat and bread, but empty pockets forbade. Tipsy men drank up their wages in the bar- rooms; and in many cold dark chambers little children huddled under the thin blankets, trying to forget their misery in sleep.

No nice dinners filled the air with savory smells, no gay trees dropped toys and bonbons into eager hands, no little stockings hung in rows beside the chimney-piece ready to be filled, no happy sounds of music, gay voices, and dancing feet were heard; and there were no signs of Christmas anywhere.

"Don't they have any in this place?" asked Effie, shivering, as she held fast the spirit's hand, following where he led her. "We come to bring it. Let me show you our best workers." And the spirit pointed to some sweet-faced men and women who came stealing into the poor houses, working such beautiful miracles that Effie could only stand and watch.

Some slipped money into the empty pockets, and sent the happy

15

mothers to buy all the comforts they needed; others led the drunken men out of temptation, and took them home to find safer pleasures there. Fires were kindled on cold hearths, tables spread as if by magic, and warm clothes wrapped round shivering limbs. Flowers suddenly bloomed in the chambers of the sick; old people found themselves remembered; sad hearts were consoled by a tender word, and wicked ones softened by the story of Him who forgave all sin.

But the sweetest work was for the children; and Effie held her breath to watch these human fairies hang up and fill the little stockings without which a child's Christmas is not perfect, putting in things that once she would have thought very humble presents, but which now seemed beautiful and precious because these poor babies had nothing.

"That is so beautiful! I wish I could make merry Christmases as these good people do, and be loved and thanked as they are," said Effie, softly, as she watched the busy men and women do their work and steal away without thinking of any reward but their own satisfaction.

"You can if you will. I have shown you the way. Try it, and see how happy your own holiday will be hereafter."

As he spoke, the spirit seemed to put his arms about her, and vanished with a kiss.

"Oh, stay and show me more!" cried Effie, trying to hold him fast.

"Darling, wake up, and tell me why you are smiling in your sleep," said a voice in her ear; and opening her eyes, there was mamma bending over her, and morning sunshine streaming into the room.

"Are they all gone? Did you hear the bells? Wasn't it splendid?" she asked, rubbing her eyes, and looking about her for the pretty child who was so real and sweet.

"You have been dreaming at a great rate,--talking in your sleep, laughing, and clapping your hands as if you were cheering some one.

16

Tell me what was so splendid," said mamma, smoothing the tumbled hair and lifting up the sleepy head. Then, while she was being dressed, Effie told her dream, and Nursey thought it very wonderful; but mamma smiled to see how curiously things the child had thought, read, heard, and seen through the day were mixed up in her sleep.

"The spirit said I could work lovely miracles if I tried; but I don't know how to begin, for I have no magic candle to make feasts appear, and light up groves of Christmas trees, as he did," said Effie, sorrowfully.

"Yes, you have. We will do it! we will do it!" And clapping her hands, mamma suddenly began to dance all over the room as if she had lost her wits.

"How? how? You must tell me, mamma," cried Effie, dancing after her, and ready to believe anything possible when she remembered the adventures of the past night.

"I've got it! I've got it!--the new idea. A splendid one, if I can only carry it out!" And mamma waltzed the little girl round till her curls flew wildly in the air, while Nursey laughed as if she would die.

"Tell me! tell me!" shrieked Effie. "No, no; it is a surprise,--a grand surprise for Christmas day!" sung mamma, evidently charmed with her happy thought. "Now, come to breakfast; for we must work like bees if we want to play spirits tomorrow. You and Nursey will go out shopping, and get heaps of things, while I arrange matters behind the scenes."

They were running downstairs as mamma spoke, and Effie called out breathlessly,--

"It won't be a surprise; for I know you are going to ask some poor children here, and have a tree or something. It won't be like my dream; for they had ever so many trees, and more children than we can find anywhere."

17

"There will be no tree, no party, no dinner, in this house at all, and no presents for you. Won't that be a surprise?" And mamma laughed at Effie's bewildered face.

"Do it. I shall like it, I think; and I won't ask any questions, so it will all burst upon me when the time comes," she said; and she ate her breakfast thoughtfully, for this really would be a new sort of Christmas.

All that morning Effie trotted after Nursey in and out of shops, buying dozens of barking dogs, woolly lambs, and squeaking birds; tiny tea-sets, gay picture-books, mittens and hoods, dolls and candy. Parcel after parcel was sent home; but when Effie returned she saw no trace of them, though she peeped everywhere. Nursey chuckled, but wouldn't give a hint, and went out again in the afternoon with a long list of more things to buy; while Effie wandered forlornly about the house, missing the usual merry stir that went before the Christmas dinner and the evening fun.

As for mamma, she was quite invisible all day, and came in at night so tired that she could only lie on the sofa to rest, smiling as if some very pleasant thought made her happy in spite of weariness.

"Is the surprise going on all right?" asked Effie, anxiously; for it seemed an immense time to wait till another evening came.

"Beautifully! better than I expected; for several of my good friends are helping, or I couldn't have done it as I wish. I know you will like it, dear, and long remember this new way of making Christmas merry."

Mamma gave her a very tender kiss, and Effie went to bed.

The next day was a very strange one; for when she woke there was no stocking to examine, no pile of gifts under her napkin, no one said "Merry Christmas!" to her, and the dinner was just as usual to her. Mamma vanished again, and Nursey kept wiping her eyes and saying: "The dear things! It's the prettiest idea I ever heard of. No one but your blessed ma could have done it." "Do stop, Nursey, or I shall go crazy because I don't know the secret!" cried Effie, more than once; and she kept her eye on the clock, for at seven in the evening the surprise was to come off.

The longed-for hour arrived at last, and the child was too excited to ask questions when Nurse put on her cloak and hood, led her to the carriage, and they drove away, leaving their house the one dark and silent one in the row. "I feel like the girls in the fairy tales who are led off to strange places and see fine things," said Effie, in a whisper, as they jingled through the gay streets.

"Ah, my deary, it is like a fairy tale, I do assure you, and you will see finer things than most children will tonight. Steady, now, and do just as I tell you, and don't say one word whatever you see," answered Nursey, quite quivering with excitement as she patted a large box in her lap, and nodded and laughed with twinkling eyes.

They drove into a dark yard, and Effie was led through a back door to a little room, where Nurse coolly proceeded to take off not only her cloak and hood, but her dress and shoes also. Effie stared and bit her lips, but kept still until out of the box came a little white fur coat and boots, a wreath of holly leaves and berries, and a candle with a frill of gold paper round it. A long "Oh!" escaped her then; and when she was dressed and saw herself in the glass, she started back, exclaiming, "Why, Nursey, I look like the spirit in my dream!"

"So you do; and that's the part you are to play, my pretty! Now whist, while I blind your eyes and put you in your place."

"Shall I be afraid?" whispered Effie, full of wonder; for as they went out she heard the sound of many voices, the tramp of many feet, and, in spite of the bandage, was sure a great light shone upon her when she stopped.

"You needn't be; I shall stand close by, and your ma will be there."

After the handkerchief was tied about her eyes, Nurse led Effie up some steps, and placed her on a high platform, where something like leaves touched her head, and the soft snap of lamps seemed to fill the air. Music began as soon as Nurse clapped her hands, the voices outside sounded nearer, and the tramp was evidently coming up the stairs.

"Now, my precious, look and see how you and your dear ma have made a merry Christmas for them that needed it!"

Off went the bandage; and for a minute Effie really did think she was asleep again, for she actually stood in "a grove of Christmas trees," all gay and shining as in her vision. Twelve on a side, in two rows down the room, stood the little pines, each on its low table; and behind Effie a taller one rose to the roof, hung with wreaths of popcorn, apples, oranges, horns of candy, and cakes of all sorts, from sugary hearts to gingerbread Jumbos. On the smaller trees she saw many of her own discarded toys and those Nursey bought, as well as heaps that seemed to have rained down straight from that delightful Christmas country where she felt as if she was again.

"How splendid! Who is it for? What is that noise? Where is mamma?" cried Effie, pale with pleasure and surprise, as she stood looking down the brilliant little street from her high place.

Before Nurse could answer, the doors at the lower end flew open, and in marched twenty-four little blue-gowned orphan girls, singing sweetly, until amazement changed the song to cries of joy and wonder as the shining spectacle appeared. While they stood staring with round eyes at the wilderness of pretty things about them, mamma stepped up beside Effie, and holding her hand fast to give her courage, told the story of the dream in a few simple words, ending in this way:--

"So my little girl wanted to be a Christmas spirit too, and make this a happy day for those who had not as many pleasures and comforts as she has. She likes surprises, and we planned this for you all. She shall play the good fairy, and give each of you something from this tree, after which every one will find her own name on a small tree, and can go to enjoy it in her own way. March by, my dears, and let us fill your hands."

Nobody told them to do it, but all the hands were clapped heartily before a single child stirred; then one by one they came to look up wonderingly at the pretty giver of the feast as she leaned down to offer them great yellow oranges, red apples, bunches of grapes, bonbons, and cakes, till all were gone, and a double row of smiling faces turned toward her as the children filed back to their places in the orderly way they had been taught.

Then each was led to her own tree by the good ladies who had helped mamma with all their hearts; and the happy hubbub that arose would have satisfied even Santa Claus himself,--shrieks of joy, dances of delight, laughter and tears (for some tender little things could not bear so much pleasure at once, and sobbed with mouths full of candy and hands full of toys). How they ran to show one another the new treasures! how they peeped and tasted, pulled and pinched, until the air was full of queer noises, the floor covered with papers, and the little trees left bare of all but candles!

"I don't think heaven can be any gooder than this," sighed one small girl, as she looked about her in a blissful maze, holding her full apron with one hand, while she luxuriously carried sugar-plums to her mouth with the other.

"Is that a truly angel up there?" asked another, fascinated by the little white figure with the wreath on its shining hair, who in some mysterious way had been the cause of all this merry-making.

"I wish I dared to go and kiss her for this splendid party," said a lame child, leaning on her crutch, as she stood near the steps, wondering how it seemed to sit in a mother's lap, as Effie was doing, while she watched the happy scene before her. Effie heard her, and remembering Tiny Tim, ran down and put her arms about the pale child, kissing the wistful face, as she said sweetly, "You may; but mamma deserves the thanks. She did it all; I only dreamed about it."

Lame Katy felt as if "a truly angel" was embracing her, and could only stammer out her thanks, while the other children ran to see the pretty spirit, and touch her soft dress, until she stood in a crowd of blue gowns laughing as they held up their gifts for her to see and admire.

Mamma leaned down and whispered one word to the older girls; and suddenly they all took hands to dance round Effie, singing as they skipped.

It was a pretty sight, and the ladies found it hard to break up the happy revel; but it was late for small people, and too much fun is a mistake. So the girls fell into line, and marched before Effie and mamma again, to say goodnight with such grateful little faces that the eyes of those who looked grew dim with tears. Mamma kissed every one; and many a hungry childish heart felt as if the touch of those tender lips was their best gift. Effie shook so many small hands that her own tingled; and when Katy came she pressed a small doll into Effie's hand, whispering, "You didn't have a single present, and we had lots. Do keep that; it's the prettiest thing I got."

"I will," answered Effie, and held it fast until the last smiling face was gone, the surprise all over, and she safe in her own bed, too tired and happy for anything but sleep.

"Mamma, it was a beautiful surprise, and I thank you so much! I don't see how you did it; but I like it best of all the Christmases I ever had, and mean to make one every year. I had my splendid big present, and here is the dear little one to keep for love of poor Katy; so even that part of my wish came true."

And Effie fell asleep with a happy smile on her lips, her one humble gift still in her hand, and a new love for Christmas in her heart that never changed through a long life spent in doing good.

Cousin Tribulation's Story

By Louisa May Alcott

Dear Merrys:--As a subject appropriate to the season, I want to tell you about a New Year's breakfast which I had when I was a little girl. What do you think it was? A slice of dry bread and an apple. This is how it happened, and it is a true story, every word.

As we came down to breakfast that morning, with very shiny faces and spandy clean aprons, we found father alone in the dining-room.

"Happy New Year, papa! Where is mother?" we cried.

"A little boy came begging and said they were starving at home, so your mother went to see and--ah, here she is."

As papa spoke, in came mamma, looking very cold, rather sad, and very much excited.

"Children, don't begin till you hear what I have to say," she cried; and we sat staring at her, with the breakfast untouched before us.

"Not far away from here, lies a poor woman with a little new-born baby. Six children are huddled into one bed to keep from freezing, for they have no fire. There is nothing to eat over there; and the oldest boy came here to tell me they were starving this bitter cold day. My little girls, will you give them your breakfast, as a New Year's gift?"

We sat silent a minute, and looked at the nice, hot porridge, creamy milk, and good bread and butter; for we were brought up like English children, and never drank tea or coffee, or ate anything but porridge for our breakfast.

"I wish we'd eaten it up," thought I, for I was rather a selfish child, and very hungry.

"I'm so glad you come before we began," said Nan, cheerfully.

"May I go and help carry it to the poor, little children?" asked Beth, who had the tenderest heart that ever beat under a pinafore.

"I can carry the lassy pot," said little May, proudly giving the thing she loved best.

"And I shall take all the porridge," I burst in, heartily ashamed of my first feeling.

"You shall put on your things and help me, and when we come back, we'll get something to eat," said mother, beginning to pile the bread and butter into a big basket.

We were soon ready, and the procession set out. First, papa, with a basket of wood on one arm and coal on the other; mamma next, with a bundle of warm things and the teapot; Nan and I carried a pail of hot porridge between us, and each a pitcher of milk; Beth brought some cold meat, May the "lassy pot," and her old hood and boots; and Betsey, the girl, brought up the rear with a bag of potatoes and some meal.

Fortunately it was early, and we went along back streets, so few people saw us, and no one laughed at the funny party.

What a poor, bare, miserable place it was, to be sure,--broken windows, no fire, ragged clothes, wailing baby, sick mother, and a pile of pale, hungry children cuddled under one quilt, trying to keep warm. How the big eyes stared and the blue lips smiled as we came in!

"Ah, mein Gott! it is the good angels that come to us!" cried the poor woman, with tears of joy.

"Funny angels, in woollen hoods and red mittens," said I; and they all laughed.

Then we fell to work, and in fifteen minutes, it really did seem as if fairies had been at work there. Papa made a splendid fire in the old fireplace and stopped up the broken window with his own hat and coat. Mamma set the shivering children round the fire, and wrapped the poor woman in warm things. Betsey and the rest of us spread the table, and fed the starving little ones.

"Das ist gute!" "Oh, nice!" "Der angel--Kinder!" cried the poor things as they ate and smiled and basked in the warm blaze. We had never been called "angel-children" before, and we thought it very charming, especially I who had often been told I was "a regular Sancho." What fun it was! Papa, with a towel for an apron, fed the smallest child; mamma dressed the poor little new-born baby as tenderly as if it had been her own. Betsey gave the mother gruel and tea, and comforted her with assurance of better days for all. Nan, Lu, Beth, and May flew about among the seven children, talking and laughing and trying to understand their funny, broken English. It was a very happy breakfast, though we didn't get any of it; and when we came away, leaving them all so comfortable, and promising to bring clothes and food by and by, I think there were not in all the hungry little girls who gave away their breakfast, and contented themselves with a bit of bread and an apple of New Year's day.

Tilly's Christmas

By Louisa May Alcott

"I'm so glad to-morrow is Christmas, because I'm going to have lots of presents."

"So am I glad, though I don't expect any presents but a pair of mittens."

"And so am I; but I shan't have any presents at all."

As the three little girls trudged home from school they said these things, and as Tilly spoke, both the others looked at her with pity and some surprise, for she spoke cheerfully, and they wondered how she could be happy when she was so poor she could have no presents on Christmas.

"Don't you wish you could find a purse full of money right here in the path?" said Kate, the child who was going to have "lots of presents."

"Oh, don't I, if I could keep it honestly!" and Tilly's eyes shone at the very thought.

"What would you buy?" asked Bessy, rubbing her cold hands, and longing for her mittens.

"I'd buy a pair of large, warm blankets, a load of wood, a shawl for mother, and a pair of shoes for me; and if there was enough left, I'd give Bessy a new hat, and then she needn't wear Ben's old felt one," answered Tilly.

The girls laughed at that ; but Bessy pulled the funny hat over her ears, and said she was much obliged, but she'd rather have candy.

"Let's look, and may be we can find a purse. People are always going about with money at Christmas time, and some one may lose it here," said Kate.

So, as they went along the snowy road, they looked about them, half in earnest, half in fun. Suddenly Tilly sprang forward, exclaiming,

"I see it! I've found it!"

The others followed, but all stopped disappointed; for it wasn't a purse, it was only a little bird. It lay upon the snow with its wings spread and feebly fluttering, as if too weak to fly. Its little feet were benumbed with cold; its once bright eyes were dull with pain, and instead of a blithe song, it could only utter a faint chirp, now and then, as if crying for help.

"Nothing but a stupid old robin; how provoking!" cried Kate, sitting down to rest.

"I shan't touch it. I found one once, and took care of it, and the ungrateful thing flew away the minute it was well," said Bessy, creeping under Kate's shawl, and putting her hands under her chin to warm them.

"Poor little birdie! How pitiful he looks, and how glad he must be to see some one coming to help him! I'll take him up gently, and carry him home to mother. Don't be frightened, dear, I'm your friend;" and Tilly knelt down in the snow, stretching her hand to the bird with the tenderest pity in her face.

Kate and Bessy laughed.

"Don't stop for that thing; it's getting late and cold: let's go on and look for the purse," they said, moving away.

"You wouldn't leave it to die?' cried Tilly.

"I'd rather have the bird than the money, so I shan't look any more. The purse wouldn't be mine, and I should only be tempted to keep it; but this poor thing will thank and love me, and I'm so glad I came in time."

Gently lifting the bird, Tilly felt its tiny cold claws cling to her hand, and saw its dim eyes brighten as it nestled down with a grateful chirp.

"Now I've got a Christmas present after all," she said, smiling, as - they walked on. " I always wanted a bird, and this one will be such a pretty pet for me!"

"He'll fly away the first chance he gets, and die anyhow; so you'd better not waste your time over him," said Bessy.

"He can't pay you for taking care of him, and my mother says it isn't worth while to help folks that can't help us," added Kate.

"My mother says, 'Do as you'd be done by;' and I'm sure I'd like any one to help me if I was dying of cold and hunger.' Love your neighbor as yourself? is another of her sayings. This bird is my little neighbor, and I'll love him and care for him, as I often wish our rich neighbor would love and care for us," answered Tilly, breathing her warm breath over the benumbed bird, who looked up at her with confiding eyes, quick to feel and know a friend.

"What a funny girl you are," said Kate; "caring for that silly bird, and talking about loving your neighbor in that sober way. Mr. King don't care a bit for you, and never will, though he knows how poor you are; so I don't think your plan amounts to much."

"I believe it, though; and shall do my part, any way. Good-night. I hope you'll have a merry Christmas, and lots of pretty things," answered Tilly, as they parted.

Her eyes were full, and she felt so poor as she went on alone toward the little old house where she lived. It would have been so pleasant to know that she was going to have some of the pretty things all children love to find in their full stockings on Christmas morning. And pleasanter still to have been able to give her mother something nice. So many comforts were needed, and there was no hope of getting them; for they could barely get food and fire.

"Never mind, birdie, we'll make the best of what we have, and be merry in spite of every thing. You shall have a happy Christmas, any way; and I know God won't forget us, if every one else does."

She stopped a minute to wipe her eyes, and lean her cheek against the bird's soft breast, finding great comfort in the little creature, though it could only love her, nothing more.

"See, mother, what a nice present I've found," she cried, going in with a cheery face that was like sunshine in the dark room.

"I'm glad of that, dearie; for I haven't been able to get my little girl any thing but a rosy apple. Poor bird! Give it some of your warm bread and milk."

"Why, mother, what a big bowlful ! I'm afraid you gave me all the milk," said Tilly, smiling over the nice, steaming supper that stood ready for her.

"I've had plenty, dear. Sit down and dry your wet feet, and put the bird in my basket on this warm flannel."

Tilly peeped into the closet and saw nothing there but dry bread.

"Mother's given me all the milk, and is going without her tea, 'cause she knows I'm hungry. Now I'll surprise her, and she shall have a good supper too. She is going to split wood, and I'll fix it while she's gone."

So Tilly put down the old tea-pot, carefully poured out a part of the milk, and from her pocket produced a great, plummy bun, that one of the school-children had given her, and she had saved for her mother. A slice of the dry bread was nicely toasted, and the bit of butter set by for her put on it. When her mother came in there was the table drawn up in a warm place, a hot cup of tea ready, and Tilly and birdie waiting for her.

Such a poor little supper, and yet such a happy one; for love, charity, and contentment were guests there, and that Christmas eve was a blither one than that up at the great house, where lights shone, fires blazed, a great tree glittered, and music sounded, as the children danced and played.

"We must go to bed early, for we've only wood enough to last over to-morrow. I shall be paid for my work the day after, and then we can get some," said Tilly's mother, as they sat by the fire.

"If my bird was only a fairy bird, and would give us three wishes, how nice it would be! Poor dear, he can't give me any thing; but it's no matter," answered Tilly, looking at the robin, who lay in the basket with his head under his wing, a mere little feathery bunch.

"He can give you one thing, Tilly, the pleasure of doing good. That is one of the sweetest things in life; and the poor can enjoy it as well as the rich."

As her mother spoke, with her tired hand softly stroking her little daughter's hair, Tilly suddenly started and pointed to the window, saying, in a frightened whisper,

"I saw a face, a man's face, looking in! It's gone now; but I truly saw it."

"Some traveller attracted by the light perhaps. I'll go and see." And Tilly's mother went to the door.

No one was there. The wind blew cold, the stars shone, the snow lay white on field and wood, and the Christmas moon was glittering in the sky.

"What sort of a face was it?" asked Tilly's mother, coming back.

"A pleasant sort of face, I think; but I was so startled I don't quite know what it was like. I wish we had a curtain there," said Tilly.

"I like to have our light shine out in the evening, for the road is dark and lonely just here, and the twinkle of our lamp is pleasant to people's eyes as they go by. We can do so little for our neighbors, I am glad to cheer the way for them. Now put these poor old shoes to dry, and go to bed, dearie; I'll come soon."

Tilly went, taking her bird with her to sleep in his basket near by, lest he should be lonely in the night.

Soon the little house was dark and still, and no one saw the Christmas spirits at their work that night.

When Tilly opened the door next morning, she gave a loud cry, clapped her hands, and then stood still, quite speechless with wonder and delight. There, before the door, lay a great pile of wood, all ready to burn, a big bundle and a basket; with a lovely nosegay of winter roses, holly, and evergreen tied to the handle.

"Oh, mother! did the fairies do it?" cried Tilly, pale with her happiness, as she seized the basket, while her mother took in the bundle.

"Yes, dear, the best and dearest fairy in the world, called 'Charity.' She walks abroad at Christmas time, does beautiful deeds like this, and does not stay to be thanked," answered her mother with full eyes, as she undid the parcel.

There they were, the warm, thick blankets, the comfortable shawl, the new shoes, and, best of all, a pretty winter hat for Bessy. The basket was full of good things to eat, and on the flowers lay a paper saying,

"For the little girl who loves her neighbor as herself."

"Mother, I really think my bird is a fairy bird, and all these splendid things come from him," said Tilly, laughing and crying with joy.

31

It really did seem so, for as she spoke, the robin flew to the table, hopped to the nosegay, and perching among the roses, began to chirp with all his little might. The sun streamed in on flowers, bird, and happy child, and no one saw a shadow glide away from the window; no one ever knew that Mr. King had seen and heard the little girls the night before, or dreamed that the rich neighbor had learned a lesson from the poor neighbor.

And Tilly's bird was a fairy bird; for by her love and tenderness to the helpless thing, she brought good gifts to herself, happiness to the unknown giver of them, and a faithful little friend who did not fly away, but stayed with her till the snow was gone, making summer for her in the winter-time.

The Little Match Girl

By Hans Christian Andersen

Most terribly cold it was; it snowed, and was nearly quite dark, and evening—the last evening of the year. In this cold and darkness there went along the street a poor little girl, bareheaded, and with naked feet. When she left home she had slippers on, it is true; but what was the good of that? They were very large slippers, which her mother had hitherto worn; so large were they; and the poor little thing lost them as she scuffled away across the street, because of two carriages that rolled by dreadfully fast.

One slipper was nowhere to be found; the other had been laid hold of by an urchin, and off he ran with it; he thought it would do capitally for a cradle when he some day or other should have children himself. So the little maiden walked on with her tiny naked feet, that were quite red and blue from cold. She carried a quantity of matches in an old apron, and she held a bundle of them in her hand. Nobody had bought anything of her the whole livelong day; no one had given her a single farthing.

She crept along trembling with cold and hunger—a very picture of sorrow, the poor little thing!

The flakes of snow covered her long fair hair, which fell in beautiful curls around her neck; but of that, of course, she never once now thought. From all the windows the candles were gleaming, and it smelt so deliciously of roast goose, for you know it was New Year's Eve; yes, of that she thought.

In a corner formed by two houses, of which one advanced more than the other, she seated herself down and cowered together. Her little feet she had drawn close up to her, but she grew colder and colder, and to go home she did not venture, for she had not sold any matches and could not bring a farthing of money: from her father she would certainly get blows, and at home it was cold too, for above her she had only the roof, through which the wind whistled, even though the largest cracks were stopped up with straw and rags.

Her little hands were almost numbed with cold. Oh! a match might afford her a world of comfort, if she only dared take a single one out of the bundle, draw it against the wall, and warm her fingers by it. She drew one out. "Rischt!" how it blazed, how it burnt! It was a warm, bright flame, like a candle, as she held her hands over it: it was a wonderful light. It seemed really to the little maiden as though she were sitting before a large iron stove, with burnished brass feet and a brass ornament at top. The fire burned with such blessed influence; it warmed so delightfully. The little girl had already stretched out her feet to warm them too; but—the small flame went out, the stove vanished: she had only the remains of the burnt-out match in her hand.

She rubbed another against the wall: it burned brightly, and where the light fell on the wall, there the wall became transparent like a veil, so that she could see into the room. On the table was spread a snow-white tablecloth; upon it was a splendid porcelain service, and the roast goose was steaming famously with its stuffing of apple and dried plums. And what was still more capital to behold was, the goose hopped down from the dish, reeled about on the floor with knife and fork in its breast, till it came up to the poor little girl; when—the match went out and nothing but the thick, cold, damp wall was left behind. She lighted another match. Now there she was sitting under the most magnificent Christmas tree: it was still larger, and more decorated than the one which she had seen through the glass door in the rich merchant's house.

Thousands of lights were burning on the green branches, and gaily-colored pictures, such as she had seen in the shop-windows, looked down upon her. The little maiden stretched out her hands towards them when—the match went out. The lights of the Christmas tree rose higher and higher, she saw them now as stars in heaven; one fell down and formed a long trail of fire.

"Someone is just dead!" said the little girl; for her old grandmother, the only person who had loved her, and who was now no more, had told her, that when a star falls, a soul ascends to God.

She drew another match against the wall: it was again light, and in the lustre there stood the old grandmother, so bright and radiant, so mild, and with such an expression of love.

"Grandmother!" cried the little one. "Oh, take me with you! You go away when the match burns out; you vanish like the warm stove, like the delicious roast goose, and like the magnificent Christmas tree!" And she rubbed the whole bundle of matches quickly against the wall, for she wanted to be quite sure of keeping her grandmother near her. And the matches gave such a brilliant light that it was brighter than at noonday: never formerly had the grandmother been so beautiful and so tall. She took the little maiden, on her arm, and both flew in brightness and in joy so high, so very high, and then above was neither cold, nor hunger, nor anxiety—they were with God.

But in the corner, at the cold hour of dawn, sat the poor girl, with rosy cheeks and with a smiling mouth, leaning against the wall—frozen to death on the last evening of the old year. Stiff and stark sat the child there with her matches, of which one bundle had been burnt. "She wanted to warm herself," people said. No one had the slightest suspicion of what beautiful things she had seen; no one even dreamed of the splendor in which, with her grandmother she had entered on the joys of a new year.

The Fir Tree

By Hans Christian Andersen

Out in the woods stood a nice little Fir Tree. The place he had was a very good one: the sun shone on him: as to fresh air, there was enough of that, and round him grew many large-sized comrades, pines as well as firs. But the little Fir wanted so very much to be a grown-up tree.

He did not think of the warm sun and of the fresh air; he did not care for the little cottage children that ran about and prattled when they were in the woods looking for wild-strawberries. The children often came with a whole pitcher full of berries, or a long row of them threaded on a straw, and sat down near the young tree and said, "Oh, how pretty he is! What a nice little fir!" But this was what the Tree could not bear to hear.

At the end of a year he had shot up a good deal, and after another year he was another long bit taller; for with fir trees one can always tell by the shoots how many years old they are.

"Oh! Were I but such a high tree as the others are," sighed he. "Then I should be able to spread out my branches, and with the tops to look into the wide world! Then would the birds build nests among my branches: and when there was a breeze, I could bend with as much stateliness as the others!"

Neither the sunbeams, nor the birds, nor the red clouds which morning and evening sailed above him, gave the little Tree any pleasure.

In winter, when the snow lay glittering on the ground, a hare would often come leaping along, and jump right over the little Tree. Oh, that made him so angry! But two winters were past, and in the third the Tree was so large that the hare was obliged to go round it. "To grow and grow, to get older and be tall," thought the Tree—"that, after all, is the most delightful thing in the world!"

In autumn the wood-cutters always came and felled some of the largest trees. This happened every year; and the young Fir Tree, that had now grown to a very comely size, trembled at the sight; for the magnificent great trees fell to the earth with noise and cracking, the branches were lopped off, and the trees looked long and bare; they were hardly to be recognised; and then they were laid in carts, and the horses dragged them out of the wood.

Where did they go to? What became of them?

In spring, when the swallows and the storks came, the Tree asked them, "Don't you know where they have been taken? Have you not met them anywhere?"

The swallows did not know anything about it; but the Stork looked musing, nodded his head, and said, "Yes; I think I know; I met many ships as I was flying hither from Egypt; on the ships were magnificent masts, and I venture to assert that it was they that smelt so of fir. I may congratulate you, for they lifted themselves on high most majestically!"

"Oh, were I but old enough to fly across the sea! But how does the sea look in reality? What is it like?"

"That would take a long time to explain," said the Stork, and with these words off he went.

"Rejoice in thy growth!" said the Sunbeams. "Rejoice in thy vigorous growth, and in the fresh life that moveth within thee!"

And the Wind kissed the Tree, and the Dew wept tears over him; but the Fir understood it not.

When Christmas came, quite young trees were cut down: trees which often were not even as large or of the same age as this Fir Tree, who could never rest, but always wanted to be off. These young trees, and they were always the finest looking, retained their branches; they were laid on carts, and the horses drew them out of the wood.

"Where are they going to?" asked the Fir. "They are not taller than I; there was one indeed that was considerably shorter; and why do they retain all their branches? Whither are they taken?"

"We know! We know!" chirped the Sparrows. "We have peeped in at the windows in the town below! We know whither they are taken! The greatest splendor and the greatest magnificence one can imagine await them. We peeped through the windows, and saw them planted in the middle of the warm room and ornamented with the most splendid things, with gilded apples, with gingerbread, with toys, and many hundred lights!"

"And then?" asked the Fir Tree, trembling in every bough. "And then? What happens then?"

"We did not see anything more: it was incomparably beautiful."

"I would fain know if I am destined for so glorious a career," cried the Tree, rejoicing. "That is still better than to cross the sea! What a longing do I suffer! Were Christmas but come! I am now tall, and my branches spread like the others that were carried off last year! Oh! were I but already on the cart! Were I in the warm room with all the splendor and magnificence! Yes; then something better, something still grander, will surely follow, or wherefore should they thus ornament me? Something better, something still grander must follow—but what? Oh, how I long, how I suffer! I do not know myself what is the matter with me!"

"Rejoice in our presence!" said the Air and the Sunlight. "Rejoice in thy own fresh youth!"

But the Tree did not rejoice at all; he grew and grew, and was green both winter and summer. People that saw him said, "What a fine tree!" and towards Christmas he was one of the first that was cut down. The axe struck deep into the very pith; the Tree fell to the earth with a sigh; he felt a pang—it was like a swoon; he could not think of happiness, for he was sorrowful at being separated from his home, from the place where he had sprung up. He well knew that he should never see his dear old comrades, the little bushes and flowers around him, anymore; perhaps not even the birds! The departure was not at all agreeable.

The Tree only came to himself when he was unloaded in a court-yard with the other trees, and heard a man say, "That one is splendid! We don't want the others." Then two servants came in rich livery and carried the Fir Tree into a large and splendid drawing-room. Portraits were hanging on the walls, and near the white porcelain stove stood two large Chinese vases with lions on the covers. There, too, were large easy-chairs, silken sofas, large tables full of picture-books and full of toys, worth hundreds and hundreds of crowns—at least the children said so. And the Fir Tree was stuck upright in a cask that was filled with sand; but no one could see that it was a cask, for green cloth was hung all round it, and it stood on a large gaily-colored carpet. Oh! how the Tree quivered! What was to happen? The servants, as well as the young ladies, decorated it. On one branch there hung little nets cut out of colored paper, and each net was filled with sugarplums; and among the other boughs gilded apples and walnuts were suspended, looking as though they had grown there, and little blue and white tapers were placed among the leaves. Dolls that looked for all the world like men— the Tree had never beheld such before—were seen among the foliage, and at the very top a large star of gold tinsel was fixed. It was really splendid—beyond description splendid.

"This evening!" they all said. "How it will shine this evening!"

"Oh!" thought the Tree. "If the evening were but come! If the tapers were but lighted! And then I wonder what will happen! Perhaps the other trees from the forest will come to look at me! Perhaps the sparrows will beat against the windowpanes! I wonder if I shall take root here, and winter and summer stand covered with ornaments!"

He knew very much about the matter—but he was so impatient that for sheer longing he got a pain in his back, and this with trees is the same thing as a headache with us.

The candles were now lighted—what brightness! What splendor! The Tree trembled so in every bough that one of the tapers set fire to the foliage. It blazed up famously.

"Help! Help!" cried the young ladies, and they quickly put out the fire.

Now the Tree did not even dare tremble. What a state he was in! He was so uneasy lest he should lose something of his splendor, that he was quite bewildered amidst the glare and brightness; when suddenly both folding-doors opened and a troop of children rushed in as if they would upset the Tree. The older persons followed quietly; the little ones stood quite still. But it was only for a moment; then they shouted that the whole place re-echoed with their rejoicing; they danced round the Tree, and one present after the other was pulled off.

"What are they about?" thought the Tree. "What is to happen now!" And the lights burned down to the very branches, and as they burned down they were put out one after the other, and then the children had permission to plunder the Tree. So they fell upon it with such violence that all its branches cracked; if it had not been fixed firmly in the ground, it would certainly have tumbled down.

The children danced about with their beautiful playthings; no one looked at the Tree except the old nurse, who peeped between the branches; but it was only to see if there was a fig or an apple left that had been forgotten.

"A story! A story!" cried the children, drawing a little fat man towards the Tree. He seated himself under it and said, "Now we are in the shade, and the Tree can listen too. But I shall tell only one story. Now which will you have; that about Ivedy-Avedy, or about Humpy-

Dumpy, who tumbled downstairs, and yet after all came to the throne and married the princess?"

"Ivedy-Avedy," cried some; "Humpy-Dumpy," cried the others. There was such a bawling and screaming — the Fir Tree alone was silent, and he thought to himself, "Am I not to bawl with the rest? Am I to do nothing whatever?" for he was one of the company, and had done what he had to do.

And the man told about Humpy-Dumpy that tumbled down, who notwithstanding came to the throne, and at last married the princess. And the children clapped their hands, and cried. "Oh, go on! Do go on!" They wanted to hear about Ivedy-Avedy too, but the little man only told them about Humpy-Dumpy. The Fir Tree stood quite still and absorbed in thought; the birds in the wood had never related the like of this. "Humpy-Dumpy fell downstairs, and yet he married the princess! Yes, yes! That's the way of the world!" thought the Fir Tree, and believed it all, because the man who told the story was so good-looking. "Well, well! who knows, perhaps I may fall downstairs, too, and get a princess as wife!" And he looked forward with joy to the morrow, when he hoped to be decked out again with lights, playthings, fruits, and tinsel.

"I won't tremble to-morrow!" thought the Fir Tree. "I will enjoy to the full all my splendor! To-morrow I shall hear again the story of Humpy-Dumpy, and perhaps that of Ivedy-Avedy too." And the whole night the Tree stood still and in deep thought.

In the morning the servant and the housemaid came in.

"Now then the splendor will begin again," thought the Fir. But they dragged him out of the room, and up the stairs into the loft: and here, in a dark corner, where no daylight could enter, they left him. "What's the meaning of this?" thought the Tree. "What am I to do here? What shall I hear now, I wonder?" And he leaned against the wall lost in reverie. Time enough had he too for his reflections; for days and nights passed on, and nobody came up; and when at last somebody did come, it was only to put some great trunks in a corner, out of the way. There stood the Tree quite hidden; it seemed as if he had been entirely forgotten.

"'Tis now winter out-of-doors!" thought the Tree. "The earth is hard and covered with snow; men cannot plant me now, and therefore I have been put up here under shelter till the spring-time comes! How thoughtful that is! How kind man is, after all! If it only were not so dark here, and so terribly lonely! Not even a hare! And out in the woods it was so pleasant, when the snow was on the ground, and the hare leaped by; yes—even when he jumped over me; but I did not like it then! It is really terribly lonely here!"

"Squeak! Squeak!" said a little Mouse, at the same moment, peeping out of his hole. And then another little one came. They snuffed about the Fir Tree, and rustled among the branches.

"It is dreadfully cold," said the Mouse. "But for that, it would be delightful here, old Fir, wouldn't it?"

"I am by no means old," said the Fir Tree. "There's many a one considerably older than I am."

"Where do you come from," asked the Mice; "and what can you do?" They were so extremely curious. "Tell us about the most beautiful spot on the earth. Have you never been there? Were you never in the larder, where cheeses lie on the shelves, and hams hang from above; where one dances about on tallow candles: that place where one enters lean, and comes out again fat and portly?"

"I know no such place," said the Tree. "But I know the wood, where the sun shines and where the little birds sing." And then he told all about his youth; and the little Mice had never heard the like before; and they listened and said, "Well, to be sure! How much you have seen! How happy you must have been!"

"I!" said the Fir Tree, thinking over what he had himself related.

"Yes, in reality those were happy times." And then he told about Christmas-eve, when he was decked out with cakes and candles.

"Oh," said the little Mice, "how fortunate you have been, old Fir Tree!"

"I am by no means old," said he. "I came from the wood this winter; I am in my prime, and am only rather short for my age."

"What delightful stories you know," said the Mice: and the next night they came with four other little Mice, who were to hear what the Tree recounted: and the more he related, the more he remembered himself; and it appeared as if those times had really been happy times. "But they may still come—they may still come! Humpy-Dumpy fell downstairs, and yet he got a princess!" and he thought at the moment of a nice little Birch Tree growing out in the woods: to the Fir, that would be a real charming princess.

"Who is Humpy-Dumpy?" asked the Mice. So then the Fir Tree told the whole fairy tale, for he could remember every single word of it; and the little Mice jumped for joy up to the very top of the Tree. Next night two more Mice came, and on Sunday two Rats even; but they said the stories were not interesting, which vexed the little Mice; and they, too, now began to think them not so very amusing either.

"Do you know only one story?" asked the Rats.

"Only that one," answered the Tree. "I heard it on my happiest evening; but I did not then know how happy I was."

"It is a very stupid story! Don't you know one about bacon and tallow candles? Can't you tell any larder stories?"

"No," said the Tree.

"Then good-bye," said the Rats; and they went home.

At last the little Mice stayed away also; and the Tree sighed: "After all, it was very pleasant when the sleek little Mice sat round me, and listened to what I told them. Now that too is over. But I will take good care to enjoy myself when I am brought out again."

But when was that to be? Why, one morning there came a quantity of people and set to work in the loft. The trunks were moved, the tree was pulled out and thrown—rather hard, it is true—down on the floor, but a man drew him towards the stairs, where the daylight shone.

"Now a merry life will begin again," thought the Tree. He felt the fresh air, the first sunbeam—and now he was out in the courtyard. All passed so quickly, there was so much going on around him, the Tree quite forgot to look to himself. The court adjoined a garden, and all was in flower; the roses hung so fresh and odorous over the balustrade, the lindens were in blossom, the Swallows flew by, and said, "Quirre-vit! My husband is come!" but it was not the Fir Tree that they meant.

"Now, then, I shall really enjoy life," said he exultingly, and spread out his branches; but, alas, they were all withered and yellow! It was in a corner that he lay, among weeds and nettles. The golden star of tinsel was still on the top of the Tree, and glittered in the sunshine.

In the court-yard some of the merry children were playing who had danced at Christmas round the Fir Tree, and were so glad at the sight of him. One of the youngest ran and tore off the golden star.

"Only look what is still on the ugly old Christmas tree!" said he, trampling on the branches, so that they all cracked beneath his feet.

And the Tree beheld all the beauty of the flowers, and the freshness in the garden; he beheld himself, and wished he had remained in his dark corner in the loft; he thought of his first youth in the wood, of the merry Christmas-eve, and of the little Mice who had listened with so much pleasure to the story of Humpy-Dumpy.

"'Tis over—'tis past!" said the poor Tree. "Had I but rejoiced when I had reason to do so! But now 'tis past, 'tis past!"

44

And the gardener's boy chopped the Tree into small pieces; there was a whole heap lying there. The wood flamed up splendidly under the large brewing copper, and it sighed so deeply! Each sigh was like a shot.

The boys played about in the court, and the youngest wore the gold star on his breast which the Tree had had on the happiest evening of his life. However, that was over now—the Tree gone, the story at an end. All, all was over—every tale must end at last.

The Snow Man

By Hans Christian Andersen

"IT is so delightfully cold," said the Snow Man, "that it makes my whole body crackle. This is just the kind of wind to blow life into one. How that great red thing up there is staring at me!" He meant the sun, who was just setting. "It shall not make me wink. I shall manage to keep the pieces."

He had two triangular pieces of tile in his head, instead of eyes; his mouth was made of an old broken rake, and was, of course, furnished with teeth. He had been brought into existence amidst the joyous shouts of boys, the jingling of sleigh-bells, and the slashing of whips. The sun went down, and the full moon rose, large, round, and clear, shining in the deep blue.

"There it comes again, from the other side," said the Snow Man, who supposed the sun was showing himself once more. "Ah, I have cured him of staring, though; now he may hang up there, and shine, that I may see myself. If I only knew how to manage to move away from this place,- I should so like to move. If I could, I would slide along yonder on the ice, as I have seen the boys do; but I don't understand how; I don't even know how to run."

"Away, away," barked the old yard-dog. He was quite hoarse, and could not pronounce "Bow wow" properly. He had once been an indoor dog, and lay by the fire, and he had been hoarse ever since. "The sun will make you run some day. I saw him, last winter, make your predecessor run, and his predecessor before him. Away, away, they all have to go."

"I don't understand you, comrade," said the Snow Man. "Is that thing up yonder to teach me to run? I saw it running itself a little while ago, and now it has come creeping up from the other side.

"You know nothing at all," replied the yard-dog; "but then, you've only lately been patched up. What you see yonder is the moon, and the one before it was the sun. It will come again to-morrow, and most likely teach you to run down into the ditch by the well; for I think the weather is going to change. I can feel such pricks and stabs in my left leg; I am sure there is going to be a change."

"I don't understand him," said the Snow Man to himself; "but I have a feeling that he is talking of something very disagreeable. The one who stared so just now, and whom he calls the sun, is not my friend; I can feel that too."

"Away, away," barked the yard-dog, and then he turned round three times, and crept into his kennel to sleep.

There was really a change in the weather. Towards morning, a thick fog covered the whole country round, and a keen wind arose, so that the cold seemed to freeze one's bones; but when the sun rose, the sight was splendid. Trees and bushes were covered with hoar frost, and looked like a forest of white coral; while on every twig glittered frozen dew-drops. The many delicate forms concealed in summer by luxuriant foliage, were now clearly defined, and looked like glittering lace-work. From every twig glistened a white radiance. The birch, waving in the wind, looked full of life, like trees in summer; and its appearance was wondrously beautiful. And where the sun shone, how everything glittered and sparkled, as if diamond dust had been strewn about; while the snowy carpet of the earth appeared as if covered with diamonds, from which countless lights gleamed, whiter than even the snow itself.

"This is really beautiful," said a young girl, who had come into the garden with a young man; and they both stood still near the Snow Man, and contemplated the glittering scene. "Summer cannot show a more beautiful sight," she exclaimed, while her eyes sparkled.

"And we can't have such a fellow as this in the summer time," replied the young man, pointing to the Snow Man; "he is capital."

The girl laughed, and nodded at the Snow Man, and then tripped away over the snow with her friend. The snow creaked and crackled beneath her feet, as if she had been treading on starch.

"Who are these two?" asked the Snow Man of the yard-dog. "You have been here longer than I have; do you know them?"

"Of course I know them," replied the yard-dog; "she has stroked my back many times, and he has given me a bone of meat. I never bite those two."

"But what are they?" asked the Snow Man.

"They are lovers," he replied; "they will go and live in the same kennel by-and-by, and gnaw at the same bone. Away, away!"

"Are they the same kind of beings as you and I?" asked the Snow Man.

"Well, they belong to the same master," retorted the yard-dog. "Certainly people who were only born yesterday know very little. I can see that in you. I have age and experience. I know every one here in the house, and I know there was once a time when I did not lie out here in the cold, fastened to a chain. Away, away!"

"The cold is delightful," said the Snow Man; "but do tell me tell me; only you must not clank your chain so; for it jars all through me when you do that."

"Away, away!" barked the yard-dog; "I'll tell you; they said I was a pretty little fellow once; then I used to lie in a velvet-covered chair, up at the master's house, and sit in the mistress's lap. They used to kiss my nose, and wipe my paws with an embroidered handkerchief, and I was called 'Ami, dear Ami, sweet Ami.' But after a while I grew too big for them, and they sent me away to the housekeeper's room; so I came to live on the lower story. You can look into the room from where you stand, and see where I was master once; for I was indeed master to the housekeeper. It was certainly a smaller room than those up stairs; but I was more comfortable; for I was not being continually taken hold of and pulled about by the children as I had been. I received quite as good food, or even better. I had my own cushion, and there was a stove- it is the finest thing in the world at this season of the year. I used to go under the stove, and lie down quite beneath it. Ah, I still dream of that stove. Away, away!"

"Does a stove look beautiful?" asked the Snow Man, "is it at all like me?"

"It is just the reverse of you,' said the dog; "it's as black as a crow, and has a long neck and a brass knob; it eats firewood, so that fire spurts out of its mouth. We should keep on one side, or under it, to be comfortable. You can see it through the window, from where you stand."

Then the Snow Man looked, and saw a bright polished thing with a brazen knob, and fire gleaming from the lower part of it. The Snow Man felt quite a strange sensation come over him; it was very odd, he knew not what it meant, and he could not account for it. But there are people who are not men of snow, who understand what it is. "'And why did you leave her?" asked the Snow Man, for it seemed to him that the stove must be of the female sex. "How could you give up such a comfortable place?"

"I was obliged," replied the yard-dog. "They turned me out of doors, and chained me up here. I had bitten the youngest of my master's sons in the leg, because he kicked away the bone I was gnawing. 'Bone for bone,' I thought; but they were so angry, and from that time I have been fastened with a chain, and lost my bone. Don't you hear how hoarse I am. Away, away! I can't talk any more like other dogs. Away, away, that is the end of it all."

But the Snow Man was no longer listening. He was looking into the housekeeper's room on the lower storey; where the stove stood on its four iron legs, looking about the same size as the Snow Man himself.

"What a strange crackling I feel within me," he said. "Shall I ever get in there? It is an innocent wish, and innocent wishes are sure to be fulfilled. I must go in there and lean against her, even if I have to break the window."

"You must never go in there," said the yard-dog, "for if you approach the stove, you'll melt away, away."

"I might as well go," said the Snow Man, "for I think I am breaking up as it is."

During the whole day the Snow Man stood looking in through the window, and in the twilight hour the room became still more inviting, for from the stove came a gentle glow, not like the sun or the moon; no, only the bright light which gleams from a stove when it has been well fed. When the door of the stove was opened, the flames darted out of its mouth; this is customary with all stoves. The light of the flames fell directly on the face and breast of the Snow Man with a ruddy gleam. "I can endure it no longer," said he; "how beautiful it looks when it stretches out its tongue?"

The night was long, but did not appear so to the Snow Man, who stood there enjoying his own reflections, and crackling with the cold. In the morning, the window-panes of the housekeeper's room were covered with ice. They were the most beautiful ice-flowers any Snow Man could desire, but they concealed the stove. These window-panes would not thaw, and he could see nothing of the stove, which he pictured to himself, as if it had been a lovely human being. The snow crackled and the wind whistled around him; it was just the kind of frosty weather a Snow Man might thoroughly enjoy. But he did not enjoy it; how, indeed, could he enjoy anything when he was "stove sick?"

"That is terrible disease for a Snow Man," said the yard-dog; "I have suffered from it myself, but I got over it. Away, away," he barked and then he added, "the weather is going to change." And the weather did change; it began to thaw. As the warmth increased, the Snow Man decreased. He said nothing and made no complaint, which is a sure sign. One morning he broke, and sunk down altogether; and, behold, where he had stood, something like a broomstick remained sticking up in the ground. It was the pole round which the boys had built him up. "Ah, now I understand why he had such a great longing for the stove," said the yard-dog. "Why, there's the shovel that is used for cleaning out the stove, fastened to the pole." The Snow Man had a stove scraper in his body; that was what moved him so. "But it's all over now. Away, away." And soon the winter passed. "Away, away," barked the hoarse yard-dog. But the girls in the house sang,

"Come from your fragrant home, green thyme;
Stretch your soft branches, willow-tree;
The months are bringing the sweet spring-time,
When the lark in the sky sings joyfully.
Come gentle sun, while the cuckoo sings,
And I'll mock his note in my wanderings."

And nobody thought any more of the Snow Man.

THE END

Goody Santa Claus on a Sleigh Ride

By Katharine Lee Bates

Santa, must I tease in vain, Deer? Let me go and hold the reindeer,
While you clamber down the chimneys. Don't look savage as a Turk!
Why should you have all the glory of the joyous Christmas story,
And poor little Goody Santa Claus have nothing but the work?

It would be so very cozy, you and I, all round and rosy,
Looking like two loving snowballs in our fuzzy Arctic furs,
Tucked in warm and snug together, whisking through the winter
weather
Where the tinkle of the sleigh-bells is the only sound that stirs.

Goody Santa Claus on a Sleigh Ride: Mrs. Claus
You just sit here and grow chubby off the goodies in my cubby
From December to December, till your white beard sweeps your
knees;
For you must allow, my Goodman, that you're but a lazy woodman
And rely on me to foster all our fruitful Christmas trees.

While your Saintship waxes holy, year by year, and roly-poly,
Blessed by all the lads and lassies in the limits of the land,
While your toes at home you're toasting, then poor Goody must go
posting
Out to plant and prune and garner, where our fir-tree forests stand.

Oh! but when the toil is sorest how I love our fir-tree forest,
Heart of light and heart of beauty in the Northland cold and dim,
All with gifts and candles laden to delight a boy or maiden,
And its dark-green branches ever murmuring the Christmas hymn!

Yet ask young Jack Frost, our neighbor, who but Goody has the labor,
Feeding roots with milk and honey that the bonbons may be sweet!

Who but Goody knows the reason why the playthings bloom in season
And the ripened toys and trinkets rattle gaily to her feet!

From the time the dollies budded, wiry-boned and saw-dust blooded,
With their waxen eyelids winking when the wind the tree-tops plied,
Have I rested for a minute, until now your pack has in it
All the bright, abundant harvest of the merry Christmastide?

Santa, wouldn't it be pleasant to surprise me with a present?
And this ride behind the reindeer is the boon your Goody begs;
Think how hard my extra work is, tending the Thanksgiving turkeys
And our flocks of rainbow chickens — those that lay the Easter eggs.

Home to womankind is suited? Nonsense, Goodman! Let our fruited
Orchards answer for the value of a woman out-of-doors.
Why then bid me chase the thunder, while the roof you're safely
under,
All to fashion fire-crackers with the lighting in their cores?

See! I've fetched my snow-flake bonnet, with the sunrise ribbons on
it;
I've not worn it since we fled from Fairyland our wedding day;
How we sped through iceberg porches with the Northern Lights for
torches!
You were young and slender, Santa, and we had this very sleigh.

Jump in quick then? That's my bonny. Hey down derry! Nonny nonny!
While I tie your fur cap closer, I will kiss your ruddy chin.
I'm so pleased I fall to singing, just as sleigh-bells take to ringing!
Are the cloud-spun lap-robes ready? Tirra-lirra! Tuck me in.

Off across the starlight Norland, where no plant adorns the moorland
Save the ruby-berried holly and the frolic mistletoe!
Oh, but this is Christmas revel! Off across the frosted level
Where the reindeers' hoofs strike sparkles from the crispy, crackling
snow!

There's the Man i' the Moon before us, bound to lead the Christmas chorus
With the music of the sky-waves rippling round his silver shell —
Glimmering boat that leans and tarries with the weight of dreams she carries
To the cots of happy children. Gentle sailor, steer her well!

Now we pass through dusky portals to the drowsy land of mortals;
Snow-enfolded, silent cities stretch about us dim and far.
Oh! how sound the world is sleeping, midnight watch no shepherd keeping,
Though an angel-face shines gladly down from every golden star.

Here's a roof. I'll hold the reindeer. I suppose this weather-vane, Dear,
Some one set here just on purpose for our teams to fasten to.
There's its gilded cock, — the gaby! — wants to crow and tell the baby
We are come. Be careful, Santa! Don't get smothered in the flue.

Back so soon? No chimney-swallow dives but where his mate can follow.
Bend your cold ear, Sweetheart Santa, down to catch my whisper faint:
Would it be so very shocking if your Goody filled a stocking
Just for once? Oh, dear! Forgive me. Frowns do not become a Saint.

I will peep in at the skylights, where the moon sheds tender twilights
Equally down silken chambers and down attics bare and bleak.
Let me show with hailstone candies these two dreaming boys — the dandies
In their frilled and fluted nighties, rosy cheek to rosy cheek!

What! No gift for this poor garret? Take a sunset sash and wear it
O'er the rags, my pale-faced lassie, till thy father smiles again.
He's a poet, but — oh, cruel! he has neither light nor fuel.

54

Here's a fallen star to write by, and a music-box of rain.

So our sprightly reindeer clamber, with their fairy sleigh of amber,
On from roof to roof , the woven shades of night about us drawn.
On from roof to roof we twinkle, all the silver bells a-tinkle,
Till blooms in yonder blessèd East the rose of Christmas dawn.

Now the pack is fairly rifled, and poor Santa's well-nigh stifled;
Yet you would not let your Goody fill a single baby-sock;
Yes, I know the task takes brain, Dear. I can only hold the reindeer,
And so see me climb down chimney — it would give your nerves a
shock.

Wait! There's yet a tiny fellow, smiling lips and curls so yellow
You would think a truant sunbeam played in them all night. He spins
Giant tops, a flies kites higher than the gold cathedral spire
In his creams — the orphan bairnie, trustful little Tatterkins.

Santa, don't pass by the urchin! Shake the pack, and deeply search in
All your pockets. There is always one toy more. I told you so.
Up again? Why, what's the trouble? On your eyelash winks the bubble
Mortals call a tear, I fancy. Holes in stocking, heel and toe?

Goodman, though your speech is crusty now and then there's nothing
rusty
In your heart. A child's least sorrow makes your wet eyes glisten, too;
But I'll mend that sock so nearly it shall hold your gifts completely.
Take the reins and let me show you what a woman's wit can do.

Puff! I'm up again, my Deary, flushed a bit and somewhat weary,
With my wedding snow-flake bonnet worse for many a sooty knock;
But be glad you let me wheedle, since, an icicle for needle,
Threaded with the last pale moonbeam, I have darned the laddie's
sock.

Then I tucked a paint-box in it ('twas no easy task to win it

From the Artist of the Autumn Leaves) and frost-fruits white and
sweet,
With the toys your pocket misses — oh! and kisses upon kisses
To cherish safe from evil paths the motherless small feet.

Chirrup! chirrup! There's a patter of soft footsteps and a clatter
Of child voices. Speed it, reindeer, up the sparkling Arctic Hill!
Merry Christmas, little people! Joy-bells ring in every steeple,
And Goody's gladdest of the glad. I've had my own sweet will.

A Kidnapped Santa Claus

By L. Frank Baum

Santa Claus lives in the Laughing Valley, where stands the big, rambling castle in which his toys are manufactured. His workmen, selected from the ryls, knooks, pixies and fairies, live with him, and every one is as busy as can be from one year's end to another.

It is called the Laughing Valley because everything there is happy and gay. The brook chuckles to itself as it leaps rollicking between its green banks; the wind whistles merrily in the trees; the sunbeams dance lightly over the soft grass, and the violets and wild flowers look smilingly up from their green nests. To laugh one needs to be happy; to be happy one needs to be content. And throughout the Laughing Valley of Santa Claus contentment reigns supreme.

On one side is the mighty Forest of Burzee. At the other side stands the huge mountain that contains the Caves of the Daemons. And between them the Valley lies smiling and peaceful.

One would think that our good old Santa Claus, who devotes his days to making children happy, would have no enemies on all the earth; and, as a matter of fact, for a long period of time he encountered nothing but love wherever he might go.

But the Daemons who live in the mountain caves grew to hate Santa Claus very much, and all for the simple reason that he made children happy.

The Caves of the Daemons are five in number. A broad pathway leads up to the first cave, which is a finely arched cavern at the foot of the mountain, the entrance being beautifully carved and decorated. In it resides the Daemon of Selfishness. Back of this is another cavern inhabited by the Daemon of Envy. The cave of the Daemon of Hatred is next in order, and through this one passes to the home of the Daemon of Malice--situated in a dark and fearful cave in the very heart of the mountain. I do not know what lies beyond this. Some say there are terrible pitfalls leading to death and destruction, and this may very well be true. However, from each one of the four caves mentioned there is a small, narrow tunnel leading to the fifth cave--a cozy little room occupied by the Daemon of Repentance. And as the rocky floors of these passages are well worn by the track of passing feet, I judge that many wanderers in the Caves of the Daemons have escaped through the tunnels to the abode of the Daemon of Repentance, who is said to be a pleasant sort of fellow who gladly opens for one a little door admitting you into fresh air and sunshine again.

Well, these Daemons of the Caves, thinking they had great cause to dislike old Santa Claus, held a meeting one day to discuss the matter.

"I'm really getting lonesome," said the Daemon of Selfishness. "For Santa Claus distributes so many pretty Christmas gifts to all the children that they become happy and generous, through his example, and keep away from my cave."

"I'm having the same trouble," rejoined the Daemon of Envy. "The little ones seem quite content with Santa Claus, and there are few, indeed, that I can coax to become envious."

"And that makes it bad for me!" declared the Daemon of Hatred. "For if no children pass through the Caves of Selfishness and Envy, none can get to MY cavern."

"Or to mine," added the Daemon of Malice.

"For my part," said the Daemon of Repentance, "it is easily seen that if children do not visit your caves they have no need to visit mine; so that I am quite as neglected as you are."

"And all because of this person they call Santa Claus!" exclaimed the

Daemon of Envy. "He is simply ruining our business, and something must be done at once."

To this they readily agreed; but what to do was another and more difficult matter to settle. They knew that Santa Claus worked all through the year at his castle in the Laughing Valley, preparing the gifts he was to distribute on Christmas Eve; and at first they resolved to try to tempt him into their caves, that they might lead him on to the terrible pitfalls that ended in destruction.

So the very next day, while Santa Claus was busily at work, surrounded by his little band of assistants, the Daemon of Selfishness came to him and said:

"These toys are wonderfully bright and pretty. Why do you not keep them for yourself? It's a pity to give them to those noisy boys and fretful girls, who break and destroy them so quickly.

"Nonsense!" cried the old graybeard, his bright eyes twinkling merrily as he turned toward the tempting Daemon. "The boys and girls are never so noisy and fretful after receiving my presents, and if I can make them happy for one day in the year I am quite content."

So the Daemon went back to the others, who awaited him in their caves, and said:

"I have failed, for Santa Claus is not at all selfish."

The following day the Daemon of Envy visited Santa Claus. Said he: "The toy shops are full of playthings quite as pretty as those you are making. What a shame it is that they should interfere with your business! They make toys by machinery much quicker than you can make them by hand; and they sell them for money, while you get nothing at all for your work."

But Santa Claus refused to be envious of the toy shops.

"I can supply the little ones but once a year--on Christmas Eve," he answered; "for the children are many, and I am but one. And as my work is one of love and kindness I would be ashamed to receive money for my little gifts. But throughout all the year the children must be amused in some way, and so the toy shops are able to bring much happiness to my little friends. I like the toy shops, and am glad to see them prosper."

In spite of the second rebuff, the Daemon of Hatred thought he would try to influence Santa Claus. So the next day he entered the busy workshop and said:

"Good morning, Santa! I have bad news for you."

"Then run away, like a good fellow," answered Santa Claus. "Bad news is something that should be kept secret and never told."

"You cannot escape this, however," declared the Daemon; "for in the world are a good many who do not believe in Santa Claus, and these you are bound to hate bitterly, since they have so wronged you."

"Stuff and rubbish!" cried Santa.

"And there are others who resent your making children happy and who sneer at you and call you a foolish old rattlepate! You are quite right to hate such base slanderers, and you ought to be revenged upon them for their evil words."

"But I don't hate 'em!" exclaimed Santa Claus positively. "Such people do me no real harm, but merely render themselves and their children unhappy. Poor things! I'd much rather help them any day than injure them."

Indeed, the Daemons could not tempt old Santa Claus in any way. On the contrary, he was shrewd enough to see that their object in visiting him was to make mischief and trouble, and his cheery laughter disconcerted the evil ones and showed to them the folly of such an undertaking. So they abandoned honeyed words and determined to use force.

It was well known that no harm can come to Santa Claus while he is in the Laughing Valley, for the fairies, and ryls, and knooks all protect him. But on Christmas Eve he drives his reindeer out into the big world, carrying a sleighload of toys and pretty gifts to the children; and this was the time and the occasion when his enemies had the best chance to injure him. So the Daemons laid their plans and awaited the arrival of Christmas Eve.

The moon shone big and white in the sky, and the snow lay crisp and sparkling on the ground as Santa Claus cracked his whip and sped away out of the Valley into the great world beyond. The roomy sleigh was packed full with huge sacks of toys, and as the reindeer dashed onward our jolly old Santa laughed and whistled and sang for very joy. For in all his merry life this was the one day in the year when he was happiest--the day he lovingly bestowed the treasures of his workshop upon the little children.

It would be a busy night for him, he well knew. As he whistled and shouted and cracked his whip again, he reviewed in mind all the towns and cities and farmhouses where he was expected, and figured that he had just enough presents to go around and make every child happy. The reindeer knew exactly what was expected of them, and dashed along so swiftly that their feet scarcely seemed to touch the snow-covered ground.

Suddenly a strange thing happened: a rope shot through the moonlight and a big noose that was in the end of it settled over the arms and body of Santa Claus and drew tight. Before he could resist or even cry out he was jerked from the seat of the sleigh and tumbled head foremost into a snowbank, while the reindeer rushed onward with the load of toys and carried it quickly out of sight and sound.

Such a surprising experience confused old Santa for a moment, and when he had collected his senses he found that the wicked Daemons had pulled him from the snowdrift and bound him tightly with many coils of the stout rope. And then they carried the kidnapped Santa Claus away to their mountain, where they thrust the prisoner into a secret cave and chained him to the rocky wall so that he could not escape.

"Ha, ha!" laughed the Daemons, rubbing their hands together with cruel glee. "What will the children do now? How they will cry and scold and storm when they find there are no toys in their stockings and no gifts on their Christmas trees! And what a lot of punishment they will receive from their parents, and how they will flock to our Caves of Selfishness, and Envy, and Hatred, and Malice! We have done a mighty clever thing, we Daemons of the Caves!"

Now it so chanced that on this Christmas Eve the good Santa Claus had taken with him in his sleigh Nuter the Ryl, Peter the Knook, Kilter the Pixie, and a small fairy named Wisk--his four favorite assistants. These little people he had often found very useful in helping him to distribute his gifts to the children, and when their master was so suddenly dragged from the sleigh they were all snugly tucked underneath the seat, where the sharp wind could not reach them.

The tiny immortals knew nothing of the capture of Santa Claus until some time after he had disappeared. But finally they missed his cheery voice, and as their master always sang or whistled on his journeys, the silence warned them that something was wrong.

Little Wisk stuck out his head from underneath the seat and found Santa Claus gone and no one to direct the flight of the reindeer.

"Whoa!" he called out, and the deer obediently slackened speed and came to a halt.

Peter and Nuter and Kilter all jumped upon the seat and looked back over the track made by the sleigh. But Santa Claus had been left miles and miles behind.

"What shall we do?" asked Wisk anxiously, all the mirth and mischief banished from his wee face by this great calamity.

"We must go back at once and find our master," said Nuter the Ryl, who thought and spoke with much deliberation.

"No, no!" exclaimed Peter the Knook, who, cross and crabbed though he was, might always be depended upon in an emergency. "If we delay, or go back, there will not be time to get the toys to the children before morning; and that would grieve Santa Claus more than anything else."

"It is certain that some wicked creatures have captured him," added Kilter thoughtfully, "and their object must be to make the children unhappy. So our first duty is to get the toys distributed as carefully as if Santa Claus were himself present. Afterward we can search for our master and easily secure his freedom."

This seemed such good and sensible advice that the others at once resolved to adopt it. So Peter the Knook called to the reindeer, and the faithful animals again sprang forward and dashed over hill and valley, through forest and plain, until they came to the houses wherein children lay sleeping and dreaming of the pretty gifts they would find on Christmas morning.

The little immortals had set themselves a difficult task; for although they had assisted Santa Claus on many of his journeys, their master had always directed and guided them and told them exactly what he wished them to do. But now they had to distribute the toys according to their own judgment, and they did not understand children as well as did old Santa. So it is no wonder they made some laughable errors.

Mamie Brown, who wanted a doll, got a drum instead; and a drum is of no use to a girl who loves dolls. And Charlie Smith, who delights to romp and play out of doors, and who wanted some new rubber boots to keep his feet dry, received a sewing box filled with colored worsteds and threads and needles, which made him so provoked that he thoughtlessly called our dear Santa Claus a fraud.

Had there been many such mistakes the Daemons would have accomplished their evil purpose and made the children unhappy. But the little friends of the absent Santa Claus labored faithfully and intelligently to carry out their master's ideas, and they made fewer errors than might be expected under such unusual circumstances.

And, although they worked as swiftly as possible, day had begun to break before the toys and other presents were all distributed; so for the first time in many years the reindeer trotted into the Laughing Valley, on their return, in broad daylight, with the brilliant sun peeping over the edge of the forest to prove they were far behind their accustomed hours.

Having put the deer in the stable, the little folk began to wonder how they might rescue their master; and they realized they must discover, first of all, what had happened to him and where he was.

So Wisk the Fairy transported himself to the bower of the Fairy Queen, which was located deep in the heart of the Forest of Burzee; and once there, it did not take him long to find out all about the naughty Daemons and how they had kidnapped the good Santa Claus to prevent his making children happy. The Fairy Queen also promised her assistance, and then, fortified by this powerful support, Wisk flew back to where Nuter and Peter and Kilter awaited him, and the four counseled together and laid plans to rescue their master from his enemies.

It is possible that Santa Claus was not as merry as usual during the night that succeeded his capture. For although he had faith in the judgment of his little friends he could not avoid a certain amount of worry, and an anxious look would creep at times into his kind old eyes as he thought of the disappointment that might await his dear little children. And the Daemons, who guarded him by turns, one after another, did not neglect to taunt him with contemptuous words in his helpless condition.

When Christmas Day dawned the Daemon of Malice was guarding the prisoner, and his tongue was sharper than that of any of the others.

"The children are waking up, Santa!" he cried. "They are waking up to find their stockings empty! Ho, ho! How they will quarrel, and wail, and stamp their feet in anger! Our caves will be full today, old Santa! Our caves are sure to be full!"

But to this, as to other like taunts, Santa Claus answered nothing. He was much grieved by his capture, it is true; but his courage did not forsake him. And, finding that the prisoner would not reply to his jeers, the Daemon of Malice presently went away, and sent the Daemon of Repentance to take his place.

This last personage was not so disagreeable as the others. He had gentle and refined features, and his voice was soft and pleasant in tone.

"My brother Daemons do not trust me overmuch," said he, as he entered the cavern; "but it is morning, now, and the mischief is done. You cannot visit the children again for another year."

"That is true," answered Santa Claus, almost cheerfully; "Christmas Eve is past, and for the first time in centuries I have not visited my children."

"The little ones will be greatly disappointed," murmured the Daemon of Repentance, almost regretfully; "but that cannot be helped now. Their grief is likely to make the children selfish and envious and hateful, and if they come to the Caves of the Daemons today I shall get a chance to lead some of them to my Cave of Repentance."

"Do you never repent, yourself?" asked Santa Claus, curiously.

"Oh, yes, indeed," answered the Daemon. "I am even now repenting that I assisted in your capture. Of course it is too late to remedy the evil that has been done; but repentance, you know, can come only after an

65

evil thought or deed, for in the beginning there is nothing to repent of."

"So I understand," said Santa Claus. "Those who avoid evil need never visit your cave."

"As a rule, that is true," replied the Daemon; "yet you, who have done no evil, are about to visit my cave at once; for to prove that I sincerely regret my share in your capture I am going to permit you to escape."

This speech greatly surprised the prisoner, until he reflected that it was just what might be expected of the Daemon of Repentance. The fellow at once busied himself untying the knots that bound Santa Claus and unlocking the chains that fastened him to the wall. Then he led the way through a long tunnel until they both emerged in the Cave of Repentance.

"I hope you will forgive me," said the Daemon pleadingly. "I am not really a bad person, you know; and I believe I accomplish a great deal of good in the world."

With this he opened a back door that let in a flood of sunshine, and Santa Claus sniffed the fresh air gratefully.

"I bear no malice," said he to the Daemon, in a gentle voice; "and I am sure the world would be a dreary place without you. So, good morning, and a Merry Christmas to you!"

With these words he stepped out to greet the bright morning, and a moment later he was trudging along, whistling softly to himself, on his way to his home in the Laughing Valley.

Marching over the snow toward the mountain was a vast army, made up of the most curious creatures imaginable. There were numberless knooks from the forest, as rough and crooked in appearance as the gnarled branches of the trees they ministered to. And there were dainty ryls from the fields, each one bearing the emblem of the flower or plant it guarded. Behind these were many ranks of pixies, gnomes and nymphs, and in the rear a thousand beautiful fairies floated along in gorgeous array.

This wonderful army was led by Wisk, Peter, Nuter, and Kilter, who had assembled it to rescue Santa Claus from captivity and to punish the Daemons who had dared to take him away from his beloved children.

And, although they looked so bright and peaceful, the little immortals were armed with powers that would be very terrible to those who had incurred their anger. Woe to the Daemons of the Caves if this mighty army of vengeance ever met them!

But lo! coming to meet his loyal friends appeared the imposing form of Santa Claus, his white beard floating in the breeze and his bright eyes sparkling with pleasure at this proof of the love and veneration he had inspired in the hearts of the most powerful creatures in existence.

And while they clustered around him and danced with glee at his safe return, he gave them earnest thanks for their support. But Wisk, and Nuter, and Peter, and Kilter, he embraced affectionately.

"It is useless to pursue the Daemons," said Santa Claus to the army. "They have their place in the world, and can never be destroyed. But that is a great pity, nevertheless," he continued musingly.

So the fairies, and knooks, and pixies, and ryls all escorted the good man to his castle, and there left him to talk over the events of the night with his little assistants.

Wisk had already rendered himself invisible and flown through the big world to see how the children were getting along on this bright Christmas morning; and by the time he returned, Peter had finished telling Santa Claus of how they had distributed the toys.

"We really did very well," cried the fairy, in a pleased voice; "for I found little unhappiness among the children this morning. Still, you must not get captured again, my dear master; for we might not be so

67

fortunate another time in carrying out your ideas."

He then related the mistakes that had been made, and which he had not discovered until his tour of inspection. And Santa Claus at once sent him with rubber boots for Charlie Smith, and a doll for Mamie Brown; so that even those two disappointed ones became happy.

As for the wicked Daemons of the Caves, they were filled with anger and chagrin when they found that their clever capture of Santa Claus had come to naught. Indeed, no one on that Christmas Day appeared to be at all selfish, or envious, or hateful. And, realizing that while the children's saint had so many powerful friends it was folly to oppose him, the Daemons never again attempted to interfere with his journeys on Christmas Eve.

Little Bun Rabbit

By L. Frank Baum

"Oh, Little Bun Rabbit, so soft and so shy,
Say, what do you see with your big, round eye?"
"On Christmas we rabbits," says Bunny so shy,
"Keep watch to see Santa go galloping by."

Little Dorothy had passed all the few years of her life in the country, and being the only child upon the farm she was allowed to roam about the meadows and woods as she pleased. On the bright summer mornings Dorothy's mother would tie a sun-bonnet under the girl's chin, and then she romped away to the fields to amuse herself in her own way.

She came to know every flower that grew, and to call them by name, and she always stepped very carefully to avoid treading on them, for Dorothy was a kind-hearted child and did not like to crush the pretty flowers that bloomed in her path. And she was also very fond of all the animals, and learned to know them well, and even to understand their language, which very few people can do. And the animals loved Dorothy in turn, for the word passed around amongst them that she could be trusted to do them no harm. For the horse, whose soft nose Dorothy often gently stroked, told the cow of her kindness, and the cow told the dog, and the dog told the cat, and the cat told her black kitten, and the black kitten told the rabbit when one day they met in the turnip patch.

Therefore when the rabbit, which is the most timid of all animals and the most difficult to get acquainted with, looked out of a small bush at the edge of the wood one day and saw Dorothy standing a little way off, he did not scamper away, as is his custom, but sat very still and met the gaze of her sweet eyes boldly, although perhaps his heart beat a little faster than usual.

Dorothy herself was afraid she might frighten him away, so she kept very quiet for a time, leaning silently against a tree and smiling encouragement at her timorous companion until the rabbit became reassured and blinked his big eyes at her thoughtfully. For he was as much interested in the little girl as she in him, since it was the first time he had dared to meet a person face to face.

Finally Dorothy ventured to speak, so she asked, very softly and slowly,

"Oh, Little Bun Rabbit, so soft and so shy,
Say, what do you see with your big, round eye?"

"Many things," answered the rabbit, who was pleased to hear the girl speak in his own language; "in summer-time I see the clover-leaves that I love to feed upon and the cabbages at the end of the farmer's garden. I see the cool bushes where I can hide from my enemies, and I see the dogs and the men long before they can see me, or know that I am near, and therefore I am able to keep out of their way."

"Is that the reason your eyes are so big?" asked Dorothy.

"I suppose so," returned the rabbit; "you see we have only our eyes and our ears and our legs to defend ourselves with. We cannot fight, but we can always run away, and that is a much better way to save our lives than by fighting."

"Where is your home, bunny?" enquired the girl.

"I live in the ground, far down in a cool, pleasant hole I have dug in the midst of the forest. At the bottom of the hole is the nicest little room you can imagine, and there I have made a soft bed to rest in at night. When I meet an enemy I run to my hole and jump in, and there I stay until all danger is over."

"You have told me what you see in summer," continued Dorothy, who was greatly interested in the rabbit's account of himself, "but what do you see in the winter?"

"In winter we rabbits," said Bunny so shy, "Keep watch to see Santa go galloping by."

"And do you ever see him?" asked the girl, eagerly.

"Oh, yes; every winter. I am not afraid of him, nor of his reindeer. And it is such fun to see him come dashing along, cracking his whip and calling out cheerily to his reindeer, who are able to run even swifter than we rabbits. And Santa Claus, when he sees me, always gives me a nod and a smile, and then I look after him and his big load of toys which he is carrying to the children, until he has galloped away out of sight. I like to see the toys, for they are so bright and pretty, and every year there is something new amongst them. Once I visited Santa, and saw him make the toys."

"Oh, tell me about it!" pleaded Dorothy.

"It was one morning after Christmas," said the rabbit, who seemed to enjoy talking, now that he had overcome his fear of Dorothy, "and I was sitting by the road-side when Santa Claus came riding back in his empty sleigh. He does not come home quite so fast as he goes, and when he saw me he stopped for a word.

"'You look very pretty this morning, Bun Rabbit,' he said, in his jolly way; 'I think the babies would love to have you to play with.'

"'I don't doubt it, your honor,' I answered; 'but they 'd soon kill me with handling, even if they did not scare me to death; for babies are very rough with their playthings.'

"'That is true,' replied Santa Claus; 'and yet you are so soft and pretty it is a pity the babies can't have you. Still, as they would abuse a live rabbit I think I shall make them some toy rabbits, which they cannot hurt; so if you will jump into my sleigh with me and ride home to my castle for a few days, I 'll see if I can't make some toy rabbits just like you."

"Of course I consented, for we all like to please old Santa, and a minute later I had jumped into the sleigh beside him and we were dashing away at full speed toward his castle. I enjoyed the ride very much, but I enjoyed the castle far more; for it was one of the loveliest places you could imagine. It stood on the top of a high mountain and is built of gold and silver bricks, and the windows are pure diamond crystals. The rooms are big and high, and there is a soft carpet upon every floor and many strange things scattered around to amuse one. Santa Claus lives there all alone, except for old Mother Hubbard, who cooks the meals for him; and her cupboard is never bare now, I can promise you! At the top of the castle there is one big room, and that is Santa's work-shop, where he makes the toys. On one side is his work-bench, with plenty of saws and hammers and jack-knives; and on another side is the paint-bench, with paints of every color and brushes of every size and shape. And in other places are great shelves, where the toys are put to dry and keep new and bright until Christmas comes and it is time to load them all into his sleigh.

"After Mother Hubbard had given me a good dinner, and I had eaten some of the most delicious clover I have ever tasted, Santa took me up into his work-room and sat me upon the table.

"'If I can only make rabbits half as nice as you are,' he said, 'the little ones will be delighted.' Then he lit a big pipe and began to smoke, and soon he took a roll of soft fur from a shelf in a corner and commenced to cut it out in the shape of a rabbit. He smoked and whistled all the time he was working, and he talked to me in such a jolly way that I sat perfectly still and allowed him to measure my ears and my legs so that he could cut the fur into the proper form.

"'Why, I 've got your nose too long, Bunny,' he said once; and so he snipped a little off the fur he was cutting, so that the toy rabbit's nose should be like mine. And again he said, 'Good gracious! the ears are too short entirely!' So he had to get a needle and thread and sew on more fur to the ears, so that they might be the right size. But after a time it was all finished, and then he stuffed the fur full of sawdust and sewed it up neatly; after which he put in some glass eyes that made the toy rabbit look wonderfully life-like. When it was all done he put it on the table beside me, and at first I did n't know whether I was the live rabbit or the toy rabbit, we were so much alike.

"'It's a very good job,' said Santa, nodding his head at us pleasantly; 'and I shall have to make a lot of these rabbits, for the little children are sure to be greatly pleased with them.'

"So he immediately began to make another, and this time he cut the fur just the right size, so that it was even better than the first rabbit.

"'I must put a squeak in it,' said Santa.

"So he took a box of squeaks from a shelf and put one into the rabbit before he sewed it up. When it was all finished he pressed the toy rabbit with his thumb, and it squeaked so naturally that I jumped off the table, fearing at first the new rabbit was alive. Old Santa laughed merrily at this, and I soon recovered from my fright and was pleased to think the babies were to have such pretty playthings.

"'After this,' said Santa Claus, 'I can make rabbits without having you for a pattern; but if you like you may stay a few days longer in my castle and amuse yourself."

"I thanked him and decided to stay. So for several days I watched him making all kinds of toys, and I wondered to see how quickly he made them, and how many new things he invented.

"'I almost wish I was a child,' I said to him one day, 'for then I too could have playthings.'

73

"'Ah, you can run about all day, in summer and in winter, and enjoy yourself in your own way,' said Santa; 'but the poor little children are obliged to stay in the house in the winter and on rainy days in the summer, and then they must have toys to amuse them and keep them contented.'"

"I knew this was true, so I only said, admiringly, 'You must be the quickest and the best workman in all the world, Santa.'

"'I suppose I am,' he answered; 'but then, you see, I have been making toys for hundreds of years, and I make so many it is no wonder I am skillful. And now, if you are ready to go home, I 'll hitch up the reindeer and take you back again.'

"'Oh, no,' said I, 'I prefer to run by myself, for I can easily find the way and I want to see the country.'

"'If that is the case,' replied Santa, 'I must give you a magic collar to wear, so that you will come to no harm.'

"So, after Mother Hubbard had given me a good meal of turnips and sliced cabbage, Santa Claus put the magic collar around my neck and I started for home. I took my time on the journey, for I knew nothing could harm me, and I saw a good many strange sights before I got back to this place again."

"But what became of the magic collar?" asked Dorothy, who had listened with breathless interest to the rabbit's story.

"After I got home," replied the rabbit, "the collar disappeared from around my neck, and I knew Santa had called it back to himself again. He did not give it to me, you see; he merely let me take it on my journey to protect me. The next Christmas, when I watched by the road-side to see Santa, I was pleased to notice a great many of the toy rabbits sticking out of the loaded sleigh. The babies must have liked them, too, for every year since I have seen them amongst the toys.

"Santa never forgets me, and every time he passes he calls out, in his jolly voice,

"'A merry Christmas to you, Bun Rabbit! The babies still love you dearly.'"

The Rabbit paused, and Dorothy was just about to ask another question when Bunny raised his head and seemed to hear something coming.

"What is it?" enquired the girl.

"It's the farmer's big shepherd dog," answered the Rabbit, "and I must be going before he sees me, or I shall shall [both shalls in original] have to run for my life. So good bye, Dorothy; I hope we shall meet again, and then I will gladly tell you more of my adventures."

The next instant he had sprung into the wood, and all that Dorothy could see of him was a gray streak darting in and out amongst the trees.

The Christmas Cuckoo

By Frances Browne (Adapted)

Once upon a time there stood in the midst of a bleak moor, in the North Country, a certain village. All its inhabitants were poor, for their fields were barren, and they had little trade; but the poorest of them all were two brothers called Scrub and Spare, who followed the cobbler's craft. Their hut was built of clay and wattles. The door was low and always open, for there was no window. The roof did not entirely keep out the rain and the only thing comfortable was a wide fireplace, for which the brothers could never find wood enough to make sufficient fire. There they worked in most brotherly friendship, though with little encouragement.

On one unlucky day a new cobbler arrived in the village. He had lived in the capital city of the kingdom and, by his own account, cobbled for the queen and the princesses. His awls were sharp, his lasts were new; he set up his stall in a neat cottage with two windows. The villagers soon found out that one patch of his would outwear two of the brothers'. In short, all the mending left Scrub and Spare, and went to the new cobbler.

The season had been wet and cold, their barley did not ripen well, and the cabbages never half- closed in the garden. So the brothers were poor that winter, and when Christmas came they had nothing to feast on but a barley loaf and a piece of rusty bacon. Worse than that, the snow was very deep and they could get no firewood.

Their hut stood at the end of the village; beyond it spread the bleak moor, now all white and silent. But that moor had once been a forest; great roots of old trees were still to be found in it, loosened from the soil and laid bare by the winds and rains. One of these, a rough, gnarled log, lay hard by their door, the half of it above the snow, and Spare said to his brother: --

"Shall we sit here cold on Christmas while the great root lies yonder? Let us chop it up for firewood, the work will make us warm."

"No," said Scrub, "it's not right to chop wood on Christmas; besides, that root is too hard to be broken with any hatchet."

"Hard or not, we must have a fire," replied Spare. "Come, brother, help me in with it. Poor as we are there is nobody in the village will have such a yule log as ours."

Scrub liked a little grandeur, and, in hopes of having a fine yule log, both brothers strained and strove with all their might till, between pulling and pushing, the great old root was safe on the hearth, and beginning to crackle and blaze with the red embers.

In high glee the cobblers sat down to their bread and bacon. The door was shut, for there was nothing but cold moonlight and snow outside; but the hut, strewn with fir boughs and ornamented with holly, looked cheerful as the ruddy blaze flared up and rejoiced their hearts.

Then suddenly from out the blazing root they heard: "Cuckoo! cuckoo!" as plain as ever the spring-bird's voice came over the moor on a May morning.

"What is that?" said Scrub, terribly frightened; "it is something bad!"

"Maybe not," said Spare.

And out of the deep hole at the side of the root, which the fire had not reached, flew a large, gray cuckoo, and lit on the table before them. Much as the cobblers had been surprised, they were still more so when it said: --

"Good gentlemen, what season is this?"

"It's Christmas," said Spare.

"Then a merry Christmas to you!" said the cuckoo. "I went to sleep in the hollow of that old root one evening last summer, and never woke till the heat of your fire made me think it was summer again. But now since you have burned my lodging, let me stay in your hut till the spring comes round, -- I only want a hole to sleep in, and when I go on my travels next summer be assured I will bring you some present for your trouble."

"Stay and welcome," said Spare, while Scrub sat wondering if it were something bad or not.

"I'll make you a good warm hole in the thatch," said Spare. "But you must be hungry after that long sleep, -- here is a slice of barley bread. Come help us to keep Christmas!"

The cuckoo ate up the slice, drank water from a brown jug, and flew into a snug hole which Spare scooped for it in the thatch of the hut.

Scrub said he was afraid it would n't be lucky; but as it slept on and the days passed he forgot his fears.

So the snow melted, the heavy rains came, the cold grew less, the days lengthened, and one sunny morning the brothers were awakened by the cuckoo shouting its own cry to let them know the spring had come.

"Now I'm going on my travels," said the bird, "over the world to tell men of the spring. There is no country where trees bud, or flowers bloom, that I will not cry in before the year goes round. Give me another slice of barley bread to help me on my journey, and tell me what present I shall bring you at the twelvemonth's end."

Scrub would have been angry with his brother for cutting so large a slice, their store of barley being low, but his mind was occupied with what present it would be most prudent to ask for.

"There are two trees hard by the well that lies at the world's end," said the cuckoo; "one of them is called the golden tree, for its leaves are all of beaten gold. Every winter they fall into the well with a sound like scattered coin, and I know not what becomes of them. As for the other, it is always green like a laurel. Some call it the wise, and some the merry, tree. Its leaves never fall, but they that get one of them keep a blithe heart in spite of all misfortunes, and can make themselves as merry in a hut as in a palace."

"Good master cuckoo, bring me a leaf off that tree!" cried Spare.

"Now, brother, don't be a fool!" said Scrub; "think of the leaves of beaten gold! Dear master cuckoo, bring me one of them!"

Before another word could be spoken the cuckoo had flown out of the open door, and was shouting its spring cry over moor and meadow.

The brothers were poorer than ever that year. Nobody would send them a single shoe to mend, and Scrub and Spare would have left the village but for their barley-field and their cabbage- garden. They sowed their barley, planted their cabbage, and, now that their trade was gone, worked in the rich villagers' fields to make out a scanty living.

So the seasons came and passed; spring, summer, harvest, and winter followed each other as they have done from the beginning. At the end of the latter Scrub and Spare had grown so poor and ragged that their old neighbors forgot to invite them to wedding feasts or merrymakings, and the brothers thought the cuckoo had forgotten them, too, when at daybreak on the first of April they heard a hard beak knocking at their door, and a voice crying: --

"Cuckoo! cuckoo! Let me in with my presents!"

Spare ran to open the door, and in came the cuckoo, carrying on one side of its bill a golden leaf larger than that of any tree in the North Country; and in the other side of its bill, one like that of the common laurel, only it had a fresher green.

"Here," it said, giving the gold to Scrub and the green to Spare, "it is a long carriage from the world's end. Give me a slice of barley bread, for I must tell the North Country that the spring has come."

Scrub did not grudge the thickness of that slice, though it was cut from their last loaf. So much gold had never been in the cobbler's hands before, and he could not help exulting over his brother.

"See the wisdom of my choice," he said, holding up the large leaf of gold. "As for yours, as good might be plucked from any hedge, I wonder a sensible bird would carry the like so far."

"Good master cobbler," cried the cuckoo, finishing its slice, "your conclusions are more hasty than courteous. If your brother is disappointed this time, I go on the same journey every year, and for your hospitable entertainment will think it no trouble to bring each of you whichever leaf you desire."

"Darling cuckoo," cried Scrub, "bring me a golden one."

And Spare, looking up from the green leaf on which he gazed as though it were a crown-jewel, said: --

"Be sure to bring me one from the merry tree."

And away flew the cuckoo.

"This is the feast of All Fools, and it ought to be your birthday," said Scrub. "Did ever man fling away such an opportunity of getting rich? Much good your merry leaves will do in the midst of rags and poverty!"

But Spare laughed at him, and answered with quaint old proverbs concerning the cares that come with gold, till Scrub, at length getting angry, vowed his brother was not fit to live with a respectable man; and taking his lasts, his awls, and his golden leaf, he left the wattle hut, and went to tell the villagers.

They were astonished at the folly of Spare, and charmed with Scrub's good sense, particularly when he showed them the golden leaf, and told that the cuckoo would bring him one every spring.

The new cobbler immediately took him into partnership; the greatest people sent him their shoes to mend. Fairfeather, a beautiful village maiden, smiled graciously upon him; and in the course of that summer they were married, with a grand wedding feast, at which the whole village danced except Spare, who was not invited, because the bride could not bear his low-mindedness, and his brother thought him a disgrace to the family.

As for Scrub he established himself with Fairfeather in a cottage close by that of the new cobbler, and quite as fine. There he mended shoes to everybody's satisfaction, had a scarlet coat and a fat goose for dinner on holidays. Fairfeather, too, had a crimson gown, and fine blue ribbons; but neither she nor Scrub was content, for to buy this grandeur the golden leaf had to be broken and parted With piece by piece, so the last morsel was gone before the cuckoo came with another.

Spare lived on in the old hut, and worked in the cabbage-garden. [Scrub had got the barley-field because he was the elder.] Every day his coat grew more ragged, and the hut more weather- beaten; but people remarked that he never looked sad or sour. And the wonder was that, from the time any one began to keep his company, he or she grew kinder, happier, and content.

Every first of April the cuckoo came tapping at their doors with the golden leaf for Scrub, and the green for Spare. Fairfeather would have entertained it nobly with wheaten bread and honey, for she had some notion of persuading it to bring two golden leaves instead of one; but the cuckoo flew away to eat barley bread with Spare, saying it was not fit company for fine people, and liked the old hut where it slept so snugly from Christmas till spring.

Scrub spent the golden leaves, and remained always discontented; and Spare kept the merry ones.

I do not know how many years passed in this manner, when a certain great lord, who owned that village, came to the neighborhood. His castle stood on the moor. It was ancient and strong, with high towers and a deep moat. All the country as far as one could see from the highest turret belonged to its lord; but he had not been there for twenty years, and would not have come then only he was melancholy. And there he lived in a very bad temper. The servants said nothing would please him, and the villagers put on their worst clothes lest he should raise their rents.

But one day in the harvest-time His Lordship chanced to meet Spare gathering water-cresses at a meadow stream, and fell into talk with the cobbler. How it was nobody could tell, but from that hour the great lord cast away his melancholy. He forgot all his woes, and went about with a noble train, hunting, fishing, and making merry in his hall, where all travelers were entertained, and all the poor were welcome.

This strange story spread through the North Country, and great company came to the cobbler's hut, -- rich men who had lost their money, poor men who had lost their friends, beauties who had grown old, wits who had gone out of fashion, -- all came to talk with Spare, and, whatever their troubles had been, all went home merry.

The rich gave him presents, the poor gave him thanks. Spare's coat ceased to be ragged, he had bacon with his cabbage, and the villagers began to think there was some sense in him.

By this time his fame had reached the capital city, and even the court. There were a great many discontented people there; and the king had lately fallen into ill humor because a neighboring princess, with seven islands for her dowry, would not marry his eldest son.

So a royal messenger was sent to Spare, with a velvet mantle, a diamond ring, and a command that he should repair to court immediately.

"To-morrow is the first of April," said Spare, "and I will go with you two hours after sunrise."

The messenger lodged all night at the castle, and the cuckoo came at sunrise with the merry leaf.

"Court is a fine place," it said, when the cobbler told it he was going, "but I cannot come there; they would lay snares and catch me; so be careful of the leaves I have brought you, and give me a farewell slice of barley bread."

Spare was sorry to part with the cuckoo, little as he had of its company, but he gave it a slice which would have broken Scrub's heart in former times, it was so thick and large. And having sewed up the leaves in the lining of his leather doublet, he set out with the messenger on his way to court.

His coming caused great surprise there. Everybody wondered what the king could see in such a common-looking man; but scarcely had His Majesty conversed with him half an hour, when the princess and her seven islands were forgotten and orders given that a feast for all comers should be spread in the banquet hall.

The princes of the blood, the great lords and ladies, the ministers of state, after that discoursed with Spare, and the more they talked the lighter grew their hearts, so that such changes had never been seen at court.

The lords forgot their spites and the ladies their envies, the princes and ministers made friends among themselves, and the judges showed no favor.

As for Spare, he had a chamber assigned him in the palace, and a seat at the king's table. One sent him rich robes, and another costly jewels; but in the midst of all his grandeur he still wore the leathern doublet, and continued to live at the king's court, happy and honored, and making all others merry and content.

Christmas Greetings from a Fairy to a Child

By Lewis Carroll

Lady dear, if Fairies may
For a moment lay aside
Cunning tricks and elfish play,
'Tis at happy Christmas-tide.

We have heard the children say—
Gentle children, whom we love—
Long ago, on Christmas Day,
Came a message from above.

Still, as Christmas-tide comes round,
They remember it again—
Echo still the joyful sound
"Peace on earth, good-will to men!"

Yet the hearts must childlike be
Where such heavenly guests abide:
Unto children, in their glee,
All the year is Christmas-tide!

Thus, forgetting tricks and play
For a moment, Lady dear,
We would wish you, if we may,
Merry Christmas, glad New Year!

The Christmas Fairy of Strasburg: A German Folk-Tale

By J. Stirling Coyne (Adapted)

Once, long ago, there lived near the ancient city of Strasburg, on the river Rhine, a young and handsome count, whose name was Otto. As the years flew by he remained unwed, and never so much as cast a glance at the fair maidens of the country round; for this reason people began to call him "Stone-Heart."

It chanced that Count Otto, on one Christmas Eve, ordered that a great hunt should take place in the forest surrounding his castle. He and his guests and his many retainers rode forth, and the chase became more and more exciting. It led through thickets, and over pathless tracts of forest, until at length Count Otto found himself separated from his companions.

He rode on by himself until he came to a spring of clear, bubbling water, known to the people around as the "Fairy Well." Here Count Otto dismounted. He bent over the spring and began to lave his hands in the sparkling tide, but to his wonder he found that though the weather was cold and frosty, the water was warm and delightfully caressing. He felt a glow of joy pass through his veins, and, as he plunged his hands deeper, he fancied that his right hand was grasped by another, soft and small, which gently slipped from his finger the gold ring he always wore. And, lo! when he drew out his hand, the gold ring was gone.

Full of wonder at this mysterious event, the count mounted his horse and returned to his castle, resolving in his mind that the very next day he would have the Fairy Well emptied by his servants.

He retired to his room, and, throwing himself just as he was upon his couch, tried to sleep; but the strangeness of the adventure kept him restless and wakeful.

Suddenly he heard the hoarse baying of the watch-hounds in the courtyard, and then the creaking of the drawbridge, as though it were being lowered. Then came to his ear the patter of many small feet on the stone staircase, and next he heard indistinctly the sound of light footsteps in the chamber adjoining his own.

Count Otto sprang from his couch, and as he did so there sounded a strain of delicious music, and the door of his chamber was flung open. Hurrying into the next room, he found himself in the midst of numberless Fairy beings, clad in gay and sparkling robes. They paid no heed to him, but began to dance, and laugh, and sing, to the sound of mysterious music.

In the center of the apartment stood a splendid Christmas Tree, the first ever seen in that country. Instead of toys and candles there hung on its lighted boughs diamond stars, pearl necklaces, bracelets of gold ornamented with colored jewels, aigrettes of rubies and sapphires, silken belts embroidered with Oriental pearls, and daggers mounted in gold and studded with the rarest gems. The whole tree swayed, sparkled, and glittered in the radiance of its many lights.

Count Otto stood speechless, gazing at all this wonder, when suddenly the Fairies stopped dancing and fell back, to make room for a lady of dazzling beauty who came slowly toward him.

She wore on her raven-black tresses a golden diadem set with jewels. Her hair flowed down upon a robe of rosy satin and creamy velvet. She stretched out two small, white hands to the count and addressed him in sweet, alluring tones:—

"Dear Count Otto," said she, "I come to return your Christmas visit. I am Ernestine, the Queen of the Fairies. I bring you something you lost in the Fairy Well."

And as she spoke she drew from her bosom a golden casket, set with diamonds, and placed it in his hands. He opened it eagerly and found within his lost gold ring.

Carried away by the wonder of it all, and overcome by an irresistible impulse, the count pressed the Fairy Ernestine to his heart, while she, holding him by the hand, drew him into the magic mazes of the dance. The mysterious music floated through the room, and the rest of that Fairy company circled and whirled around the Fairy Queen and Count Otto, and then gradually dissolved into a mist of many colors, leaving the count and his beautiful guest alone.

Then the young man, forgetting all his former coldness toward the maidens of the country round about, fell on his knees before the Fairy and besought her to become his bride. At last she consented on the condition that he should never speak the word "death" in her presence.

The next day the wedding of Count Otto and Ernestine, Queen of the Fairies, was celebrated with great pomp and magnificence, and the two continued to live happily for many years.

Now it happened on a time, that the count and his Fairy wife were to hunt in the forest around the castle. The horses were saddled and bridled, and standing at the door, the company waited, and the count paced the hall in great impatience; but still the Fairy Ernestine tarried long in her chamber. At length she appeared at the door of the hall, and the count addressed her in anger.

"You have kept us waiting so long," he cried, "that you would make a good messenger to send for Death!"

Scarcely had he spoken the forbidden and fatal word, when the Fairy, uttering a wild cry, vanished from his sight. In vain Count Otto, overwhelmed with grief and remorse, searched the castle and the Fairy Well, no trace could he find of his beautiful, lost wife but the imprint of her delicate hand set in the stone arch above the castle gate.

Years passed by, and the Fairy Ernestine did not return. The count continued to grieve. Every Christmas Eve he set up a lighted tree in the room where he had first met the Fairy, hoping in vain that she would return to him.

Time passed and the count died. The castle fell into ruins. But to this day may be seen above the massive gate, deeply sunken in the stone arch, the impress of a small and delicate hand.

And such, say the good folk of Strasburg, was the origin of the Christmas Tree.

A Christmas Tree

By Charles Dickens

I have been looking on, this evening, at a merry company of children assembled round that pretty German toy, a Christmas Tree. The tree was planted in the middle of a great round table, and towered high above their heads. It was brilliantly lighted by a multitude of little tapers; and everywhere sparkled and glittered with bright objects. There were rosy-cheeked dolls, hiding behind the green leaves; and there were real watches (with movable hands, at least, and an endless capacity of being wound up) dangling from innumerable twigs; there were French-polished tables, chairs, bedsteads, wardrobes, eight-day clocks, and various other articles of domestic furniture (wonderfully made, in tin, at Wolverhampton), perched among the boughs, as if in preparation for some fairy housekeeping; there were jolly, broad-faced little men, much more agreeable in appearance than many real men-- and no wonder, for their heads took off, and showed them to be full of sugar-plums; there were fiddles and drums; there were tambourines, books, work-boxes, paint-boxes, sweetmeat-boxes, peep-show boxes, and all kinds of boxes; there were trinkets for the elder girls, far brighter than any grown-up gold and jewels; there were baskets and pincushions in all devices; there were guns, swords, and banners; there were witches standing in enchanted rings of pasteboard, to tell fortunes; there were teetotums, humming-tops, needle-cases, pen-wipers, smelling-bottles, conversation-cards, bouquet-holders; real fruit, made artificially dazzling with gold leaf; imitation apples, pears, and walnuts, crammed with surprises; in short, as a pretty child, before me, delightedly whispered to another pretty child, her bosom friend, "There was everything, and more." This motley collection of odd objects, clustering on the tree like magic fruit, and flashing back the bright looks directed towards it from every side--some of the diamond-eyes admiring it were hardly on a level with the table, and a few were languishing in timid wonder on the bosoms of pretty mothers, aunts, and nurses--made a lively realisation of the fancies of childhood; and set me thinking how all the trees that grow and all the things that come into existence on the earth, have their wild adornments at that well-remembered time.

Being now at home again, and alone, the only person in the house awake, my thoughts are drawn back, by a fascination which I do not care to resist, to my own childhood. I begin to consider, what do we all remember best upon the branches of the Christmas Tree of our own young Christmas days, by which we climbed to real life.

Straight, in the middle of the room, cramped in the freedom of its growth by no encircling walls or soon-reached ceiling, a shadowy tree arises; and, looking up into the dreamy brightness of its top-- for I observe in this tree the singular property that it appears to grow downward towards the earth--I look into my youngest Christmas recollections!

All toys at first, I find. Up yonder, among the green holly and red berries, is the Tumbler with his hands in his pockets, who wouldn't lie down, but whenever he was put upon the floor, persisted in rolling his fat body about, until he rolled himself still, and brought those lobster eyes of his to bear upon me--when I affected to laugh very much, but in my heart of hearts was extremely doubtful of him. Close beside him is that infernal snuff-box, out of which there sprang a demoniacal Counsellor in a black gown, with an obnoxious head of hair, and a red cloth mouth, wide open, who was not to be endured on any terms, but could not be put away either; for he used suddenly, in a highly magnified state, to fly out of Mammoth Snuff-boxes in dreams, when least expected. Nor is the frog with cobbler's wax on his tail, far off; for there was no knowing where he wouldn't jump; and when he flew over the candle, and came upon one's hand with that spotted back--red on a green ground--he was horrible. The cardboard lady in a blue-silk skirt, who was stood up against the candlestick to dance, and whom I see on the same branch, was milder, and was beautiful; but I can't say as much

90

for the larger cardboard man, who used to be hung against the wall and pulled by a string; there was a sinister expression in that nose of his; and when he got his legs round his neck (which he very often did), he was ghastly, and not a creature to be alone with.

When did that dreadful Mask first look at me? Who put it on, and why was I so frightened that the sight of it is an era in my life? It is not a hideous visage in itself; it is even meant to be droll, why then were its stolid features so intolerable? Surely not because it hid the wearer's face. An apron would have done as much; and though I should have preferred even the apron away, it would not have been absolutely insupportable, like the mask. Was it the immovability of the mask? The doll's face was immovable, but I was not afraid of HER. Perhaps that fixed and set change coming over a real face, infused into my quickened heart some remote suggestion and dread of the universal change that is to come on every face, and make it still? Nothing reconciled me to it. No drummers, from whom proceeded a melancholy chirping on the turning of a handle; no regiment of soldiers, with a mute band, taken out of a box, and fitted, one by one, upon a stiff and lazy little set of lazy-tongs; no old woman, made of wires and a brown-paper composition, cutting up a pie for two small children; could give me a permanent comfort, for a long time. Nor was it any satisfaction to be shown the Mask, and see that it was made of paper, or to have it locked up and be assured that no one wore it. The mere recollection of that fixed face, the mere knowledge of its existence anywhere, was sufficient to awake me in the night all perspiration and horror, with, "O I know it's coming! O the mask!"

I never wondered what the dear old donkey with the panniers--there he is! was made of, then! His hide was real to the touch, I recollect. And the great black horse with the round red spots all over him--the horse that I could even get upon--I never wondered what had brought him to that strange condition, or thought that such a horse was not commonly seen at Newmarket. The four horses of no colour, next to him, that went into the waggon of cheeses, and could be taken out and stabled under the piano, appear to have bits of fur-tippet for their tails, and other bits for their manes, and to stand on pegs instead of legs, but it was not so when they were brought home for a Christmas present. They were all right, then; neither was their harness unceremoniously nailed into their chests, as appears to be the case now. The tinkling works of the music-cart, I DID find out, to be made of quill tooth-picks and wire; and I always thought that little tumbler in his shirt sleeves, perpetually swarming up one side of a wooden frame, and coming down, head foremost, on the other, rather a weak-minded person--though good-natured; but the Jacob's Ladder, next him, made of little squares of red wood, that went flapping and clattering over one another, each developing a different picture, and the whole enlivened by small bells, was a mighty marvel and a great delight.

Ah! The Doll's house!--of which I was not proprietor, but where I visited. I don't admire the Houses of Parliament half so much as that stone-fronted mansion with real glass windows, and door-steps, and a real balcony--greener than I ever see now, except at watering places; and even they afford but a poor imitation. And though it DID open all at once, the entire house-front (which was a blow, I admit, as cancelling the fiction of a staircase), it was but to shut it up again, and I could believe. Even open, there were three distinct rooms in it: a sitting-room and bed-room, elegantly furnished, and best of all, a kitchen, with uncommonly soft fire- irons, a plentiful assortment of diminutive utensils--oh, the warming-pan!--and a tin man-cook in profile, who was always going to fry two fish. What Barmecide justice have I done to the noble feasts wherein the set of wooden platters figured, each with its own peculiar delicacy, as a ham or turkey, glued tight on to it, and garnished with something green, which I recollect as moss! Could all the Temperance Societies of these later days, united, give me such a tea-drinking as I have had through the means of yonder little set of blue crockery, which really would hold liquid (it ran out of the small wooden cask, I recollect, and tasted of matches), and which made tea, nectar.

And if the two legs of the ineffectual little sugar-tongs did tumble over one another, and want purpose, like Punch's hands, what does it matter? And if I did once shriek out, as a poisoned child, and strike the fashionable company with consternation, by reason of having drunk a little teaspoon, inadvertently dissolved in too hot tea, I was never the worse for it, except by a powder!

Upon the next branches of the tree, lower down, hard by the green roller and miniature gardening-tools, how thick the books begin to hang. Thin books, in themselves, at first, but many of them, and with deliciously smooth covers of bright red or green. What fat black letters to begin with! "A was an archer, and shot at a frog." Of course he was. He was an apple-pie also, and there he is! He was a good many things in his time, was A, and so were most of his friends, except X, who had so little versatility, that I never knew him to get beyond Xerxes or Xantippe--like Y, who was always confined to a Yacht or a Yew Tree; and Z condemned for ever to be a Zebra or a Zany. But, now, the very tree itself changes, and becomes a bean-stalk--the marvellous bean-stalk up which Jack climbed to the Giant's house! And now, those dreadfully interesting, double-headed giants, with their clubs over their shoulders, begin to stride along the boughs in a perfect throng, dragging knights and ladies home for dinner by the hair of their heads. And Jack--how noble, with his sword of sharpness, and his shoes of swiftness! Again those old meditations come upon me as I gaze up at him; and I debate within myself whether there was more than one Jack (which I am loth to believe possible), or only one genuine original admirable Jack, who achieved all the recorded exploits.

Good for Christmas-time is the ruddy colour of the cloak, in which-- the tree making a forest of itself for her to trip through, with her basket- -Little Red Riding-Hood comes to me one Christmas Eve to give me information of the cruelty and treachery of that dissembling Wolf who ate her grandmother, without making any impression on his appetite, and then ate her, after making that ferocious joke about his teeth. She was my first love. I felt that if I could have married Little Red Riding-Hood, I should have known perfect bliss. But, it was not to be; and there was nothing for it but to look out the Wolf in the Noah's Ark there, and put him late in the procession on the table, as a monster who was to be degraded. O the wonderful Noah's Ark! It was not found seaworthy when put in a washing-tub, and the animals were crammed in at the roof, and needed to have their legs well shaken down before they could be got in, even there- -and then, ten to one but they began to tumble out at the door, which was but imperfectly fastened with a wire latch--but what was THAT against it! Consider the noble fly, a size or two smaller than the elephant: the lady-bird, the butterfly--all triumphs of art! Consider the goose, whose feet were so small, and whose balance was so indifferent, that he usually tumbled forward, and knocked down all the animal creation. Consider Noah and his family, like idiotic tobacco-stoppers; and how the leopard stuck to warm little fingers; and how the tails of the larger animals used gradually to resolve themselves into frayed bits of string!

Hush! Again a forest, and somebody up in a tree--not Robin Hood, not Valentine, not the Yellow Dwarf (I have passed him and all Mother Bunch's wonders, without mention), but an Eastern King with a glittering scimitar and turban. By Allah! two Eastern Kings, for I see another, looking over his shoulder! Down upon the grass, at the tree's foot, lies the full length of a coal-black Giant, stretched asleep, with his head in a lady's lap; and near them is a glass box, fastened with four locks of shining steel, in which he keeps the lady prisoner when he is awake. I see the four keys at his girdle now. The lady makes signs to the two kings in the tree, who softly descend. It is the setting-in of the bright Arabian Nights.

Oh, now all common things become uncommon and enchanted to me. All lamps are wonderful; all rings are talismans. Common flower-pots are full of treasure, with a little earth scattered on the top; trees are for Ali Baba to hide in; beef-steaks are to throw down into the Valley of

Diamonds, that the precious stones may stick to them, and be carried by the eagles to their nests, whence the traders, with loud cries, will scare them. Tarts are made, according to the recipe of the Vizier's son of Bussorah, who turned pastrycook after he was set down in his drawers at the gate of Damascus; cobblers are all Mustaphas, and in the habit of sewing up people cut into four pieces, to whom they are taken blind-fold.

Any iron ring let into stone is the entrance to a cave which only waits for the magician, and the little fire, and the necromancy, that will make the earth shake. All the dates imported come from the same tree as that unlucky date, with whose shell the merchant knocked out the eye of the genie's invisible son. All olives are of the stock of that fresh fruit, concerning which the Commander of the Faithful overheard the boy conduct the fictitious trial of the fraudulent olive merchant; all apples are akin to the apple purchased (with two others) from the Sultan's gardener for three sequins, and which the tall black slave stole from the child. All dogs are associated with the dog, really a transformed man, who jumped upon the baker's counter, and put his paw on the piece of bad money. All rice recalls the rice which the awful lady, who was a ghoule, could only peck by grains, because of her nightly feasts in the burial-place. My very rocking-horse,--there he is, with his nostrils turned completely inside-out, indicative of Blood!--should have a peg in his neck, by virtue thereof to fly away with me, as the wooden horse did with the Prince of Persia, in the sight of all his father's Court.

Yes, on every object that I recognise among those upper branches of my Christmas Tree, I see this fairy light! When I wake in bed, at daybreak, on the cold, dark, winter mornings, the white snow dimly beheld, outside, through the frost on the window-pane, I hear Dinarzade. "Sister, sister, if you are yet awake, I pray you finish the history of the Young King of the Black Islands." Scheherazade replies, "If my lord the Sultan will suffer me to live another day, sister, I will not only finish that, but tell you a more wonderful story yet." Then, the gracious Sultan goes out, giving no orders for the execution, and we all three breathe again.

At this height of my tree I begin to see, cowering among the leaves--it may be born of turkey, or of pudding, or mince pie, or of these many fancies, jumbled with Robinson Crusoe on his desert island, Philip Quarll among the monkeys, Sandford and Merton with Mr. Barlow, Mother Bunch, and the Mask--or it may be the result of indigestion, assisted by imagination and over-doctoring--a prodigious nightmare. It is so exceedingly indistinct, that I don't know why it's frightful--but I know it is. I can only make out that it is an immense array of shapeless things, which appear to be planted on a vast exaggeration of the lazy-tongs that used to bear the toy soldiers, and to be slowly coming close to my eyes, and receding to an immeasurable distance. When it comes closest, it is worse. In connection with it I descry remembrances of winter nights incredibly long; of being sent early to bed, as a punishment for some small offence, and waking in two hours, with a sensation of having been asleep two nights; of the laden hopelessness of morning ever dawning; and the oppression of a weight of remorse.

And now, I see a wonderful row of little lights rise smoothly out of the ground, before a vast green curtain. Now, a bell rings--a magic bell, which still sounds in my ears unlike all other bells--and music plays, amidst a buzz of voices, and a fragrant smell of orange-peel and oil. Anon, the magic bell commands the music to cease, and the great green curtain rolls itself up majestically, and The Play begins! The devoted dog of Montargis avenges the death of his master, foully murdered in the Forest of Bondy; and a humorous Peasant with a red nose and a very little hat, whom I take from this hour forth to my bosom as a friend (I think he was a Waiter or an Hostler at a village Inn, but many years have passed since he and I have met), remarks that the sassigassity of that dog is indeed surprising; and evermore this jocular conceit will live in my remembrance fresh and unfading, overtopping all possible jokes, unto the end of time. Or now, I learn with bitter tears how poor Jane

Shore, dressed all in white, and with her brown hair hanging down, went starving through the streets; or how George Barnwell killed the worthiest uncle that ever man had, and was afterwards so sorry for it that he ought to have been let off. Comes swift to comfort me, the Pantomime--stupendous Phenomenon!--when clowns are shot from loaded mortars into the great chandelier, bright constellation that it is; when Harlequins, covered all over with scales of pure gold, twist and sparkle, like amazing fish; when Pantaloon (whom I deem it no irreverence to compare in my own mind to my grandfather) puts red-hot pokers in his pocket, and cries "Here's somebody coming!" or taxes the Clown with petty larceny, by saying, "Now, I sawed you do it!" when Everything is capable, with the greatest ease, of being changed into Anything; and "Nothing is, but thinking makes it so." Now, too, I perceive my first experience of the dreary sensation-- often to return in after-life--of being unable, next day, to get back to the dull, settled world; of wanting to live for ever in the bright atmosphere I have quitted; of doting on the little Fairy, with the wand like a celestial Barber's Pole, and pining for a Fairy immortality along with her. Ah, she comes back, in many shapes, as my eye wanders down the branches of my Christmas Tree, and goes as often, and has never yet stayed by me!

Out of this delight springs the toy-theatre,--there it is, with its familiar proscenium, and ladies in feathers, in the boxes!--and all its attendant occupation with paste and glue, and gum, and water colours, in the getting-up of The Miller and his Men, and Elizabeth, or the Exile of Siberia. In spite of a few besetting accidents and failures (particularly an unreasonable disposition in the respectable Kelmar, and some others, to become faint in the legs, and double up, at exciting points of the drama), a teeming world of fancies so suggestive and all-embracing, that, far below it on my Christmas Tree, I see dark, dirty, real Theatres in the day-time, adorned with these associations as with the freshest garlands of the rarest flowers, and charming me yet.

But hark! The Waits are playing, and they break my childish sleep!

What images do I associate with the Christmas music as I see them set forth on the Christmas Tree? Known before all the others, keeping far apart from all the others, they gather round my little bed. An angel, speaking to a group of shepherds in a field; some travellers, with eyes uplifted, following a star; a baby in a manger; a child in a spacious temple, talking with grave men; a solemn figure, with a mild and beautiful face, raising a dead girl by the hand; again, near a city gate, calling back the son of a widow, on his bier, to life; a crowd of people looking through the opened roof of a chamber where he sits, and letting down a sick person on a bed, with ropes; the same, in a tempest, walking on the water to a ship; again, on a sea-shore, teaching a great multitude; again, with a child upon his knee, and other children round; again, restoring sight to the blind, speech to the dumb, hearing to the deaf, health to the sick, strength to the lame, knowledge to the ignorant; again, dying upon a Cross, watched by armed soldiers, a thick darkness coming on, the earth beginning to shake, and only one voice heard, "Forgive them, for they know not what they do."

Still, on the lower and maturer branches of the Tree, Christmas associations cluster thick. School-books shut up; Ovid and Virgil silenced; the Rule of Three, with its cool impertinent inquiries, long disposed of; Terence and Plautus acted no more, in an arena of huddled desks and forms, all chipped, and notched, and inked; cricket-bats, stumps, and balls, left higher up, with the smell of trodden grass and the softened noise of shouts in the evening air; the tree is still fresh, still gay. If I no more come home at Christmas-time, there will be boys and girls (thank Heaven!) while the World lasts; and they do! Yonder they dance and play upon the branches of my Tree, God bless them, merrily, and my heart dances and plays too!

And I do come home at Christmas. We all do, or we all should. We all come home, or ought to come home, for a short holiday--the longer, the better--from the great boarding-school, where we are for ever working at our arithmetical slates, to take, and give a rest. As to going a visiting, where can we not go, if we will; where have we not been, when we would; starting our fancy from our Christmas Tree!

Away into the winter prospect. There are many such upon the tree! On, by low-lying, misty grounds, through fens and fogs, up long hills, winding dark as caverns between thick plantations, almost shutting out the sparkling stars; so, out on broad heights, until we stop at last, with sudden silence, at an avenue. The gate-bell has a deep, half-awful sound in the frosty air; the gate swings open on its hinges; and, as we drive up to a great house, the glancing lights grow larger in the windows, and the opposing rows of trees seem to fall solemnly back on either side, to give us place. At intervals, all day, a frightened hare has shot across this whitened turf; or the distant clatter of a herd of deer trampling the hard frost, has, for the minute, crushed the silence too. Their watchful eyes beneath the fern may be shining now, if we could see them, like the icy dewdrops on the leaves; but they are still, and all is still. And so, the lights growing larger, and the trees falling back before us, and closing up again behind us, as if to forbid retreat, we come to the house.

There is probably a smell of roasted chestnuts and other good comfortable things all the time, for we are telling Winter Stories-- Ghost Stories, or more shame for us--round the Christmas fire; and we have never stirred, except to draw a little nearer to it. But, no matter for that. We came to the house, and it is an old house, full of great chimneys where wood is burnt on ancient dogs upon the hearth, and grim portraits (some of them with grim legends, too) lower distrustfully from the oaken panels of the walls. We are a middle-aged nobleman, and we make a generous supper with our host and hostess and their guests--it being Christmas-time, and the old house full of company--and then we go to bed. Our room is a very old room. It is hung with tapestry. We don't like the portrait of a cavalier in green, over the fireplace. There are great black beams in the ceiling, and there is a great black bedstead, supported at the foot by two great black figures, who seem to have come off a couple of tombs in the old baronial church in the park, for our particular accommodation. But, we are not a superstitious nobleman, and we don't mind. Well! we dismiss our servant, lock the door, and sit before the fire in our dressing-gown, musing about a great many things. At length we go to bed. Well! we can't sleep. We toss and tumble, and can't sleep. The embers on the hearth burn fitfully and make the room look ghostly. We can't help peeping out over the counterpane, at the two black figures and the cavalier--that wicked- looking cavalier--in green. In the flickering light they seem to advance and retire: which, though we are not by any means a superstitious nobleman, is not agreeable. Well! we get nervous-- more and more nervous. We say "This is very foolish, but we can't stand this; we'll pretend to be ill, and knock up somebody." Well! we are just going to do it, when the locked door opens, and there comes in a young woman, deadly pale, and with long fair hair, who glides to the fire, and sits down in the chair we have left there, wringing her hands. Then, we notice that her clothes are wet. Our tongue cleaves to the roof of our mouth, and we can't speak; but, we observe her accurately. Her clothes are wet; her long hair is dabbled with moist mud; she is dressed in the fashion of two hundred years ago; and she has at her girdle a bunch of rusty keys. Well! there she sits, and we can't even faint, we are in such a state about it. Presently she gets up, and tries all the locks in the room with the rusty keys, which won't fit one of them; then, she fixes her eyes on the portrait of the cavalier in green, and says, in a low, terrible voice, "The stags know it!" After that, she wrings her hands again, passes the bedside, and goes out at the door. We hurry on our dressing-gown, seize our pistols (we always travel with pistols), and are following, when we find the door locked. We turn the key, look out into the dark gallery; no one there. We wander away, and try to find our servant. Can't be done. We pace the gallery till daybreak; then return to our deserted room, fall asleep, and are awakened by our servant (nothing ever haunts him) and the shining sun. Well! we make a wretched breakfast, and all the company say we look queer. After breakfast, we go over the house with our host, and then we take him to the portrait of the cavalier in green, and then it all comes out. He was false to a young housekeeper once attached to that family, and famous for her beauty, who drowned herself in a pond, and whose body was discovered, after a long time, because the stags refused to drink of the water. Since which, it has been whispered that she traverses the house at midnight (but goes especially to that room where the cavalier in green was wont to sleep), trying the old locks with the rusty keys. Well! we tell our host of what we have seen, and a shade comes over his features, and he begs it may be hushed up; and so it is. But, it's all true; and we said so, before we died (we are dead now) to many responsible people.

There is no end to the old houses, with resounding galleries, and dismal state-bedchambers, and haunted wings shut up for many years, through which we may ramble, with an agreeable creeping up our back, and encounter any number of ghosts, but (it is worthy of remark perhaps) reducible to a very few general types and classes; for, ghosts have little originality, and "walk" in a beaten track. Thus, it comes to pass, that a certain room in a certain old hall, where a certain bad lord, baronet, knight, or gentleman, shot himself, has certain planks in the floor from which the blood WILL NOT be taken out. You may scrape and scrape, as the present owner has done, or plane and plane, as his father did, or scrub and scrub, as his grandfather did, or burn and burn with strong acids, as his great- grandfather did, but, there the blood will still be--no redder and no paler--no more and no less--always just the same. Thus, in such another house there is a haunted door, that never will keep open; or another door that never will keep shut, or a haunted sound of a spinning-wheel, or a hammer, or a footstep, or a cry, or a sigh, or a horse's tramp, or the rattling of a chain. Or else, there is a turret-clock, which, at the midnight hour, strikes thirteen when the head of the family is going to die; or a shadowy, immovable black carriage which at such a time is always seen by somebody, waiting near the great gates in the stable-yard. Or thus, it came to pass how Lady Mary went to pay a visit at a large wild house in the Scottish Highlands, and, being fatigued with her long journey, retired to bed early, and innocently said, next morning, at the breakfast-table, "How odd, to have so late a party last night, in this remote place, and not to tell me of it, before I went to bed!" Then, every one asked Lady Mary what she meant? Then, Lady Mary replied, "Why, all night long, the carriages were driving round and round the terrace, underneath my window!" Then, the owner of the house turned pale, and so did his Lady, and Charles Macdoodle of Macdoodle signed to Lady Mary to say no more, and every one was silent. After breakfast, Charles Macdoodle told Lady Mary that it was a tradition in the family that those rumbling carriages on the terrace betokened death. And so it proved, for, two months afterwards, the Lady of the mansion died. And Lady Mary, who was a Maid of Honour at Court, often told this story to the old Queen Charlotte; by this token that the old King always said, "Eh, eh? What, what? Ghosts, ghosts? No such thing, no such thing!" And never left off saying so, until he went to bed.

Or, a friend of somebody's whom most of us know, when he was a young man at college, had a particular friend, with whom he made the compact that, if it were possible for the Spirit to return to this earth after its separation from the body, he of the twain who first died, should reappear to the other. In course of time, this compact was forgotten by our friend; the two young men having progressed in life, and taken diverging paths that were wide asunder. But, one night, many years afterwards, our friend being in the North of England, and staying for the night in an inn, on the Yorkshire Moors, happened to look out of bed; and there, in the moonlight, leaning on a bureau near the window, steadfastly regarding him, saw his old college friend! The appearance being solemnly addressed, replied, in a kind of whisper, but very audibly, "Do not come near me. I am dead. I am here to redeem my promise. I come from another world, but may not disclose its secrets!" Then, the whole form becoming paler, melted, as it were, into the moonlight, and faded away.

Or, there was the daughter of the first occupier of the picturesque

Elizabethan house, so famous in our neighbourhood. You have heard about her? No! Why, SHE went out one summer evening at twilight, when she was a beautiful girl, just seventeen years of age, to gather flowers in the garden; and presently came running, terrified, into the hall to her father, saying, "Oh, dear father, I have met myself!" He took her in his arms, and told her it was fancy, but she said, "Oh no! I met myself in the broad walk, and I was pale and gathering withered flowers, and I turned my head, and held them up!" And, that night, she died; and a picture of her story was begun, though never finished, and they say it is somewhere in the house to this day, with its face to the wall.

Or, the uncle of my brother's wife was riding home on horseback, one mellow evening at sunset, when, in a green lane close to his own house, he saw a man standing before him, in the very centre of a narrow way. "Why does that man in the cloak stand there!" he thought. "Does he want me to ride over him?" But the figure never moved. He felt a strange sensation at seeing it so still, but slackened his trot and rode forward. When he was so close to it, as almost to touch it with his stirrup, his horse shied, and the figure glided up the bank, in a curious, unearthly manner--backward, and without seeming to use its feet--and was gone. The uncle of my brother's wife, exclaiming, "Good Heaven! It's my cousin Harry, from Bombay!" put spurs to his horse, which was suddenly in a profuse sweat, and, wondering at such strange behaviour, dashed round to the front of his house. There, he saw the same figure, just passing in at the long French window of the drawing-room, opening on the ground. He threw his bridle to a servant, and hastened in after it. His sister was sitting there, alone. "Alice, where's my cousin Harry?" "Your cousin Harry, John?" "Yes. From Bombay. I met him in the lane just now, and saw him enter here, this instant." Not a creature had been seen by any one; and in that hour and minute, as it afterwards appeared, this cousin died in India.

Or, it was a certain sensible old maiden lady, who died at ninety-nine, and retained her faculties to the last, who really did see the Orphan Boy; a story which has often been incorrectly told, but, of which the real truth is this--because it is, in fact, a story belonging to our family--and she was a connexion of our family. When she was about forty years of age, and still an uncommonly fine woman (her lover died young, which was the reason why she never married, though she had many offers), she went to stay at a place in Kent, which her brother, an Indian-Merchant, had newly bought. There was a story that this place had once been held in trust by the guardian of a young boy; who was himself the next heir, and who killed the young boy by harsh and cruel treatment. She knew nothing of that. It has been said that there was a Cage in her bedroom in which the guardian used to put the boy. There was no such thing. There was only a closet. She went to bed, made no alarm whatever in the night, and in the morning said composedly to her maid when she came in, "Who is the pretty forlorn-looking child who has been peeping out of that closet all night?" The maid replied by giving a loud scream, and instantly decamping. She was surprised; but she was a woman of remarkable strength of mind, and she dressed herself and went downstairs, and closeted herself with her brother. "Now, Walter," she said, "I have been disturbed all night by a pretty, forlorn-looking boy, who has been constantly peeping out of that closet in my room, which I can't open. This is some trick." "I am afraid not, Charlotte," said he, "for it is the legend of the house. It is the Orphan Boy. What did he do?" "He opened the door softly," said she, "and peeped out. Sometimes, he came a step or two into the room. Then, I called to him, to encourage him, and he shrunk, and shuddered, and crept in again, and shut the door." "The closet has no communication, Charlotte," said her brother, "with any other part of the house, and it's nailed up." This was undeniably true, and it took two carpenters a whole forenoon to get it open, for examination. Then, she was satisfied that she had seen the Orphan Boy. But, the wild and terrible part of the story is, that he was also seen by three of her brother's sons, in succession, who all died young. On the occasion of each child being taken ill, he came home in a heat, twelve hours before, and said, Oh, Mamma, he had been playing under a particular oak-tree, in a certain meadow, with a strange boy--a pretty, forlorn-looking boy, who was very timid, and made signs! From fatal experience, the parents came to know that this was the Orphan Boy, and that the course of that child whom he chose for his little playmate was surely run.

Legion is the name of the German castles, where we sit up alone to wait for the Spectre--where we are shown into a room, made comparatively cheerful for our reception--where we glance round at the shadows, thrown on the blank walls by the crackling fire--where we feel very lonely when the village innkeeper and his pretty daughter have retired, after laying down a fresh store of wood upon the hearth, and setting forth on the small table such supper-cheer as a cold roast capon, bread, grapes, and a flask of old Rhine wine- -where the reverberating doors close on their retreat, one after another, like so many peals of sullen thunder--and where, about the small hours of the night, we come into the knowledge of divers supernatural mysteries. Legion is the name of the haunted German students, in whose society we draw yet nearer to the fire, while the schoolboy in the corner opens his eyes wide and round, and flies off the footstool he has chosen for his seat, when the door accidentally blows open. Vast is the crop of such fruit, shining on our Christmas Tree; in blossom, almost at the very top; ripening all down the boughs!

Among the later toys and fancies hanging there--as idle often and less pure--be the images once associated with the sweet old Waits, the softened music in the night, ever unalterable! Encircled by the social thoughts of Christmas-time, still let the benignant figure of my childhood stand unchanged! In every cheerful image and suggestion that the season brings, may the bright star that rested above the poor roof, be the star of all the Christian World! A moment's pause, O vanishing tree, of which the lower boughs are dark to me as yet, and let me look once more! I know there are blank spaces on thy branches,

105

where eyes that I have loved have shone and smiled; from which they are departed. But, far above, I see the raiser of the dead girl, and the Widow's Son; and God is good! If Age be hiding for me in the unseen portion of thy downward growth, O may I, with a grey head, turn a child's heart to that figure yet, and a child's trustfulness and confidence!

Now, the tree is decorated with bright merriment, and song, and dance, and cheerfulness. And they are welcome. Innocent and welcome be they ever held, beneath the branches of the Christmas Tree, which cast no gloomy shadow! But, as it sinks into the ground, I hear a whisper going through the leaves. "This, in commemoration of the law of love and kindness, mercy and compassion. This, in remembrance of Me!"

Christmas at Fezziwig's Warehouse

By Charles Dickens

"Yo Ho! my boys," said Fezziwig. "No more work to-night! Christmas Eve, Dick! Christmas, Ebenezer! Let's have the shutters up!" cried old Fezziwig with a sharp clap of his hands, "before a man can say Jack Robinson. . . ."

"Hilli-ho!" cried old Fezziwig, skipping down from the high desk with wonderful agility. "Clear away, my lads, and let's have lots of room here! Hilli-ho, Dick! Cheer-up, Ebenezer!"

Clear away! There was nothing they wouldn't have cleared away, or couldn't have cleared away with old Fezziwig looking on. It was done in a minute. Every movable was packed off, as if it were dismissed from public life forevermore; the floor was swept and watered, the lamps were trimmed, fuel was heaped upon the fire; and the warehouse was as snug, and warm, and dry, and bright a ballroom as you would desire to see on a winter's night.

In came a fiddler with a music book, and went up to the lofty desk and made an orchestra of it and tuned like fifty stomach-aches. In came Mrs. Fezziwig, one vast substantial smile. In came the three Misses Fezziwig, beaming and lovable. In came the six followers whose hearts they broke. In came all the young men and women employed in the business. In came the housemaid with her cousin the baker. In came the cook with her brother's particular friend the milkman. In came the boy from over the way, who was suspected of not having board enough from his master, trying to hide himself behind the girl from next door but one who was proved to have had her ears pulled by her mistress; in they all came, anyhow and everyhow. Away they all went, twenty couple at once; hands half round and back again the other way; down the middle and up again; round and round in various stages of affectionate grouping, old top couple always turning up in the wrong place; new top couple starting off again, as soon as they got there; all top couples at last, and not a bottom one to help them.

When this result was brought about the fiddler struck up "Sir Roger de Coverley." Then old Fezziwig stood out to dance with Mrs. Fezziwig. Top couple, too, with a good stiff piece of work cut out for them; three or four and twenty pairs of partners; people who were not to be trifled with; people who would dance and had no notion of walking.

But if they had been thrice as many--oh, four times as many--old Fezziwig would have been a match for them, and so would Mrs. Fezziwig. As to her, she was worthy to be his partner in every sense of the term. If that's not high praise, tell me higher and I'll use it. A positive light appeared to issue from Fezziwig's calves. They shone in every part of the dance like moons. You couldn't have predicted at any given time what would become of them next. And when old Fezziwig and Mrs. Fezziwig had gone all through the dance, advance and retire; both hands to your partner, bow and courtesy, corkscrew, thread the needle, and back again to your place; Fezziwig "cut"--cut so deftly that he appeared to wink with his legs, and came upon his feet again with a stagger.

When the clock struck eleven the domestic ball broke up. Mr. and Mrs. Fezziwig took their stations, one on either side of the door, and shaking hands with every person individually, as he or she went out, wished him or her a Merry Christmas!

The Gift of the Magi

By O. Henry

ONE dollar and eighty-seven cents. That was all. And sixty cents of it was in pennies. Pennies saved one and two at a time by bulldozing the grocer and the vegetable man and the butcher until one's cheeks burned with the silent imputation of parsimony that such close dealing implied. Three times Della counted it. One dollar and eighty-seven cents. And the next day would be Christmas.

There was clearly nothing to do but flop down on the shabby little couch and howl. So Della did it. Which instigates the moral reflection that life is made up of sobs, sniffles, and smiles, with sniffles predominating.

While the mistress of the home is gradually subsiding from the first stage to the second, take a look at the home. A furnished flat at $8 per week. It did not exactly beggar description, but it certainly had that word on the lookout for the mendicancy squad.

In the vestibule below was a letter-box into which no letter would go, and an electric button from which no mortal finger could coax a ring. Also appertaining thereunto was a card bearing the name "Mr. James Dillingham Young."

The "Dillingham" had been flung to the breeze during a former period of prosperity when its possessor was being paid $30 per week. Now, when the income was shrunk to $20, though, they were thinking seriously of contracting to a modest and unassuming D. But whenever Mr. James Dillingham Young came home and reached his flat above he was called "Jim" and greatly hugged by Mrs. James Dillingham Young, already introduced to you as Della. Which is all very good.

Della finished her cry and attended to her cheeks with the powder rag. She stood by the window and looked out dully at a gray cat walking a gray fence in a gray backyard. Tomorrow would be Christmas Day, and she had only $1.87 with which to buy Jim a present. She had been saving every penny she could for months, with this result. Twenty dollars a week doesn't go far. Expenses had been greater than she had calculated. They always are. Only $1.87 to buy a present for Jim. Her Jim. Many a happy hour she had spent planning for something nice for him. Something fine and rare and sterling—something just a little bit near to being worthy of the honor of being owned by Jim.

There was a pier glass between the windows of the room. Perhaps you have seen a pier glass in an $8 flat. A very thin and very agile person may, by observing his reflection in a rapid sequence of longitudinal strips, obtain a fairly accurate conception of his looks. Della, being slender, had mastered the art.

Suddenly she whirled from the window and stood before the glass. Her eyes were shining brilliantly, but her face had lost its color within twenty seconds. Rapidly she pulled down her hair and let it fall to its full length.

Now, there were two possessions of the James Dillingham Youngs in which they both took a mighty pride. One was Jim's gold watch that had been his father's and his grandfather's. The other was Della's hair. Had the queen of Sheba lived in the flat across the airshaft, Della would have let her hair hang out the window some day to dry just to depreciate Her Majesty's jewels and gifts. Had King Solomon been the janitor, with all his treasures piled up in the basement, Jim would have pulled out his watch every time he passed, just to see him pluck at his beard from envy.

So now Della's beautiful hair fell about her rippling and shining like a cascade of brown waters. It reached below her knee and made itself almost a garment for her. And then she did it up again nervously and quickly. Once she faltered for a minute and stood still while a tear or

110

two splashed on the worn red carpet.

On went her old brown jacket; on went her old brown hat. With a whirl of skirts and with the brilliant sparkle still in her eyes, she fluttered out the door and down the stairs to the street.

Where she stopped the sign read: "Mme. Sofronie. Hair Goods of All Kinds." One flight up Della ran, and collected herself, panting. Madame, large, too white, chilly, hardly looked the "Sofronie."

"Will you buy my hair?" asked Della.

"I buy hair," said Madame. "Take yer hat off and let's have a sight at the looks of it."

Down rippled the brown cascade.

"Twenty dollars," said Madame, lifting the mass with a practised hand.

"Give it to me quick," said Della.

Oh, and the next two hours tripped by on rosy wings. Forget the hashed metaphor. She was ransacking the stores for Jim's present.

She found it at last. It surely had been made for Jim and no one else. There was no other like it in any of the stores, and she had turned all of them inside out. It was a platinum fob chain simple and chaste in design, properly proclaiming its value by substance alone and not by meretricious ornamentation—as all good things should do. It was even worthy of The Watch. As soon as she saw it she knew that it must be Jim's. It was like him. Quietness and value—the description applied to both. Twenty-one dollars they took from her for it, and she hurried home with the 87 cents. With that chain on his watch Jim might be properly anxious about the time in any company. Grand as the watch was, he sometimes looked at it on the sly on account of the old leather strap that he used in place of a chain.

When Della reached home her intoxication gave way a little to prudence and reason. She got out her curling irons and lighted the gas and went to work repairing the ravages made by generosity added to love. Which is always a tremendous task, dear friends—a mammoth task.

Within forty minutes her head was covered with tiny, close-lying curls that made her look wonderfully like a truant schoolboy. She looked at her reflection in the mirror long, carefully, and critically.

"If Jim doesn't kill me," she said to herself, "before he takes a second look at me, he'll say I look like a Coney Island chorus girl. But what could I do—oh! what could I do with a dollar and eighty-seven cents?"

At 7 o'clock the coffee was made and the frying-pan was on the back of the stove hot and ready to cook the chops.

Jim was never late. Della doubled the fob chain in her hand and sat on the corner of the table near the door that he always entered. Then she heard his step on the stair away down on the first flight, and she turned white for just a moment. She had a habit of saying a little silent prayer about the simplest everyday things, and now she whispered: "Please God, make him think I am still pretty."

The door opened and Jim stepped in and closed it. He looked thin and very serious. Poor fellow, he was only twenty-two—and to be burdened with a family! He needed a new overcoat and he was without gloves.

Jim stopped inside the door, as immovable as a setter at the scent of quail. His eyes were fixed upon Della, and there was an expression in them that she could not read, and it terrified her. It was not anger, nor surprise, nor disapproval, nor horror, nor any of the sentiments that she had been prepared for. He simply stared at her fixedly with that peculiar expression on his face.

Della wriggled off the table and went for him.

"Jim, darling," she cried, "don't look at me that way. I had my hair cut off and sold because I couldn't have lived through Christmas without giving you a present. It'll grow out again—you won't mind, will you? I just had to do it. My hair grows awfully fast. Say 'Merry Christmas!' Jim, and let's be happy. You don't know what a nice—what a beautiful, nice gift I've got for you."

"You've cut off your hair?" asked Jim, laboriously, as if he had not arrived at that patent fact yet even after the hardest mental labor.

"Cut it off and sold it," said Della. "Don't you like me just as well, anyhow? I'm me without my hair, ain't I?"

Jim looked about the room curiously.

"You say your hair is gone?" he said, with an air almost of idiocy.

"You needn't look for it," said Della. "It's sold, I tell you—sold and gone, too. It's Christmas Eve, boy. Be good to me, for it went for you. Maybe the hairs of my head were numbered," she went on with sudden serious sweetness, "but nobody could ever count my love for you. Shall I put the chops on, Jim?"

Out of his trance Jim seemed quickly to wake. He enfolded his Della. For ten seconds let us regard with discreet scrutiny some inconsequential object in the other direction. Eight dollars a week or a million a year—what is the difference? A mathematician or a wit would give you the wrong answer. The magi brought valuable gifts, but that was not among them. This dark assertion will be illuminated later on.

Jim drew a package from his overcoat pocket and threw it upon the table.

"Don't make any mistake, Dell," he said, "about me. I don't think there's anything in the way of a haircut or a shave or a shampoo that could make me like my girl any less. But if you'll unwrap that package you may see why you had me going a while at first."

113

White fingers and nimble tore at the string and paper. And then an ecstatic scream of joy; and then, alas! a quick feminine change to hysterical tears and wails, necessitating the immediate employment of all the comforting powers of the lord of the flat.

For there lay The Combs—the set of combs, side and back, that Della had worshipped long in a Broadway window. Beautiful combs, pure tortoise shell, with jewelled rims—just the shade to wear in the beautiful vanished hair. They were expensive combs, she knew, and her heart had simply craved and yearned over them without the least hope of possession. And now, they were hers, but the tresses that should have adorned the coveted adornments were gone.

But she hugged them to her bosom, and at length she was able to look up with dim eyes and a smile and say: "My hair grows so fast, Jim!"

And then Della leaped up like a little singed cat and cried, "Oh, oh!"

Jim had not yet seen his beautiful present. She held it out to him eagerly upon her open palm. The dull precious metal seemed to flash with a reflection of her bright and ardent spirit.

"Isn't it a dandy, Jim? I hunted all over town to find it. You'll have to look at the time a hundred times a day now. Give me your watch. I want to see how it looks on it."

Instead of obeying, Jim tumbled down on the couch and put his hands under the back of his head and smiled.

"Dell," said he, "let's put our Christmas presents away and keep 'em a while. They're too nice to use just at present. I sold the watch to get the money to buy your combs. And now suppose you put the chops on."

The magi, as you know, were wise men—wonderfully wise men—who brought gifts to the Babe in the manger. They invented the art of giving Christmas presents. Being wise, their gifts were no doubt wise ones, possibly bearing the privilege of exchange in case of duplication. And here I have lamely related to you the uneventful chronicle of two foolish children in a flat who most unwisely sacrificed for each other the greatest treasures of their house. But in a last word to the wise of these days let it be said that of all who give gifts these two were the wisest. Of all who give and receive gifts, such as they are wisest. Everywhere they are wisest. They are the magi.

Whistling Dick's Christmas Stocking

By O. Henry

It was with much caution that Whistling Dick slid back the door of the box-car, for Article 5716, City Ordinances, authorized (perhaps unconstitutionally) arrest on suspicion, and he was familiar of old with this ordinance. So, before climbing out, he surveyed the field with all the care of a good general.

He saw no change since his last visit to this big, alms-giving, long-suffering city of the South, the cold weather paradise of the tramps. The levee where his freight-car stood was pimpled with dark bulks of merchandise. The breeze reeked with the well-remembered, sickening smell of the old tarpaulins that covered bales and barrels. The dun river slipped along among the shipping with an oily gurgle. Far down toward Chalmette he could see the great bend in the stream outlined by the row of electric lights. Across the river Algiers lay, a long, irregular blot, made darker by the dawn which lightened the sky beyond. An industrious tug or two, coming for some early sailing ship, gave a few appalling toots, that seemed to be the signal for breaking day. The Italian luggers were creeping nearer their landing, laden with early vegetables and shellfish. A vague roar, subterranean in quality, from dray wheels and street cars, began to make itself heard and felt; and the ferryboats, the Mary Anns of water craft, stirred sullenly to their menial morning tasks.

Whistling Dick's red head popped suddenly back into the car. A sight too imposing and magnificent for his gaze had been added to the scene. A vast, incomparable policeman rounded a pile of rice sacks and stood within twenty yards of the car. The daily miracle of the dawn, now being performed above Algiers, received the flattering attention of this specimen of municipal official splendour. He gazed with unbiased dignity at the faintly glowing colours until, at last, he turned to them his broad back, as if convinced that legal interference was not needed, and the sunrise might proceed unchecked. So he turned his face to the rice bags, and, drawing a flat flask from an inside pocket, he placed it to his lips and regarded the firmament.

Whistling Dick, professional tramp, possessed a half-friendly acquaintance with this officer. They had met several times before on the levee at night, for the officer, himself a lover of music, had been attracted by the exquisite whistling of the shiftless vagabond. Still, he did not care, under the present circumstances, to renew the acquaintance. There is a difference between meeting a policeman on a lonely wharf and whistling a few operatic airs with him, and being caught by him crawling out of a freight-car. So Dick waited, as even a New Orleans policeman must move on some time--perhaps it is a retributive law of nature--and before long "Big Fritz" majestically disappeared between the trains of cars.

Whistling Dick waited as long as his judgment advised, and then slid swiftly to the ground. Assuming as far as possible the air of an honest labourer who seeks his daily toil, he moved across the network of railway lines, with the intention of making his way by quiet Girod Street to a certain bench in Lafayette Square, where, according to appointment, he hoped to rejoin a pal known as "Slick," this adventurous pilgrim having preceded him by one day in a cattle-car into which a loose slat had enticed him.

As Whistling Dick picked his way where night still lingered among the big, reeking, musty warehouses, he gave way to the habit that had won for him his title. Subdued, yet clear, with each note as true and liquid as a bobolink's, his whistle tinkled about the dim, cold mountains of brick like drops of rain falling into a hidden pool. He followed an air, but it swam mistily into a swirling current of improvisation. You could cull out the trill of mountain brooks, the staccato of green rushes shivering above chilly lagoons, the pipe of sleepy birds.

Rounding a corner, the whistler collided with a mountain of blue and brass.

"So," observed the mountain calmly, "You are already pack. Und dere vill not pe frost before two veeks yet! Und you haf forgotten how to vistle. Dere was a valse note in dot last bar."

"Watcher know about it?" said Whistling Dick, with tentative familiarity; "you wit yer little Gherman-band nixcumrous chunes. Watcher know about music? Pick yer ears, and listen agin. Here's de way I whistled it--see?"

He puckered his lips, but the big policeman held up his hand.

"Shtop," he said, "und learn der right way. Und learn also dot a rolling shtone can't vistle for a cent."

Big Fritz's heavy moustache rounded into a circle, and from its depths came a sound deep and mellow as that from a flute. He repeated a few bars of the air the tramp had been whistling. The rendition was cold, but correct, and he emphasized the note he had taken exception to.

"Dot p is p natural, und not p vlat. Py der vay, you petter pe glad I meet you. Von hour later, und I vould half to put you in a gage to vistle mit der chail pirds. Der orders are to bull all der pums after sunrise."

"To which?"

"To bull der pums--eferybody mitout fisible means. Dirty days is der price, or fifteen tollars."

"Is dat straight, or a game you givin' me?"

"It's der pest tip you efer had. I gif it to you pecause I pelief you are not so bad as der rest. Und pecause you gan visl 'Der Freisechutz' bezzer dan I myself gan. Don't run against any more bolicemans aroundt der corners, but go away from town a few tays. Good-pye."

118

So Madame Orleans had at last grown weary of the strange and ruffled brood that came yearly to nestle beneath her charitable pinions.

After the big policeman had departed, Whistling Dick stood for an irresolute minute, feeling all the outraged indignation of a delinquent tenant who is ordered to vacate his premises. He had pictured to himself a day of dreamful ease when he should have joined his pal; a day of lounging on the wharf, munching the bananas and cocoanuts scattered in unloading the fruit steamers; and then a feast along the free-lunch counters from which the easy-going owners were too good-natured or too generous to drive him away, and afterward a pipe in one of the little flowery parks and a snooze in some shady corner of the wharf. But here was a stern order to exile, and one that he knew must be obeyed. So, with a wary eye open from the gleam of brass buttons, he began his retreat toward a rural refuge. A few days in the country need not necessarily prove disastrous. Beyond the possibility of a slight nip of frost, there was no formidable evil to be looked for.

However, it was with a depressed spirit that Whistling Dick passed the old French market on his chosen route down the river. For safety's sake he still presented to the world his portrayal of the part of the worthy artisan on his way to labour. A stall-keeper in the market, undeceived, hailed him by the generic name of his ilk, and "Jack" halted, taken by surprise. The vender, melted by this proof of his own acuteness, bestowed a foot of Frankfurter and half a loaf, and thus the problem of breakfast was solved.

When the streets, from topographical reasons, began to shun the river bank the exile mounted to the top of the levee, and on its well-trodden path pursued his way. The suburban eye regarded him with cold suspicion, individuals reflected the stern spirit of the city's heartless edict. He missed the seclusion of the crowded town and the safety he could always find in the multitude.

At Chalmette, six miles upon his desultory way, there suddenly

119

menaced him a vast and bewildering industry. A new port was being established; the dock was being built, compresses were going up; picks and shovels and barrows struck at him like serpents from every side. An arrogant foreman bore down upon him, estimating his muscles with the eye of a recruiting-sergeant. Brown men and black men all about him were toiling away. He fled in terror.

By noon he had reached the country of the plantations, the great, sad, silent levels bordering the mighty river. He overlooked fields of sugar-cane so vast that their farthest limits melted into the sky. The sugar-making season was well advanced, and the cutters were at work; the waggons creaked drearily after them; the Negro teamsters inspired the mules to greater speed with mellow and sonorous imprecations. Dark-green groves, blurred by the blue of distance, showed where the plantation-houses stood. The tall chimneys of the sugar-mills caught the eye miles distant, like lighthouses at sea.

At a certain point Whistling Dick's unerring nose caught the scent of frying fish. Like a pointer to a quail, he made his way down the levee side straight to the camp of a credulous and ancient fisherman, whom he charmed with song and story, so that he dined like an admiral, and then like a philosopher annihilated the worst three hours of the day by a nap under the trees.

When he awoke and again continued his hegira, a frosty sparkle in the air had succeeded the drowsy warmth of the day, and as this portent of a chilly night translated itself to the brain of Sir Peregrine, he lengthened his stride and bethought him of shelter. He travelled a road that faithfully followed the convolutions of the levee, running along its base, but whither he knew not. Bushes and rank grass crowded it to the wheel ruts, and out of this ambuscade the pests of the lowlands swarmed after him, humming a keen, vicious soprano. And as the night grew nearer, although colder, the whine of the mosquitoes became a greedy, petulant snarl that shut out all other sounds. To his right, against the heavens, he saw a green light moving, and, accompanying it, the masts and funnels of a big incoming steamer, moving as upon a screen at a magic-lantern show. And there were mysterious marshes at his left, out of which came queer gurgling cries and a choked croaking. The whistling vagrant struck up a merry warble to offset these melancholy influences, and it is likely that never before, since Pan himself jigged it on his reeds, had such sounds been heard in those depressing solitudes.

A distant clatter in the rear quickly developed into the swift beat of horses' hoofs, and Whistling Dick stepped aside into the dew-wet grass to clear the track. Turning his head, he saw approaching a fine team of stylish grays drawing a double surrey. A stout man with a white moustache occupied the front seat, giving all his attention to the rigid lines in his hands. Behind him sat a placid, middle-aged lady and a brilliant-looking girl hardly arrived at young ladyhood. The lap-robe had slipped partly from the knees of the gentleman driving, and Whistling Dick saw two stout canvas bags between his feet--bags such as, while loafing in cities, he had seen warily transferred between express waggons and bank doors. The remaining space in the vehicle was filled with parcels of various sizes and shapes.

As the surrey swept even with the sidetracked tramp, the bright-eyed girl, seized by some merry, madcap impulse, leaned out toward him with a sweet, dazzling smile, and cried, "Mer-ry Christ-mas!" in a shrill, plaintive treble.

Such a thing had not often happened to Whistling Dick, and he felt handicapped in devising the correct response. But lacking time for reflection, he let his instinct decide, and snatching off his battered derby, he rapidly extended it at arm's length, and drew it back with a continuous motion, and shouted a loud, but ceremonious, "Ah, there!" after the flying surrey.

The sudden movement of the girl had caused one of the parcels to become unwrapped, and something limp and black fell from it into the road. The tramp picked it up, and found it to be a new black silk stocking, long and fine and slender. It crunched crisply, and yet with a luxurious softness, between his fingers.

"Ther bloomin' little skeezicks!" said Whistling Dick, with a broad grin bisecting his freckled face. "W't d' yer think of dat, now! Mer-ry Chris-mus! Sounded like a cuckoo clock, da'ts what she did. Dem guys is swells, too, bet yer life, an' der old 'un stacks dem sacks of dough down under his trotters like dey was common as dried apples. Been shoppin' for Chrismus, and de kid's lost one of her new socks w'ot she was goin' to hold up Santy wid. De bloomin' little skeezicks! Wit' her 'Mer-ry Chris-mus!' W'ot d' yer t'ink! Same as to say, 'Hello, Jack, how goes it?' and as swell as Fift' Av'noo, and as easy as a blowout in Cincinnat."

Whistling Dick folded the stocking carefully, and stuffed it into his pocket.

It was nearly two hours later when he came upon signs of habitation. The buildings of an extensive plantation were brought into view by a turn in the road. He easily selected the planter's residence in a large square building with two wings, with numerous good-sized, well-lighted windows, and broad verandas running around its full extent. it was set upon a smooth lawn, which was faintly lit by the far-reaching rays of the lamps within. A noble grove surrounded it, and old-fashioned shrubbery grew thickly about the walks and fences. The quarters of the hands and the mill buildings were situated at a distance in the rear.

The road was now enclosed on each side by a fence, and presently, as Whistling Dick drew nearer the house, he suddenly stopped and sniffed the air.

"If dere ain't a hobo stew cookin' somewhere in dis immediate precint," he said to himself, "me nose as quit tellin' de trut'."

Without hesitation he climbed the fence to windward. He found himself in an apparently disused lot, where piles of old bricks were stacked, and rejected, decaying lumber. In a corner he saw the faint glow of a fire that had become little more than a bed of living coals, and he thought he could see some dim human forms sitting or lying about it. He drew nearer, and by the light of a little blaze that suddenly flared up he saw plainly the fat figure of a ragged man in an old brown sweater and cap.

"Dat man," said Whistling Dick to himself softly, "is a dead ringer for Boston Harry. I'll try him wit de high sign."

He whistled one or two bars of a rag-time melody, and the air was immediately taken up, and then quickly ended with a peculiar run. The first whistler walked confidently up to the fire. The fat man looked up, and spake in a loud, asthmatic wheeze:

"Gents, the unexpected but welcome addition to our circle is Mr. Whistling Dick, an old friend of mine for whom I fully vouches. The waiter will lay another cover at once. Mr. W. D. will join us at supper, during which function he will enlighten us in regard to the circumstances that gave us the pleasure of his company."

"Chewin' de stuffin' out 'n de dictionary, as usual, Boston," said Whistling Dick; "but t'anks all de same for de invitashun. I guess I finds meself here about de same way as yous guys. A cop gimme de tip dis mornin'. Yous workin' on dis farm?"

"A guest," said Boston, sternly, "shouldn't never insult his entertainers until he's filled up wid grub. 'Tain't good business sense. Workin'!--but I will restrain myself. We five--me, Deaf Pete, Blinky, Goggles, and Indiana Tom--got put on to this scheme of Noo Orleans to work visiting gentlemen upon her dirty streets, and we hit the road last evening just as the tender hues of twilight had flopped down upon the daisies and things. Blinky, pass the empty oyster-can at your left to the empty gentleman at your right."

For the next ten minutes the gang of roadsters paid their undivided attention to the supper. In an old five-gallon kerosene can they had cooked a stew of potatoes, meat, and onions, which they partook of from smaller cans they had found scattered about the vacant lot.

Whistling Dick had known Boston Harry of old, and knew him to be one of the shrewdest and most successful of his brotherhood. He looked like a prosperous stock-drover or solid merchant from some country village. He was stout and hale, with a ruddy, always smoothly shaven face. His clothes were strong and neat, and he gave special attention to his decent-appearing shoes. During the past ten years he had acquired a reputation for working a larger number of successfully managed confidence games than any of his acquaintances, and he had not a day's work to be counted against him. It was rumoured among his associates that he had saved a considerable amount of money. The four other men were fair specimens of the slinking, ill-clad, noisome genus who carried their labels of "suspicious" in plain view.

After the bottom of the large can had been scraped, and pipes lit at the coals, two of the men called Boston aside and spake with him lowly and mysteriously. He nodded decisively, and then said aloud to Whistling Dick:

"Listen, sonny, to some plain talky-talk. We five are on a lay. I've guaranteed you to be square, and you're to come in on the profits equal with the boys, and you've got to help. Two hundred hands on this plantation are expecting to be paid a week's wages to-morrow morning. To-morrow's Christmas, and they want to lay off. Says the boss: 'Work from five to nine in the morning to get a train load of sugar off, and I'll pay every man cash down for the week and a day extra.' They say: 'Hooray for the boss! It goes.' He drives to Noo Orleans to-day, and fetches back the cold dollars. Two thousand and seventy-four fifty is the amount. I got the figures from a man who talks too much, who got 'em from the bookkeeper. The boss of this plantation thinks he's going to pay this wealth to the hands. He's got it down wrong; he's going to pay it to us. It's going to stay in the leisure class, where it belongs. Now, half of this haul goes to me, and the other half the rest of you may divide. Why the difference? I represent the brains. It's my scheme. Here's the way we're going to get it. There's some company at supper in the house, but they'll leave about nine. They've just happened in for an hour or so. If they don't go pretty soon, we'll work the scheme anyhow. We want all night to get away good with the dollars. They're heavy. About nine o'clock Deaf Pete and Blinky'll go down the road about a quarter beyond the house, and set fire to a big cane-field there that the cutters haven't touched yet. The wind's just right to have it roaring in two minutes. The alarm'll be given, and every man Jack about the place will be down there in ten minutes, fighting fire. That'll leave the money sacks and the women alone in the house for us to handle. You've heard cane burn? Well, there's mighty few women can screech loud enough to be heard above its crackling. The thing's dead safe. The only danger is in being caught before we can get far enough away with the money. Now, if you--"

"Boston," interrupted Whistling Dick, rising to his feet, "T'anks for the grub yous fellers has given me, but I'll be movin' on now."

"What do you mean?" asked Boston, also rising.

"W'y, you can count me outer dis deal. You oughter know that. I'm on de bum all right enough, but dat other t'ing don't go wit' me. Burglary is no good. I'll say good night and many t'anks fer--"

Whistling Dick had moved away a few steps as he spoke, but he stopped very suddenly. Boston had covered him with a short revolver of roomy calibre.

"Take your seat," said the tramp leader. "I'd feel mighty proud of myself if I let you go and spoil the game. You'll stick right in this camp until we finish the job. The end of that brick pile is your limit. You go two inches beyond that, and I'll have to shoot. Better take it easy, now."

"It's my way of doin'," said Whistling Dick. "Easy goes. You can depress de muzzle of dat twelve-incher, and run 'er back on de trucks. I remains, as de newspapers says, 'in yer midst.'"

"All right," said Boston, lowering his piece, as the other returned and took his seat again on a projecting plank in a pile of timber. "Don't try to leave; that's all. I wouldn't miss this chance even if I had to shoot an old acquaintance to make it go. I don't want to hurt anybody specially, but this thousand dollars I'm going to get will fix me for fair. I'm going to drop the road, and start a saloon in a little town I know about. I'm tired of being kicked around."

Boston Harry took from his pocket a cheap silver watch, and held it near the fire.

"It's a quarter to nine," he said. "Pete, you and Blinky start. Go down the road past the house, and fire the cane in a dozen places. Then strike for the levee, and come back on it, instead of the road, so you won't meet anybody. By the time you get back the men will all be striking out for the fire, and we'll break for the house and collar the dollars. Everybody cough up what matches he's got."

The two surly tramps made a collection of all the matches in the party, Whistling Dick contributing his quota with propitiatory alacrity, and then they departed in the dim starlight in the direction of the road.

Of the three remaining vagrants, two, Goggles and Indiana Tom, reclined lazily upon convenient lumber and regarded Whistling Dick with undisguised disfavour. Boston, observing that the dissenting recruit was disposed to remain peaceably, relaxed a little of his vigilance. Whistling Dick arose presently and strolled leisurely up and down keeping carefully within the territory assigned him.

"Dis planter chap," he said, pausing before Boston Harry, "w'ot makes yer t'ink he's got de tin in de house wit' 'im?"

"I'm advised of the facts in the case," said Boston. "He drove to Noo

Orleans and got it, I say, to-day. Want to change your mind now and come in?"

"Naw, I was just askin'. Wot kind o' team did de boss drive?"

"Pair of grays."

"Double surrey?"

"Yep."

"Women folks along?"

"Wife and kid. Say, what morning paper are you trying to pump news for?"

"I was just conversin' to pass de time away. I guess dat team passed me in de road dis evenin'. Dat's all."

As Whistling Dick put his hands in his pockets and continued his curtailed beat up and down by the fire, he felt the silk stocking he had picked up in the road.

"Ther bloomin' little skeezicks," he muttered, with a grin.

As he walked up and down he could see, through a sort of natural opening or lane among the trees, the planter's residence some seventy-five yards distant. The side of the house toward him exhibited spacious, well-lighted windows through which a soft radiance streamed, illuminating the broad veranda and some extent of the lawn beneath.

"What's that you said?" asked Boston, sharply.

"Oh, nuttin' 't all," said Whistling Dick, lounging carelessly, and kicking meditatively at a little stone on the ground.

"Just as easy," continued the warbling vagrant softly to himself, "an' sociable an' swell an' sassy, wit' her 'Mer-ry Chris-mus,' Wot d'yer t'ink, now!"

* * * * *

Dinner, two hours late, was being served in the Bellemeade plantation dining-room.

The dining-room and all its appurtenances spoke of an old regime that was here continued rather than suggested to the memory. The plate was rich to the extent that its age and quaintness alone saved it from being showy; there were interesting names signed in the corners of the pictures on the walls; the viands were of the kind that bring a shine into the eyes of gourmets. The service was swift, silent, lavish, as in the days when the waiters were assets like the plate. The names by which the planter's family and their visitors addressed one another were historic in the annals of two nations. Their manners and conversation had that most difficult kind of ease--the kind that still preserves punctilio. The planter himself seemed to be the dynamo that generated the larger portion of the gaiety and wit. The younger ones at the board found it more than difficult to turn back on him his guns of raillery and banter. It is true, the young men attempted to storm his works repeatedly, incited by the hope of gaining the approbation of their fair companions; but even when they sped a well-aimed shaft, the planter forced them to feel defeat by the tremendous discomfiting thunder of the laughter with which he accompanied his retorts. At the head of the table, serene, matronly, benevolent, reigned the mistress of the house, placing here and there the right smile, the right word, the encouraging glance.

The talk of the party was too desultory, too evanescent to follow, but at last they came to the subject of the tramp nuisance, one that had of late vexed the plantations for many miles around. The planter seized the occasion to direct his good-natured fire of raillery at the mistress, accusing her of encouraging the plague. "They swarm up and down the river every winter," he said. "They overrun New Orleans, and we catch the surplus, which is generally the worst part. And, a day or two ago, Madame New Orleans, suddenly discovering that she can't go shopping without brushing her skirts against great rows of the vagabonds

128

sunning themselves on the banquettes, says to the police: 'Catch 'em all,' and the police catch a dozen or two, and the remaining three or four thousand overflow up and down the levee, and madame there,"-- pointing tragically with the carving-knife at her-- "feeds them. They won't work; they defy my overseers, and they make friends with my dogs; and you, madame, feed them before my eyes, and intimidate me when I would interfere. Tell us, please, how many to-day did you thus incite to future laziness and depredation?"

"Six, I think," said madame, with a reflective smile; "but you know two of them offered to work, for you heard them yourself."

The planter's disconcerting laugh rang out again.

"Yes, at their own trades. And one was an artificial-flower maker, and the other a glass-blower. Oh, they were looking for work! Not a hand would they consent to lift to labour of any other kind."

"And another one," continued the soft-hearted mistress, "used quite good language. It was really extraordinary for one of his class. And he carried a watch. And had lived in Boston. I don't believe they are all bad. They have always seemed to me to rather lack development. I always look upon them as children with whom wisdom has remained at a standstill while whiskers have continued to grow. We passed one this evening as we were driving home who had a face as good as it was incompetent. He was whistling the intermezzo from 'Cavalleria' and blowing the spirit of Mascagni himself into it."

A bright eyed young girl who sat at the left of the mistress leaned over, and said in a confidential undertone:

"I wonder, mamma, if that tramp we passed on the road found my stocking, and do you think he will hang it up to-night? Now I can hang up but one. Do you know why I wanted a new pair of silk stockings when I have plenty? Well, old Aunt Judy says, if you hang up two that have never been worn, Santa Claus will fill one with good things, and

Monsieur Pambe will place in the other payment for all the words you have spoken--good or bad--on the day before Christmas. That's why I've been unusually nice and polite to everyone to-day. Monsieur Pambe, you know, is a witch gentleman; he--"

The words of the young girl were interrupted by a startling thing.

Like the wraith of some burned-out shooting star, a black streak came crashing through the window-pane and upon the table, where it shivered into fragments a dozen pieces of crystal and china ware, and then glanced between the heads of the guests to the wall, imprinting therein a deep, round indentation, at which, to-day, the visitor to Bellemeade marvels as he gazes upon it and listens to this tale as it is told.

The women screamed in many keys, and the men sprang to their feet, and would have laid their hands upon their swords had not the verities of chronology forbidden.

The planter was the first to act; he sprang to the intruding missile, and held it up to view.

"By Jupiter!" he cried. "A meteoric shower of hosiery! Has communication at last been established with Mars?"

"I should say--ahem--Venus," ventured a young-gentleman visitor, looking hopefully for approbation toward the unresponsive young-lady visitors.

The planter held at arm's length the unceremonious visitor--a long dangling black stocking. "It's loaded," he announced.

As he spoke, he reversed the stocking, holding it by the toe, and down from it dropped a roundish stone, wrapped about by a piece of yellowish paper. "Now for the first interstellar message of the century!" he cried; and nodding to the company, who had crowded about him, he adjusted his glasses with provoking deliberation, and examined it closely. When he finished, he had changed from the jolly host to the practical, decisive man of business. He immediately struck a bell, and said to the silent-footed mulatto man who responded: "Go and tell Mr. Wesley to get Reeves and Maurice and about ten stout hands they can rely upon, and come to the hall door at once. Tell him to have the men arm themselves, and bring plenty of ropes and plough lines. Tell him to hurry." And then he read aloud from the paper these words:

To the Gent of de Hous:

Dere is five tuff hoboes xcept meself in the vaken lot near de road war de old brick piles is. Dey got me stuck up wid a gun see and I taken dis means of communication. 2 of der lads is gone down to set fire to de cain field below de hous and when yous fellers goes to turn de hoes on it de hole gang is goin to rob de hous of de money yoo gotto pay off wit say git a move on ye say de kid dropt dis sock on der rode tel her mery crismus de same as she told me. Ketch de bums down de rode first and den sen a relefe core to get me out of soke youres truly,

- Whistlen Dick.

There was some quiet, but rapid, mavoeuvring at Bellemeade during the ensuring half hour, which ended in five disgusted and sullen tramps being captured, and locked securely in an outhouse pending the coming of the morning and retribution. For another result, the visiting young gentlemen had secured the unqualified worship of the visiting young ladies by their distinguished and heroic conduct. For still another, behold Whistling Dick, the hero, seated at the planter's table, feasting upon viands his experience had never before included, and waited upon by admiring femininity in shapes of such beauty and "swellness" that even his ever-full mouth could scarcely prevent him from whistling. He was made to disclose in detail his adventure with the evil gang of Boston Harry, and how he cunningly wrote the note and wrapped it around the stone and placed it at the toe of the stocking, and, watching his chance, sent it silently, with a wonderful centrifugal momentum, like a comet, at one of the big lighted windows of the dining-room.

The planter vowed that the wanderer should wander no more; that his was a goodness and an honesty that should be rewarded, and that a debt of gratitude had been made that must be paid; for had he not saved them from a doubtless imminent loss, and maybe a greater calamity? He assured Whistling Dick that he might consider himself a charge upon the honour of Bellemeade; that a position suited to his powers would be found for him at once, and hinted that the way would be heartily smoothed for him to rise to as high places of emolument and trust as the plantation afforded.

But now, they said, he must be weary, and the immediate thing to consider was rest and sleep. So the mistress spoke to a servant, and Whistling Dick was conducted to a room in the wing of the house occupied by the servants. To this room, in a few minutes, was brought a portable tin bathtub filled with water, which was placed on a piece of oiled cloth upon the floor. There the vagrant was left to pass the night.

By the light of a candle he examined the room. A bed, with the covers neatly turned back, revealed snowy pillows and sheets. A worn, but clean, red carpet covered the floor. There was a dresser with a beveled mirror, a washstand with a flowered bowl and pitcher; the two or three chairs were softly upholstered. A little table held books, papers, and a day-old cluster of roses in a jar. There were towels on a rack and soap in a white dish.

Whistling Dick set his candle on a chair and placed his hat carefully under the table. After satisfying what we must suppose to have been his curiosity by a sober scrutiny, he removed his coat, folded it, and laid it upon the floor, near the wall, as far as possible from the unused bathtub. Taking his coat for a pillow, he stretched himself luxuriously upon the carpet.

When, on Christmas morning, the first streaks of dawn broke above the marshes, Whistling Dick awoke, and reached instinctively for his hat. Then he remembered that the skirts of Fortune had swept him into their folds on the night previous, and he went to the window and raised it, to let the fresh breath of the morning cool his brow and fix the yet dream-like memory of his good luck within his brain.

As he stood there, certain dread and ominous sounds pierced the fearful hollow of his ear.

The force of plantation workers, eager to complete the shortened task allotted to them, were all astir. The mighty din of the ogre Labour shook the earth, and the poor tattered and forever disguised Prince in search of his fortune held tight to the window-sill even in the enchanted castle, and trembled.

Already from the bosom of the mill came the thunder of rolling barrels of sugar, and (prison-like sounds) there was a great rattling of chains as the mules were harried with stimulant imprecations to their places by the waggon-tongues. A little vicious "dummy" engine, with a train of flat cars in tow, stewed and fumed on the plantation tap of the narrow-gauge railroad, and a toiling, hurrying, hallooing stream of workers were dimly seen in the half darkness loading the train with the weekly output of sugar. Here was a poem; an epic--nay, a tragedy-- with work, the curse of the world, for its theme.

The December air was frosty, but the sweat broke out upon Whistling Dick's face. He thrust his head out of the window, and looked down. Fifteen feet below him, against the wall of the house, he could make out that a border of flowers grew, and by that token he overhung a bed of soft earth.

Softly as a burglar goes, he clambered out upon the sill, lowered himself until he hung by his hands alone, and then dropped safely. No one seemed to be about upon this side of the house. He dodged low, and skimmed swiftly across the yard to the low fence. It was an easy matter to vault this, for a terror urged him such as lifts the gazelle over the thorn bush when the lion pursues. A crash through the dew-drenched weeds on the roadside, a clutching, slippery rush up the grassy side of the levee to the footpath at the summit, and--he was free!

The east was blushing and brightening. The wind, himself a vagrant rover, saluted his brother upon the cheek. Some wild geese, high above, gave cry. A rabbit skipped along the path before him, free to turn to the right or to the left as his mood should send him. The river slid past, and certainly no one could tell the ultimate abiding place of its waters.

A small, ruffled, brown-breasted bird, sitting upon a dog-wood sapling, began a soft, throaty, tender little piping in praise of the dew which entices foolish worms from their holes; but suddenly he stopped, and sat with his head turned sidewise, listening.

From the path along the levee there burst forth a jubilant, stirring, buoyant, thrilling whistle, loud and keen and clear as the cleanest notes of the piccolo. The soaring sound rippled and trilled and arpeggioed as the songs of wild birds do not; but it had a wild free grace that, in a way, reminded the small, brown bird of something familiar, but exactly what he could not tell. There was in it the bird call, or reveille, that all birds know; but a great waste of lavish, unmeaning things that art had added and arranged, besides, and that were quite puzzling and strange; and the little brown bird sat with his head on one side until the sound died away in the distance.

The little bird did not know that the part of that strange warbling that he understood was just what kept the warbler without his breakfast; but he knew very well that the part he did not understand did not concern him, so he gave a little flutter of his wings and swooped down like a brown bullet upon a big fat worm that was wriggling along the levee path.

Christmas Every Day

By William Dean Howells

The little girl came into her papa's study, as she always did Saturday morning before breakfast, and asked for a story. He tried to beg off that morning, for he was very busy, but she would not let him. So he began:

"Well, once there was a little pig--"

She put her hand over his mouth and stopped him at the word. She said she had heard little pig-stories till she was perfectly sick of them.

"Well, what kind of story shall I tell, then?"

"About Christmas. It's getting to be the season. It's past Thanksgiving already."

"It seems to me," her papa argued, "that I've told as often about Christmas as I have about little pigs."

"No difference! Christmas is more interesting."

"Well!" Her papa roused himself from his writing by a great effort. "Well, then, I'll tell you about the little girl that wanted it Christmas every day in the year. How would you like that?"

"First-rate!" said the little girl; and she nestled into comfortable shape in his lap, ready for listening.

"Very well, then, this little pig--Oh, what are you pounding me for?"

"Because you said little pig instead of little girl."

"I should like to know what's the difference between a little pig and a little girl that wanted it Christmas every day!"

"Papa," said the little girl, warningly, "if you don't go on, I'll give it to you!" And at this her papa darted off like lightning, and began to tell the story as fast as he could.

Well, once there was a little girl who liked Christmas so much that she wanted it to be Christmas every day in the year; and as soon as Thanksgiving was over she began to send postal-cards to the old Christmas Fairy to ask if she mightn't have it. But the old fairy never answered any of the postals; and after a while the little girl found out that the Fairy was pretty particular, and wouldn't notice anything but letters--not even correspondence cards in envelopes; but real letters on sheets of paper, and sealed outside with a monogram--or your initial, anyway. So, then, she began to send her letters; and in about three weeks--or just the day before Christmas, it was--she got a letter from the Fairy, saying she might have it Christmas every day for a year, and then they would see about having it longer.

The little girl was a good deal excited already, preparing for the old-fashioned, once-a-year Christmas that was coming the next day, and perhaps the Fairy's promise didn't make such an impression on her as it would have made at some other time. She just resolved to keep it to herself, and surprise everybody with it as it kept coming true; and then it slipped out of her mind altogether.

She had a splendid Christmas. She went to bed early, so as to let Santa Claus have a chance at the stockings, and in the morning she was up the first of anybody and went and felt them, and found hers all lumpy with packages of candy, and oranges and grapes, and pocket-books and rubber balls, and all kinds of small presents, and her big brother's with nothing but the tongs in them, and her young lady sister's with a new silk umbrella, and her papa's and mamma's with potatoes and pieces of coal wrapped up in tissue-paper, just as they always had every Christmas. Then she waited around till the rest of the family were up, and she was the first to burst into the library, when the doors were opened, and look at the large presents laid out on the library-table--books, and portfolios, and boxes of stationery, and breastpins, and dolls, and little stoves, and dozens of handkerchiefs, and ink-stands, and skates, and snow-shovels, and photograph-frames, and little easels, and boxes of water-colors, and Turkish paste, and nougat, and candied cherries, and dolls' houses, and waterproofs--and the big Christmas-tree, lighted and standing in a waste-basket in the middle.

She had a splendid Christmas all day. She ate so much candy that she did not want any breakfast; and the whole forenoon the presents kept pouring in that the expressman had not had time to deliver the night before; and she went round giving the presents she had got for other people, and came home and ate turkey and cranberry for dinner, and plum-pudding and nuts and raisins and oranges and more candy, and then went out and coasted, and came in with a stomach-ache, crying; and her papa said he would see if his house was turned into that sort of fool's paradise another year; and they had a light supper, and pretty early everybody went to bed cross.

Here the little girl pounded her papa in the back, again.

"Well, what now? Did I say pigs?"

"You made them act like pigs."

"Well, didn't they?"

"No matter; you oughtn't to put it into a story."

"Very well, then, I'll take it all out."

Her father went on:

The little girl slept very heavily, and she slept very late, but she was wakened at last by the other children dancing round her bed with their stockings full of presents in their hands.

"What is it?" said the little girl, and she rubbed her eyes and tried to rise up in bed.

"Christmas! Christmas! Christmas!" they all shouted, and waved their stockings.

"Nonsense! It was Christmas yesterday."

Her brothers and sisters just laughed. "We don't know about that. It's Christmas to-day, anyway. You come into the library and see."

Then all at once it flashed on the little girl that the Fairy was keeping her promise, and her year of Christmases was beginning. She was dreadfully sleepy, but she sprang up like a lark--a lark that had overeaten itself and gone to bed cross--and darted into the library. There it was again! Books, and portfolios, and boxes of stationery, and breastpins--

"You needn't go over it all, papa; I guess I can remember just what was there," said the little girl.

Well, and there was the Christmas-tree blazing away, and the family picking out their presents, but looking pretty sleepy, and her father perfectly puzzled, and her mother ready to cry. "I'm sure I don't see how I'm to dispose of all these things," said her mother, and her father said it seemed to him they had had something just like it the day before, but he supposed he must have dreamed it. This struck the little girl as the best kind of a joke; and so she ate so much candy she didn't want any breakfast, and went round carrying presents, and had turkey and cranberry for dinner, and then went out and coasted, and came in with a--

"Papa!"

"Well, what now?"

"What did you promise, you forgetful thing?"

"Oh! oh yes!"

Well, the next day, it was just the same thing over again, but everybody getting crosser; and at the end of a week's time so many people had lost their tempers that you could pick up lost tempers anywhere; they perfectly strewed the ground. Even when people tried to recover their tempers they usually got somebody else's, and it made the most dreadful mix.

The little girl began to get frightened, keeping the secret all to herself; she wanted to tell her mother, but she didn't dare to; and she was ashamed to ask the Fairy to take back her gift, it seemed ungrateful and ill-bred, and she thought she would try to stand it, but she hardly knew how she could, for a whole year. So it went on and on, and it was Christmas on St. Valentine's Day and Washington's Birthday, just the same as any day, and it didn't skip even the First of April, though everything was counterfeit that day, and that was some little relief.

After a while coal and potatoes began to be awfully scarce, so many had been wrapped up in tissue-paper to fool papas and mammas with. Turkeys got to be about a thousand dollars apiece--

"Papa!"

"Well, what?"

"You're beginning to fib."

"Well, two thousand, then."

And they got to passing off almost anything for turkeys--half-grown humming-birds, and even rocs out of the Arabian Nights--the real turkeys were so scarce. And cranberries--well, they asked a diamond apiece for cranberries. All the woods and orchards were cut down for Christmas-trees, and where the woods and orchards used to be it looked just like a stubble-field, with the stumps. After a while they had to make Christmas-trees out of rags, and stuff them with bran, like old-fashioned dolls; but there were plenty of rags, because people got so poor, buying presents for one another, that they couldn't get any new clothes, and they just wore their old ones to tatters. They got so poor that everybody had to go to the poor-house, except the confectioners, and the fancy-store keepers, and the picture-book sellers, and the expressmen; and they all got so rich and proud that they would hardly wait upon a person when he came to buy. It was perfectly shameful!

Well, after it had gone on about three or four months, the little girl, whenever she came into the room in the morning and saw those great ugly, lumpy stockings dangling at the fire-place, and the disgusting presents around everywhere, used to just sit down and burst out crying. In six months she was perfectly exhausted; she couldn't even cry any more; she just lay on the lounge and rolled her eyes and panted. About the beginning of October she took to sitting down on dolls wherever she found them--French dolls, or any kind--she hated the sight of them so; and by Thanksgiving she was crazy, and just slammed her presents across the room.

By that time people didn't carry presents around nicely any more. They flung them over the fence, or through the window, or anything; and, instead of running their tongues out and taking great pains to write "For dear Papa," or "Mamma," or "Brother," or "Sister," or "Susie," or "Sammie," or "Billie," or "Bobbie," or "Jimmie," or "Jennie," or whoever it was, and troubling to get the spelling right, and then signing their names, and "Xmas, 18--," they used to write in the gift-books, "Take it, you horrid old thing!" and then go and bang it against the front door. Nearly everybody had built barns to hold their presents, but pretty soon the barns overflowed, and then they used to let them lie out in the rain, or anywhere. Sometimes the police used to come and tell them to shovel their presents off the sidewalk, or they would arrest them.

"I thought you said everybody had gone to the poor-house," interrupted the little girl.

"They did go, at first," said her papa; "but after a while the poorhouses got so full that they had to send the people back to their own houses. They tried to cry, when they got back, but they couldn't make the least sound."

"Why couldn't they?"

"Because they had lost their voices, saying 'Merry Christmas' so much. Did I tell you how it was on the Fourth of July?"

"No; how was it?" And the little girl nestled closer, in expectation of something uncommon.

Well, the night before, the boys stayed up to celebrate, as they always do, and fell asleep before twelve o'clock, as usual, expecting to be wakened by the bells and cannon. But it was nearly eight o'clock before the first boy in the United States woke up, and then he found out what the trouble was. As soon as he could get his clothes on he ran out of the house and smashed a big cannon-torpedo down on the pavement; but it didn't make any more noise than a damp wad of paper; and after he tried about twenty or thirty more, he began to pick them up and look at them. Every single torpedo was a big raisin! Then he just streaked it up-stairs, and examined his fire-crackers and toy-pistol and two-dollar collection of fireworks, and found that they were nothing but sugar and candy painted up to look like fireworks! Before ten o'clock every boy in the United States found out that his Fourth of July things had turned into Christmas things; and then they just sat down and cried--they were so mad. There are about twenty million boys in the United States, and so you can imagine what a noise they made. Some men got together before night, with a little powder that hadn't turned into purple sugar yet, and they said they would fire off one cannon, anyway. But the cannon burst into a thousand pieces, for it was nothing but rock-candy, and some of the men nearly got killed. The Fourth of July orations all turned into Christmas carols, and when anybody tried to read the Declaration, instead of saying, "When in the course of human events it becomes necessary," he was sure to sing, "God rest you, merry gentlemen." It was perfectly awful.

The little girl drew a deep sigh of satisfaction.

"And how was it at Thanksgiving?"

141

Her papa hesitated. "Well, I'm almost afraid to tell you. I'm afraid you'll think it's wicked."

"Well, tell, anyway," said the little girl.

Well, before it came Thanksgiving it had leaked out who had caused all these Christmases. The little girl had suffered so much that she had talked about it in her sleep; and after that hardly anybody would play with her. People just perfectly despised her, because if it had not been for her greediness it wouldn't have happened; and now, when it came Thanksgiving, and she wanted them to go to church, and have squash-pie and turkey, and show their gratitude, they said that all the turkeys had been eaten up for her old Christmas dinners, and if she would stop the Christmases, they would see about the gratitude. Wasn't it dreadful? And the very next day the little girl began to send letters to the Christmas Fairy, and then telegrams, to stop it. But it didn't do any good; and then she got to calling at the Fairy's house, but the girl that came to the door always said, "Not at home," or "Engaged," or "At dinner," or something like that; and so it went on till it came to the old once-a-year Christmas Eve. The little girl fell asleep, and when she woke up in the morning--

"She found it was all nothing but a dream," suggested the little girl.

"No, indeed!" said her papa. "It was all every bit true!"

"Well, what did she find out, then?"

"Why, that it wasn't Christmas at last, and wasn't ever going to be, any more. Now it's time for breakfast."

The little girl held her papa fast around the neck.

"You sha'n't go if you're going to leave it so!"

"How do you want it left?"

"Christmas once a year."

142

"All right," said her papa; and he went on again.

Well, there was the greatest rejoicing all over the country, and it extended clear up into Canada. The people met together everywhere, and kissed and cried for joy. The city carts went around and gathered up all the candy and raisins and nuts, and dumped them into the river; and it made the fish perfectly sick; and the whole United States, as far out as Alaska, was one blaze of bonfires, where the children were burning up their gift-books and presents of all kinds. They had the greatest time!

The little girl went to thank the old Fairy because she had stopped its being Christmas, and she said she hoped she would keep her promise and see that Christmas never, never came again. Then the Fairy frowned, and asked her if she was sure she knew what she meant; and the little girl asked her, Why not? and the old Fairy said that now she was behaving just as greedily as ever, and she'd better look out. This made the little girl think it all over carefully again, and she said she would be willing to have it Christmas about once in a thousand years; and then she said a hundred, and then she said ten, and at last she got down to one. Then the Fairy said that was the good old way that had pleased people ever since Christmas began, and she was agreed. Then the little girl said, "What're your shoes made of?" And the Fairy said, "Leather." And the little girl said, "Bargain's done forever," and skipped off, and hippity-hopped the whole way home, she was so glad.

"How will that do?" asked the papa.

"First-rate!" said the little girl; but she hated to have the story stop, and was rather sober. However, her mamma put her head in at the door, and asked her papa:

"Are you never coming to breakfast? What have you been telling that child?"

"Oh, just a moral tale."

The little girl caught him around the neck again.

"We know! Don't you tell what, papa! Don't you tell what!"

The Pony Engine and the Pacific Express

By William Dean Howells

Christmas Eve, after the children had hung up their stockings and got all ready for St. Nic, they climbed up on the papa's lap to kiss him good-night, and when they both got their arms round his neck, they said they were not going to bed till he told them a Christmas story. Then he saw that he would have to mind, for they were awfully severe with him, and always made him do exactly what they told him; it was the way they had brought him up. He tried his best to get out of it for a while; but after they had shaken him first this side, and then that side, and pulled him backward and forward till he did not know where he was, he began to think perhaps he had better begin. The first thing he said, after he opened his eyes, and made believe he had been asleep, or something, was, "Well, what did I leave off at?" and that made them just perfectly boiling, for they understood his tricks, and they knew he was trying to pretend that he had told part of the story already; and they said he had not left off anywhere because he had not commenced, and he saw it was no use. So he commenced.

"Once there was a little Pony Engine that used to play round the Fitchburg Depot on the side tracks, and sleep in among the big locomotives in the car-house—"

The little girl lifted her head from the papa's shoulder, where she had dropped it. "Is it a sad story, papa?"

"How is it going to end?" asked the boy.

"Well, it's got a moral," said the papa.

"Oh, all right, if it's got a moral," said the children; they had a good deal of fun with the morals the papa put to his stories. The boy added, "Go on," and the little girl prompted, "Car-house."

The papa said, "Now every time you stop me I shall have to begin all over again." But he saw that this was not going to spite them any, so he went on: "One of the locomotives was its mother, and she had got hurt once in a big smash-up, so that she couldn't run long trips any more. She was so weak in the chest you could hear her wheeze as far as you could see her. But she could work round the depot, and pull empty cars in and out, and shunt them off on the side tracks; and she was so anxious to be useful that all the other engines respected her, and they were very kind to the little Pony Engine on her account, though it was always getting in the way, and under their wheels, and everything. They all knew it was an orphan, for before its mother got hurt its father went through a bridge one dark night into an arm of the sea, and was never heard of again; he was supposed to have been drowned. The old mother locomotive used to say that it would never have happened if she had been there; but poor dear No. 236 was always so venturesome, and she had warned him against that very bridge time and again. Then she would whistle so dolefully, and sigh with her air-brakes enough to make anybody cry. You see they used to be a very happy family when they were all together, before the papa locomotive got drowned. He was very fond of the little Pony Engine, and told it stories at night after they got into the car-house, at the end of some of his long runs. It would get up on his cow-catcher, and lean its chimney up against his, and listen till it fell asleep. Then he would put it softly down, and be off again in the morning before it was awake. I tell you, those were happy days for poor No. 236. The little Pony Engine could just remember him; it was awfully proud of its papa."

The boy lifted his head and looked at the little girl, who suddenly hid her face in the papa's other shoulder. "Well, I declare, papa, she was putting up her lip."

"I wasn't, any such thing!" said the little girl. "And I don't care! So!" and then she sobbed.

"Now, never you mind," said the papa to the boy. "You'll be putting up your lip before I'm through. Well, and then she used to caution the little Pony Engine against getting in the way of the big locomotives, and told it to keep close round after her, and try to do all it could to learn about shifting empty cars. You see, she knew how ambitious the little Pony Engine was, and how it wasn't contented a bit just to grow up in the pony-engine business, and be tied down to the depot all its days. Once she happened to tell it that if it was good and always did what it was bid, perhaps a cow-catcher would grow on it some day, and then it could be a passenger locomotive. Mammas have to promise all sorts of things, and she was almost distracted when she said that."

"I don't think she ought to have deceived it, papa," said the boy. "But it ought to have known that if it was a Pony Engine to begin with, it never could have a cow-catcher."

"Couldn't it?" asked the little girl, gently.

"No; they're kind of mooley."

The little girl asked the papa, "What makes Pony Engines mooley?" for she did not choose to be told by her brother; he was only two years older than she was, anyway.

"Well; it's pretty hard to say. You see, when a locomotive is first hatched—"

"Oh, are they hatched, papa?" asked the boy.

"Well, we'll call it hatched," said the papa; but they knew he was just funning. "They're about the size of tea-kettles at first; and it's a chance whether they will have cow-catchers or not. If they keep their spouts, they will; and if their spouts drop off, they won't."

"What makes the spout ever drop off?"

"Oh, sometimes the pip, or the gapes—"

The children both began to shake the papa, and he was glad enough to go on sensibly. "Well, anyway, the mother locomotive certainly oughtn't to have deceived it. Still she had to say something, and perhaps the little Pony Engine was better employed watching its buffers with its head-light, to see whether its cow-catcher had begun to grow, than it would have been in listening to the stories of the old locomotives, and sometimes their swearing."

"Do they swear, papa?" asked the little girl, somewhat shocked, and yet pleased.

"Well, I never heard them, near by. But it sounds a good deal like swearing when you hear them on the up-grade on our hill in the night. Where was I?"

"Swearing," said the boy. "And please don't go back, now, papa."

"Well, I won't. It'll be as much as I can do to get through this story, without going over any of it again. Well, the thing that the little Pony Engine wanted to be, the most in this world, was the locomotive of the Pacific Express, that starts out every afternoon at three, you know. It intended to apply for the place as soon as its cow-catcher was grown, and it was always trying to attract the locomotive's attention, backing and filling on the track alongside of the train; and once it raced it a little piece, and beat it, before the Express locomotive was under way, and almost got in front of it on a switch. My, but its mother was scared! She just yelled to it with her whistle; and that night she sent it to sleep without a particle of coal or water in its tender.

"But the little Pony Engine didn't care. It had beaten the Pacific Express in a hundred yards, and what was to hinder it from beating it as long as it chose? The little Pony Engine could not get it out of its head. It was just like a boy who thinks he can whip a man."

The boy lifted his head. "Well, a boy can, papa, if he goes to do it the right way. Just stoop down before the man knows it, and catch him by the legs and tip him right over."

148

"Ho! I guess you see yourself!" said the little girl, scornfully.

"Well, I could!" said the boy; "and some day I'll just show you."

"Now, little cock-sparrow, now!" said the papa; and he laughed. "Well, the little Pony Engine thought he could beat the Pacific Express, anyway; and so one dark, snowy, blowy afternoon, when his mother was off pushing some empty coal cars up past the Know-Nothing crossing beyond Charlestown, he got on the track in front of the Express, and when he heard the conductor say 'All aboard,' and the starting gong struck, and the brakemen leaned out and waved to the engineer, he darted off like lightning. He had his steam up, and he just scuttled.

"Well, he was so excited for a while that he couldn't tell whether the Express was gaining on him or not; but after twenty or thirty miles, he thought he heard it pretty near. Of course the Express locomotive was drawing a heavy train of cars, and it had to make a stop or two—at Charlestown, and at Concord Junction, and at Ayer—so the Pony Engine did really gain on it a little; and when it began to be scared it gained a good deal. But the first place where it began to feel sorry, and to want its mother, was in Hoosac Tunnel. It never was in a tunnel before, and it seemed as if it would never get out. It kept thinking, What if the Pacific Express was to run over it there in the dark, and its mother off there at the Fitchburg Depot, in Boston, looking for it among the side-tracks? It gave a perfect shriek; and just then it shot out of the tunnel. There were a lot of locomotives loafing around there at North Adams, and one of them shouted out to it as it flew by, 'What's your hurry, little one?' and it just screamed back, 'Pacific Express!' and never stopped to explain. They talked in locomotive language—"

"Oh, what did it sound like?" the boy asked.

"Well, pretty queer; I'll tell you some day. It knew it had no time to fool away, and all through the long, dark night, whenever, a locomotive hailed it, it just screamed, 'Pacific Express!' and kept on. And the Express kept gaining on it. Some of the locomotives wanted to stop it, but they decided they had better not get in its way, and so it whizzed along across New York State and Ohio and Indiana, till it got to Chicago. And the Express kept gaining on it. By that time it was so hoarse it could hardly whisper, but it kept saying, 'Pacific Express! Pacific Express!' and it kept right on till it reached the Mississippi River. There it found a long train of freight cars before it on the bridge. It couldn't wait, and so it slipped down from the track to the edge of the river and jumped across, and then scrambled up the embankment to the track again."

"Papa!" said the little girl, warningly.

"Truly it did," said the papa.

"Ho! that's nothing," said the boy. "A whole train of cars did it in that Jules Verne book."

"Well," the papa went on, "after that it had a little rest, for the Express had to wait for the freight train to get off the bridge, and the Pony Engine stopped at the first station for a drink of water and a mouthful of coal, and then it flew ahead. There was a kind old locomotive at Omaha that tried to find out where it belonged, and what its mother's name was, but the Pony Engine was so bewildered it couldn't tell. And the Express kept gaining on it. On the plains it was chased by a pack of prairie wolves, but it left them far behind; and the antelopes were scared half to death. But the worst of it was when the nightmare got after it."

"The nightmare? Goodness!" said the boy.

"I've had the nightmare," said the little girl.

"Oh yes, a mere human nightmare," said the papa. "But a locomotive nightmare is a very different thing."

"Why, what's it like?" asked the boy. The little girl was almost afraid to ask.

"Well, it has only one leg, to begin with."

150

"Pshaw!"

"Wheel, I mean. And it has four cow-catchers, and four head-lights, and two boilers, and eight whistles, and it just goes whirling and screeching along. Of course it wobbles awfully; and as it's only got one wheel, it has to keep skipping from one track to the other."

"I should think it would run on the cross-ties," said the boy.

"Oh, very well, then!" said the papa. "If you know so much more about it than I do! Who's telling this story, anyway? Now I shall have to go back to the beginning. Once there was a little Pony En—"

They both put their hands over his mouth, and just fairly begged him to go on, and at last he did. "Well, it got away from the nightmare about morning, but not till the nightmare had bitten a large piece out of its tender, and then it braced up for the home-stretch. It thought that if it could once beat the Express to the Sierras, it could keep the start the rest of the way, for it could get over the mountains quicker than the Express could, and it might be in San Francisco before the Express got to Sacramento. The Express kept gaining on it. But it just zipped along the upper edge of Kansas and the lower edge of Nebraska, and on through Colorado and Utah and Nevada, and when it got to the Sierras it just stooped a little, and went over them like a goat; it did, truly; just doubled up its fore wheels under it, and jumped. And the Express kept gaining on it. By this time it couldn't say 'Pacific Express' any more, and it didn't try. It just said 'Express! Express!' and then ''Press! 'Press!' and then ''Ess! 'Ess!' and pretty soon only ''Ss! 'Ss!' And the Express kept gaining on it. Before they reached San Francisco, the Express locomotive's cow-catcher was almost touching the Pony Engine's tender; it gave one howl of anguish as it felt the Express locomotive's hot breath on the place where the nightmare had bitten the piece out, and tore through the end of the San Francisco depot, and plunged into the Pacific Ocean, and was never seen again. There, now," said the papa, trying to make the children get down, "that's all. Go to bed." The little girl was crying, and so he tried to comfort her by keeping her in his lap.

The boy cleared his throat. "What is the moral, papa?" he asked, huskily.

"Children, obey your parents," said the papa.

"And what became of the mother locomotive?" pursued the boy.

"She had a brain-fever, and never quite recovered the use of her mind again."

The boy thought awhile. "Well, I don't see what it had to do with Christmas, anyway."

"Why, it was Christmas Eve when the Pony Engine started from Boston, and Christmas afternoon when it reached San Francisco."

"Ho!" said the boy. "No locomotive could get across the continent in a day and a night, let alone a little Pony Engine."

"But this Pony Engine had to. Did you never hear of the beaver that clomb the tree?"

"No! Tell—"

"Yes, some other time."

"But how could it get across so quick? Just one day!"

"Well, perhaps it was a year. Maybe it was the next Christmas after that when it got to San Francisco."

The papa set the little girl down, and started to run out of the room, and both of the children ran after him, to pound him.

When they were in bed the boy called down-stairs to the papa, "Well, anyway, I didn't put up my lip."

THE END

Merry Christmas

By Stephen Leacock

"MY DEAR Young Friend," said Father Time, as he laid his hand gently upon my shoulder, "you are entirely wrong."

Then I looked up over my shoulder from the table at which I was sitting and I saw him.

But I had known, or felt, for at least the last half-hour that he as standing somewhere near me.

You have had, I do not doubt, good reader, more than once that strange uncanny feeling that there is some one unseen standing beside you, in a darkened room, let us say, with a dying fire, when the night has grown late, and the October wind sounds low outside, and when, through the thin curtain that we call Reality, the Unseen World starts for a moment clear upon our dreaming sense.

You have had it? Yes, I know you have. Never mind telling me about it. Stop. I don't want to hear about that strange presentiment you had the night your Aunt Eliza broke her leg. Don't let's bother with your experience. I want to tell mine.

"You are quite mistaken, my dear young friend," repeated Father Time, "quite wrong."

"Young friend?" I said, my mind, as one's mind is apt to in such a case, running to an unimportant detail. "Why do you call me young?"

"Your pardon," he answered gently — he had a gentle way with him, had Father Time. "The fault is in my failing eyes. I took you at first sight for something under a hundred."

"Under a hundred?" I expostulated. "Well, I should think so!"

"Your pardon again," said Time, "the fault is in my failing memory. I forgot. You seldom pass that nowadays, do you? Your life is very short of late."

I heard him breathe a wistful hollow sigh. Very ancient and dim he seemed as he stood beside me. But I did not turn to look upon him. I had no need to. I knew his form, in the inner and clearer sight of things, as well as every human being knows by innate instinct, the Unseen face and form of Father Time.

I could hear him murmuring beside me, "Short — short, your life is short"; till the sound of it seemed to mingle with the measured ticking of a clock somewhere in the silent house.

Then I remembered what he had said.

"How do you know that I am wrong?" I asked. "And how can you tell what I was thinking?"

"You, said it out loud," answered Father Time. "But it wouldn't have mattered, anyway. You said that Christmas was all played out and done with."

"Yes," I admitted, "that's what I said."

"And what makes you think that?" he questioned, stooping, so it seemed to me, still further over my shoulder.

"Why," I answered, "the trouble is this. I've been sitting here for hours, sitting till goodness only knows how far into the night, trying to think out something to write for a Christmas story. And it won't go. It can't be done — not in these awful days."

"A Christmas Story?"

"Yes. You see, Father Time," I explained, glad with a foolish little vanity of my trade to be able to tell him something that I thought enlightening, "all the Christmas stuff — stories and jokes and pictures — is all done, you know, in October."

I thought it would have surprised him, but I was mistaken.

"Dear me," he said, "not till October! What a rush! How well I remember in Ancient Egypt — as I think you call it — seeing them getting out their Christmas things, all cut in hieroglyphics, always two or three years ahead."

"Two or three years!" I exclaimed.

"Pooh," said Time, "that was nothing. Why in Babylon they used to get their Christmas jokes ready — all baked in clay — a whole Solar eclipse ahead of Christmas. They said, I think, that the public preferred them so."

"Egypt?" I said. "Babylon? But surely, Father Time, there was no Christmas in those days. I thought — —"

"My dear boy," he interrupted gravely, "don't you know that there has always been Christmas?"

I was silent. Father Time had moved across the room and stood beside the fireplace, leaning on the mantelpiece. The little wreaths of smoke from the fading fire seemed to mingle with his shadowy outline.

"Well," he said presently, "what is it that is wrong with Christmas?"

"Why," I answered, "all the romance, the joy, the beauty of it has gone, crushed and killed by the greed of commerce and the horrors of war. I am not, as you thought I was, a hundred years old, but I can conjure up, as anybody can, a picture of Christmas in the good old days of a hundred years ago: the quaint old-fashioned houses, standing deep among the evergreens, with the light twinkling from the windows on the snow; the warmth and comfort within; the great fire roaring on the hearth; the merry guests grouped about its blaze and the little children with their eyes dancing in the Christmas fire- light, waiting for Father Christmas in his fine mummery of red and white and cotton wool to

155

hand the presents from the yule-tide tree. I can see it," I added, "as if it were yesterday."

"It was but yesterday," said Father Time, and his voice seemed to soften with the memory of bygone years. "I remember it well."

"Ah," I continued, "that was Christmas indeed. Give me back such days as those, with the old good cheer, the old stage coaches and the gabled inns, the snapdragon and the Christmas-tree, and I'll believe again in Christmas, yes, in Father Christmas himself."

"Believe in him?" said Time quietly. "You may well do that. He happens to be standing outside in the street at this moment."

"Outside?" I exclaimed. "Why don't he come in?"

"He's afraid to," said Father Time. "He's frightened and he daren't come in unless you ask him. May I call him in?"

I signified assent, and Father Time went to the window for a moment and beckoned into the darkened street. Then I heard footsteps, clumsy and hesitant they seemed, upon the stairs. And in a moment a figure stood framed in the doorway — the figure of Father Christmas. He stood shuffling his feet, a timid, apologetic look upon his face.

How changed he was!

I had known in my mind's eye, from childhood up, the face and form of Father Christmas as well as that of Old Time himself. Everybody knows, or once knew him — a jolly little rounded man, with a great muffler wound about him, a packet of toys upon his back and with such merry, twinkling eyes and rosy cheeks as are only given by the touch of the driving snow and the rude fun of the North Wind. Why, there was once a time, not yet so long ago, when the very sound of his sleigh-bells sent the blood running warm to the heart.

But now how changed.

156

All draggled with the mud and rain he stood, as if no house had sheltered him these three years past. His old red Jersey was tattered in a dozen places, his muffler frayed and ravelled.

The bundle of toys that he dragged with him in a net seemed wet and worn till the cardboard boxes gaped asunder. There were boxes among them, I vow, that he must have been carrying these three past years.

But most of all I noted the change that had come over the face of Father Christmas. The old brave look of cheery confidence was gone. The smile that had beamed responsive to the laughing eyes of countless children around unnumbered Christmas- trees was there no more. And in the place of it there showed a look of timid apology, of apprehensiveness, as of one who has asked in vain the warmth and shelter of a human home — such a look as the harsh cruelty of this world has stamped upon the faces of its outcasts.

So stood Father Christmas shuffling upon the threshold, fumbling his poor tattered hat in his hand.

"Shall I come in?" he said, his eyes appealingly on Father Time.

"Come," said Time. He turned to speak to me, "Your room is dark. Turn up the lights. He's used to light, bright light and plenty of it. The dark has frightened him these three years past."

I turned up the lights and the bright glare revealed all the more cruelly the tattered figure before us.

Father Christmas advanced a timid step across the floor. Then he paused, as if in sudden fear.

"Is this floor mined?" he said.

"No, no," said Time soothingly. And to me he added in a murmured whisper, "He's afraid. He was blown up in a mine in No Man's Land between the trenches at Christmas-time in 1914. It broke his nerve."

"May I put my toys on that machine gun?" asked Father Christmas timidly. "It will help to keep them dry."

"It is not a machine gun," said Time gently. "See, it is only a pile of books upon the sofa." And to me he whispered, "They turned a machine gun on him in the streets of Warsaw. He thinks he sees them everywhere since then."

"It's all right, Father Christmas," I said, speaking as cheerily as I could, while I rose and stirred the fire into a blaze.

"There are no machine guns here and there are no mines. This is but the house of a poor writer."

"Ah," said Father Christmas, lowering his tattered hat still further and attempting something of a humble bow, "a writer? Are you Hans Andersen, perhaps?"

"Not quite," I answered.

"But a great writer, I do not doubt," said the old man, with a humble courtesy that he had learned, it well may be, centuries ago in the yule-tide season of his northern home. "The world owes much to its great books. I carry some of the greatest with me always. I have them here — —"

He began fumbling among the limp and tattered packages that he carried. "Look! The House that Jack Built — a marvellous, deep thing, sir — and this, The Babes in the Wood. Will you take it, sir? A poor present, but a present still — not so long ago I gave them in thousands every Christmas-time. None seem to want them now."

He looked appealingly towards Father Time, as the weak may look towards the strong, for help and guidance.

"None want them now," he repeated, and I could see the tears start in his eyes. "Why is it so? Has the world forgotten its sympathy with the lost children wandering in the wood?"

158

"All the world," I heard Time murmur with a sigh, "is wandering in the wood." But out loud he spoke to Father Christmas in cheery admonition, "Tut, tut, good Christmas," he said, "you must cheer up. Here, sit in this chair the biggest one; so — beside the fire. Let us stir it to a blaze; more wood, that's better. And listen, good old Friend, to the wind outside — almost a Christmas wind, is it not? Merry and boisterous enough, for all the evil times it stirs among."

Old Christmas seated himself beside the fire, his hands outstretched towards the flames. Something of his old-time cheeriness seemed to flicker across his features as he warmed himself at the blaze.

"That's better," he murmured. "I was cold, sir, cold, chilled to the bone. Of old I never felt it so; no matter what the wind, the world seemed warm about me. Why is it not so now?

"You see," said Time, speaking low in a whisper for my ear alone, "how sunk and broken he is? Will you not help?"

"Gladly," I answered, "if I can."

"All can," said Father Time, "every one of us."

Meantime Christmas had turned towards me a questioning eye, in which, however, there seemed to revive some little gleam of merriment.

"Have you, perhaps," he asked half timidly, "something warm to drink?"

"Something warm to drink?" I repeated.

"Ay, something warm to drink. A glass of it to drink to your health might warm my heart again, I think."

"Ah," I said, "something to drink?"

"His one failing," whispered Time, "if it is one. Forgive it him. He was used to it for centuries. Give it to him if you have it."

"I keep a little of it in the house," I said reluctantly perhaps, "in case of illness."

"Tut, tut," said Father Time, as something as near as could be to a smile passed over his shadowy face. "In case of illness! They used to say that in ancient Babylon. Here, let me pour it for him. Drink, Father Christmas, drink! "

Marvellous it was to see the old man smack his lips as he drank his glass of tea after the fashion of old Norway.

Marvellous, too, to see the way in which, with the warmth of the fire and the generous glow of the spirits, his face changed and brightened till the old-time cheerfulness beamed again upon it. He looked about him, as it were, with a new and growing interest.

"A pleasant room," he said. "And what better, sir, than the wind without and a brave fire within!"

Then his eye fell upon the mantelpiece, where lay among the litter of books and pipes a little toy horse.

"Ah," said Father Christmas almost gayly, "children in the house!"

"One," I answered, "the sweetest boy in all the world."

"I'll be bound he is!" said Father Christmas and he broke now into a merry laugh that did one's heart good to hear. "They all are! Lord bless me! The number that I have seen, and each and every one — and quite right too — the sweetest child in all the world. And how old, do you say? Two and a half all but two months except a week? The very sweetest age of all, I'll bet you say, eh, what? They all do!"

And the old man broke again into such a jolly chuckling of laughter that his snow-white locks shook upon his head.

"But stop a bit," he added. "This horse is broken. Tut, tut, a hind leg nearly off. This won't do!"

He had the toy in his lap in a moment, mending it. It was wonderful to see, for all his age, how deft his fingers were.

"Time," he said, and it was amusing to note that his voice had assumed almost an authoritative tone, "reach me that piece of string. That's right. Here, hold your finger across the knot. There! Now, then, a bit of beeswax. What? No beeswax? Tut, tut, how ill-supplied your houses are to-day. How can you mend toys, sir, without beeswax? Still, it will stand up now."

I tried to murmur by best thanks.

But Father Christmas waved my gratitude aside.

"Nonsense," he said, "that's nothing. That's my life. Perhaps the little boy would like a book too. I have them here in the packet. Here, sir, Jack and the Bean Stalk, most profound thing. I read it to myself often still. How damp it is! Pray, sir, will you let me dry my books before your fire?"

"Only too willingly," I said. "How wet and torn they are!"

Father Christmas had risen from his chair and was fumbling among his tattered packages, taking from them his children's books, all limp and draggled from the rain and wind.

"All wet and torn!" he murmured, and his voice sank again into sadness. "I have carried them these three years past. Look! These were for little children in Belgium and in Serbia, Can I get them to them, think you?"

Time gently shook his head.

"But presently, perhaps," said Father Christmas, "if I dry and mend them. Look, some of them were inscribed already! This one, see you, was written 'With father's love.' Why has it never come to him? Is it rain or tears upon the page?"

He stood bowed over his little books, his hands trembling as he turned the pages. Then he looked up, the old fear upon his face again.

"That sound!" he said. "Listen I It is guns — I hear them."

"No" no," I said, "it is nothing. Only a car passing in the street below."

"Listen," he said. "Hear that again — voices crying!"

"No, no," I answered, "not voices, only the night wind among the trees."

"My children's voices!" he exclaimed. "I hear them everywhere — they come to me in every wind — and I see them as I wander in the night and storm — my children — torn and dying in the trenches — beaten into the ground — I hear them crying from the hospitals — each one to me, still as I knew him once, a little child. Time, Time," he cried, reaching out his arms in appeal, "give me back my children!"

"They do not die in vain," Time murmured gently.

But Christmas only moaned in answer:

"Give me back my children! "

Then he sank down upon his pile of books and toys, his head buried in his arms.

"You see," said Time, "his heart is breaking, and will you not help him if you can?"

"Only too gladly," I replied. "But what is there to do?"

"This," said Father Time, "listen."

He stood before me grave and solemn, a shadowy figure but half seen though he was close beside me. The fire-light had died down, and through the curtained windows there came already the first dim brightening of dawn.

"The world that once you knew," said Father Time, "seems broken and destroyed about you. You must not let them know — the children. The cruelty and the horror and the hate that racks the world to-day — keep it from them. Some day he will know" — here Time pointed to the prostrate form of Father Christmas — "that his children, that once were, have not died in vain: that from their sacrifice shall come a nobler, better world for all to live in, a world where countless happy children shall hold bright their memory for ever. But for the children of To-day, save and spare them all you can from the evil hate and horror of the war. Later they will know and understand. Not yet. Give them. back their Merry Christmas and its kind thoughts, and its Christmas charity, till later on there shall be with it again Peace upon Earth Good Will towards Men."

His voice ceased. It seemed to vanish, as it were, in the sighing of the wind.

I looked up. Father Time and Christmas had vanished from the room. The fire was low and the day was breaking visibly outside.

"Let us begin," I murmured. "I will mend this broken horse."

I Heard the Bells On Christmas Day

By Henry Wadsworth Longfellow

I heard the bells on Christmas Day
Their old, familiar carols play,
   And wild and sweet
   The words repeat
Of peace on earth, good-will to men!

And thought how, as the day had come,
The belfries of all Christendom
   Had rolled along
   The unbroken song
Of peace on earth, good-will to men!

Till, ringing, singing on its way,
The world revolved from night to day
   A voice, a chime,
   A chant sublime
Of peace on earth, good-will to men!

Then from each black, accursed mouth,
The cannon thundered in the South,
   And with the sound
   The carols drowned
Of peace on earth, good-will to men!

It was as if an earthquake rent
The hearth-stones of a continent,
   And made forlorn
   The households born

Of peace on earth, good-will to men!

And in despair I bowed my head ;
"There is no peace on earth," I said ;
   "For hate is strong
   And mocks the song
Of peace on earth, good-will to men!"

Then pealed the bells more loud and deep:
"God is not dead ; nor doth he sleep !
   The Wrong shall fail,
   The Right prevail,
With peace on earth, good-will to men!"

The Three Kings

By Henry Wadsworth Longfellow

Three Kings came riding from far away,
  Melchior and Gaspar and Baltasar;
Three Wise Men out of the East were they,
And they travelled by night and they slept by day,
  For their guide was a beautiful, wonderful star.

The star was so beautiful, large, and clear,
  That all the other stars of the sky
Became a white mist in the atmosphere,
And by this they knew that the coming was near
  Of the Prince foretold in the prophecy.

Three caskets they bore on their saddle-bows,
  Three caskets of gold with golden keys;
Their robes were of crimson silk with rows
Of bells and pomegranates and furbelows,
  Their turbans like blossoming almond-trees.

And so the Three Kings rode into the West,
  Through the dusk of night, over hill and dell,
And sometimes they nodded with beard on breast
And sometimes talked, as they paused to rest,
  With the people they met at some wayside well.

"Of the child that is born," said Baltasar,
  "Good people, I pray you, tell us the news;
For we in the East have seen his star,
And have ridden fast, and have ridden far,

To find and worship the King of the Jews."

And the people answered, "You ask in vain;
  We know of no king but Herod the Great!"
They thought the Wise Men were men insane,
As they spurred their horses across the plain,
  Like riders in haste, and who cannot wait.

And when they came to Jerusalem,
  Herod the Great, who had heard this thing,
Sent for the Wise Men and questioned them;
And said, "Go down unto Bethlehem,
  And bring me tidings of this new king."

So they rode away; and the star stood still,
  The only one in the gray of morn
Yes, it stopped, it stood still of its own free will,
Right over Bethlehem on the hill,
  The city of David, where Christ was born.

And the Three Kings rode through the gate and the guard,
  Through the silent street, till their horses turned
And neighed as they entered the great inn-yard;
But the windows were closed, and the doors were barred,
  And only a light in the stable burned.

And cradled there in the scented hay,
  In the air made sweet by the breath of kine,
The little child in the manger lay,
The child, that would be king one day
  Of a kingdom not human but divine.

His mother Mary of Nazareth
  Sat watching beside his place of rest,
Watching the even flow of his breath,
For the joy of life and the terror of death
  Were mingled together in her breast.

They laid their offerings at his feet:
  The gold was their tribute to a King,
The frankincense, with its odor sweet,
Was for the Priest, the Paraclete,
  The myrrh for the body's burying.

And the mother wondered and bowed her head,
  And sat as still as a statue of stone;
Her heart was troubled yet comforted,
Remembering what the Angel had said
  Of an endless reign and of David's throne.

Then the Kings rode out of the city gate,
  With a clatter of hoofs in proud array;
But they went not back to Herod the Great,
For they knew his malice and feared his hate,
  And returned to their homes by another way.

Christmastide

By H. P. Lovecraft

The cottage hearth beams warm and bright,
The candles gaily glow;
The stars emit a kinder light
Above the drifted snow.

Down from the sky a magic steals
To glad the passing year,
And belfries sing with joyous peals,
For Christmastide is here!

Christmas at Red Butte

By L. M. Montgomery

"Of course Santa Claus will come," said Jimmy Martin confidently. Jimmy was ten, and at ten it is easy to be confident. "Why, he's got to come because it is Christmas Eve, and he always has come. You know that, twins."

Yes, the twins knew it and, cheered by Jimmy's superior wisdom, their doubts passed away. There had been one terrible moment when Theodora had sighed and told them they mustn't be too much disappointed if Santa Claus did not come this year because the crops had been poor, and he mightn't have had enough presents to go around.

"That doesn't make any difference to Santa Claus," scoffed Jimmy. "You know as well as I do, Theodora Prentice, that Santa Claus is rich whether the crops fail or not. They failed three years ago, before Father died, but Santa Claus came all the same. Prob'bly you don't remember it, twins, 'cause you were too little, but I do. Of course he'll come, so don't you worry a mite. And he'll bring my skates and your dolls. He knows we're expecting them, Theodora, 'cause we wrote him a letter last week, and threw it up the chimney. And there'll be candy and nuts, of course, and Mother's gone to town to buy a turkey. I tell you we're going to have a ripping Christmas."

"Well, don't use such slangy words about it, Jimmy-boy," sighed Theodora. She couldn't bear to dampen their hopes any further, and perhaps Aunt Elizabeth might manage it if the colt sold well. But Theodora had her painful doubts, and she sighed again as she looked out of the window far down the trail that wound across the prairie, red-lighted by the declining sun of the short wintry afternoon.

"Do people always sigh like that when they get to be sixteen?" asked Jimmy curiously. "You didn't sigh like that when you were only fifteen,

Theodora. I wish you wouldn't. It makes me feel funny—and it's not a nice kind of funniness either."

"It's a bad habit I've got into lately," said Theodora, trying to laugh. "Old folks are dull sometimes, you know, Jimmy-boy."

"Sixteen is awful old, isn't it?" said Jimmy reflectively. "I'll tell you what I'm going to do when I'm sixteen, Theodora. I'm going to pay off the mortgage, and buy mother a silk dress, and a piano for the twins. Won't that be elegant? I'll be able to do that 'cause I'm a man. Of course if I was only a girl I couldn't."

"I hope you'll be a good kind brave man and a real help to your mother," said Theodora softly, sitting down before the cosy fire and lifting the fat little twins into her lap.

"Oh, I'll be good to her, never you fear," assured Jimmy, squatting comfortably down on the little fur rug before the stove—the skin of the coyote his father had killed four years ago. "I believe in being good to your mother when you've only got the one. Now tell us a story, Theodora—a real jolly story, you know, with lots of fighting in it. Only please don't kill anybody. I like to hear about fighting, but I like to have all the people come out alive."

Theodora laughed, and began a story about the Riel Rebellion of '85—a story which had the double merit of being true and exciting at the same time. It was quite dark when she finished, and the twins were nodding, but Jimmy's eyes were wide open and sparkling.

"That was great," he said, drawing a long breath. "Tell us another."

"No, it's bedtime for you all," said Theodora firmly. "One story at a time is my rule, you know."

"But I want to sit up till Mother comes home," objected Jimmy.

"You can't. She may be very late, for she would have to wait to see Mr. Porter. Besides, you don't know what time Santa Claus might come—if he comes at all. If he were to drive along and see you children up instead of being sound asleep in bed, he might go right on and never call at all."

This argument was too much for Jimmy.

"All right, we'll go. But we have to hang up our stockings first. Twins, get yours."

The twins toddled off in great excitement, and brought back their Sunday stockings, which Jimmy proceeded to hang along the edge of the mantel shelf. This done, they all trooped obediently off to bed. Theodora gave another sigh, and seated herself at the window, where she could watch the moonlit prairie for Mrs. Martin's homecoming and knit at the same time.

I am afraid that you will think from all the sighing Theodora was doing that she was a very melancholy and despondent young lady. You couldn't think anything more unlike the real Theodora. She was the jolliest, bravest girl of sixteen in all Saskatchewan, as her shining brown eyes and rosy, dimpled cheeks would have told you; and her sighs were not on her own account, but simply for fear the children were going to be disappointed. She knew that they would be almost heartbroken if Santa Claus did not come, and that this would hurt the patient hardworking little mother more than all else.

Five years before this, Theodora had come to live with Uncle George and Aunt Elizabeth in the little log house at Red Butte. Her own mother had just died, and Theodora had only her big brother Donald left, and Donald had Klondike fever. The Martins were poor, but they had gladly made room for their little niece, and Theodora had lived there ever since, her aunt's right-hand girl and the beloved playmate of the children. They had been very happy until Uncle George's death two years before this Christmas Eve; but since then there had been hard times in the little log house, and though Mrs. Martin and Theodora did their best, it was a woefully hard task to make both ends meet, especially this year when their crops had been poor. Theodora and her aunt had made every sacrifice possible for the children's sake, and at least Jimmy and the twins had not felt the pinch very severely yet.

At seven Mrs. Martins bells jingled at the door and Theodora flew out. "Go right in and get warm, Auntie," she said briskly. "I'll take Ned away and unharness him."

"It's a bitterly cold night," said Mrs. Martin wearily. There was a note of discouragement in her voice that struck dismay to Theodora's heart.

"I'm afraid it means no Christmas for the children tomorrow," she thought sadly, as she led Ned away to the stable. When she returned to the kitchen Mrs. Martin was sitting by the fire, her face in her chilled hand, sobbing convulsively.

"Auntie—oh, Auntie, don't!" exclaimed Theodora impulsively. It was such a rare thing to see her plucky, resolute little aunt in tears. "You're cold and tired—I'll have a nice cup of tea for you in a trice."

"No, it isn't that," said Mrs. Martin brokenly "It was seeing those stockings hanging there. Theodora, I couldn't get a thing for the children—not a single thing. Mr. Porter would only give forty dollars for the colt, and when all the bills were paid there was barely enough left for such necessaries as we must have. I suppose I ought to feel thankful I could get those. But the thought of the children's disappointment tomorrow is more than I can bear. It would have been better to have told them long ago, but I kept building on getting more for the colt. Well, it's weak and foolish to give way like this. We'd better both take a cup of tea and go to bed. It will save fuel."

When Theodora went up to her little room her face was very thoughtful. She took a small box from her table and carried it to the window. In it was a very pretty little gold locket hung on a narrow blue ribbon. Theodora held it tenderly in her fingers, and looked out over the moonlit prairie with a very sober face. Could she give up her dear

173

locket—the locket Donald had given her just before he started for the Klondike? She had never thought she could do such a thing. It was almost the only thing she had to remind her of Donald—handsome, merry, impulsive, warmhearted Donald, who had gone away four years ago with a smile on his bonny face and splendid hope in his heart.

"Here's a locket for you, Gift o' God," he had said gaily—he had such a dear loving habit of calling her by the beautiful meaning of her name. A lump came into Theodora's throat as she remembered it. "I couldn't afford a chain too, but when I come back I'll bring you a rope of Klondike nuggets for it."

Then he had gone away. For two years letters had come from him regularly. Then he wrote that he had joined a prospecting party to a remote wilderness. After that was silence, deepening into anguish of suspense that finally ended in hopelessness. A rumour came that Donald Prentice was dead. None had returned from the expedition he had joined. Theodora had long ago given up all hope of ever seeing Donald again. Hence her locket was doubly dear to her.

But Aunt Elizabeth had always been so good and loving and kind to her. Could she not make the sacrifice for her sake? Yes, she could and would. Theodora flung up her head with a gesture that meant decision. She took out of the locket the bits of hair—her mother's and Donald's— which it contained (perhaps a tear or two fell as she did so) and then hastily donned her warmest cap and wraps. It was only three miles to Spencer; she could easily walk it in an hour and, as it was Christmas Eve, the shops would be open late. She must walk, for Ned could not be taken out again, and the mare's foot was sore. Besides, Aunt Elizabeth must not know until it was done.

As stealthily as if she were bound on some nefarious errand, Theodora slipped downstairs and out of the house. The next minute she was hurrying along the trail in the moonlight. The great dazzling prairie was around her, the mystery and splendour of the northern night all about her. It was very calm and cold, but Theodora walked so briskly that she kept warm. The trail from Red Butte to Spencer was a lonely one. Mr. Lurgan's house, halfway to town, was the only dwelling on it.

When Theodora reached Spencer she made her way at once to the only jewellery store the little town contained. Mr. Benson, its owner, had been a friend of her uncle's, and Theodora felt sure that he would buy her locket. Nevertheless her heart beat quickly, and her breath came and went uncomfortably fast as she went in. Suppose he wouldn't buy it. Then there would be no Christmas for the children at Red Butte.

"Good evening, Miss Theodora," said Mr. Benson briskly. "What can I do for you?"

"I'm afraid I'm not a very welcome sort of customer, Mr. Benson," said Theodora, with an uncertain smile. "I want to sell, not buy. Could you—will you buy this locket?"

Mr. Benson pursed up his lips, took up the locket, and examined it. "Well, I don't often buy second-hand stuff," he said, after some reflection, "but I don't mind obliging you, Miss Theodora. I'll give you four dollars for this trinket."

Theodora knew the locket had cost a great deal more than that, but four dollars would get what she wanted, and she dared not ask for more. In a few minutes the locket was in Mr. Benson's possession, and Theodora, with four crisp new bills in her purse, was hurrying to the toy store. Half an hour later she was on her way back to Red Butte, with as many parcels as she could carry—Jimmy's skates, two lovely dolls for the twins, packages of nuts and candy, and a nice plump turkey. Theodora beguiled her lonely tramp by picturing the children's joy in the morning.

About a quarter of a mile past Mr. Lurgan's house the trail curved suddenly about a bluff of poplars. As Theodora rounded the turn she halted in amazement. Almost at her feet the body of a man was lying across the road. He was clad in a big fur coat, and had a fur cap pulled well down over his forehead and ears. Almost all of him that could be seen was a full bushy beard. Theodora had no idea who he was, or where he had come from. But she realized that he was unconscious, and that he would speedily freeze to death if help were not brought. The footprints of a horse galloping across the prairie suggested a fall and a runaway, but Theodora did not waste time in speculation. She ran back at full speed to Mr. Lurgan's, and roused the household. In a few minutes Mr. Lurgan and his son had hitched a horse to a wood-sleigh, and hurried down the trail to the unfortunate man.

Theodora, knowing that her assistance was not needed, and that she ought to get home as quickly as possible, went on her way as soon as she had seen the stranger in safe keeping. When she reached the little log house she crept in, cautiously put the children's gifts in their stockings, placed the turkey on the table where Aunt Elizabeth would see it the first thing in the morning, and then slipped off to bed, a very weary but very happy girl.

The joy that reigned in the little log house the next day more than repaid Theodora for her sacrifice.

"Whoopee, didn't I tell you that Santa Claus would come all right!" shouted the delighted Jimmy. "Oh, what splendid skates!"

The twins hugged their dolls in silent rapture, but Aunt Elizabeth's face was the best of all.

Then the dinner had to be prepared, and everybody had a hand in that. Just as Theodora, after a grave peep into the oven, had announced that the turkey was done, a sleigh dashed around the house. Theodora flew to answer the knock at the door, and there stood Mr. Lurgan and a big, bewhiskered, fur-coated fellow whom Theodora recognized as the stranger she had found on the trail. But—was he a stranger? There was something oddly familiar in those merry brown eyes. Theodora felt herself growing dizzy.

"Donald!" she gasped. "Oh, Donald!"

And then she was in the big fellow's arms, laughing and crying at the same time.

Donald it was indeed. And then followed half an hour during which everybody talked at once, and the turkey would have been burned to a crisp had it not been for the presence of mind of Mr. Lurgan who, being the least excited of them all, took it out of the oven, and set it on the back of the stove.

"To think that it was you last night, and that I never dreamed it," exclaimed Theodora. "Oh, Donald, if I hadn't gone to town!"

"I'd have frozen to death, I'm afraid," said Donald soberly. "I got into Spencer on the last train last night. I felt that I must come right out—I couldn't wait till morning. But there wasn't a team to be got for love or money—it was Christmas Eve and all the livery rigs were out. So I came on horseback. Just by that bluff something frightened my horse, and he shied violently. I was half asleep and thinking of my little sister, and I went off like a shot. I suppose I struck my head against a tree. Anyway, I knew nothing more until I came to in Mr. Lurgan's kitchen. I wasn't much hurt—feel none the worse of it except for a sore head and shoulder. But, oh, Gift o' God, how you have grown! I can't realize that you are the little sister I left four years ago. I suppose you have been thinking I was dead?"

"Yes, and, oh, Donald, where have you been?"

"Well, I went way up north with a prospecting party. We had a tough time the first year, I can tell you, and some of us never came back. We weren't in a country where post offices were lying round loose either, you see. Then at last, just as we were about giving up in despair, we struck it rich. I've brought a snug little pile home with me, and things are going to look up in this log house, Gift o' God. There'll be no more worrying for you dear people over mortgages."

177

"I'm so glad—for Auntie's sake," said Theodora, with shining eyes. "But, oh, Donald, it's best of all just to have you back. I'm so perfectly happy that I don't know what to do or say."

"Well, I think you might have dinner," said Jimmy in an injured tone. "The turkey's getting stone cold, and I'm most starving. I just can't stand it another minute."

So, with a laugh, they all sat down to the table and ate the merriest Christmas dinner the little log house had ever known.

Uncle Richard's New Year Dinner

By L. M. Montgomery

Prissy Baker was in Oscar Miller's store New Year's morning, buying matches—for New Year's was not kept as a business holiday in Quincy—when her uncle, Richard Baker, came in. He did not look at Prissy, nor did she wish him a happy New Year; she would not have dared. Uncle Richard had not been on speaking terms with her or her father, his only brother, for eight years.

He was a big, ruddy, prosperous-looking man—an uncle to be proud of, Prissy thought wistfully, if only he were like other people's uncles, or, indeed, like what he used to be himself. He was the only uncle Prissy had, and when she had been a little girl they had been great friends; but that was before the quarrel, in which Prissy had had no share, to be sure, although Uncle Richard seemed to include her in his rancour.

Richard Baker, so he informed Mr. Miller, was on his way to Navarre with a load of pork.

"I didn't intend going over until the afternoon," he said, "but Joe Hemming sent word yesterday he wouldn't be buying pork after twelve today. So I have to tote my hogs over at once. I don't care about doing business New Year's morning."

"Should think New Year's would be pretty much the same as any other day to you," said Mr. Miller, for Richard Baker was a bachelor, with only old Mrs. Janeway to keep house for him.

"Well, I always like a good dinner on New Year's," said Richard Baker. "It's about the only way I can celebrate. Mrs. Janeway wanted to spend the day with her son's family over at Oriental, so I was laying out to cook my own dinner. I got everything ready in the pantry last night, 'fore I got word about the pork. I won't get back from Navarre before

179

one o'clock, so I reckon I'll have to put up with a cold bite."

After her Uncle Richard had driven away, Prissy walked thoughtfully home. She had planned to spend a nice, lazy holiday with the new book her father had given her at Christmas and a box of candy. She did not even mean to cook a dinner, for her father had had to go to town that morning to meet a friend and would be gone the whole day. There was nobody else to cook dinner for. Prissy's mother had died when Prissy was a baby. She was her father's housekeeper, and they had jolly times together.

But as she walked home, she could not help thinking about Uncle Richard. He would certainly have cold New Year cheer, enough to chill the whole coming year. She felt sorry for him, picturing him returning from Navarre, cold and hungry, to find a fireless house and an uncooked dinner in the pantry.

Suddenly an idea popped into Prissy's head. Dared she? Oh, she never could! But he would never know—there would be plenty of time—she would!

Prissy hurried home, put her matches away, took a regretful peep at her unopened book, then locked the door and started up the road to Uncle Richard's house half a mile away. She meant to go and cook Uncle Richard's dinner for him, get it all beautifully ready, then slip away before he came home. He would never suspect her of it. Prissy would not have him suspect for the world; she thought he would be more likely to throw a dinner of her cooking out of doors than to eat it.

Eight years before this, when Prissy had been nine years old, Richard and Irving Baker had quarrelled over the division of a piece of property. The fault had been mainly on Richard's side, and that very fact made him all the more unrelenting and stubborn. He had never spoken to his brother since, and he declared he never would. Prissy and her father felt very badly over it, but Uncle Richard did not seem to feel badly at all. To all appearance he had completely forgotten that there were such

180

people in the world as his brother Irving and his niece Prissy.

Prissy had no trouble in breaking into Uncle Richard's house, for the woodshed door was unfastened. She tripped into the hostile kitchen with rosy cheeks and mischief sparkling in her eyes. This was an adventure—this was fun! She would tell her father all about it when he came home at night and what a laugh they would have!

There was still a good fire in the stove, and in the pantry Prissy found the dinner in its raw state—a fine roast of fresh pork, potatoes, cabbage, turnips and the ingredients of a raisin pudding, for Richard Baker was fond of raisin puddings, and could make them as well as Mrs. Janeway could, if that was anything to boast of.

In a short time the kitchen was full of bubbling and hissings and appetizing odours. Prissy enjoyed herself hugely, and the raisin pudding, which she rather doubtfully mixed up, behaved itself beautifully.

"Uncle Richard said he'd be home by one," said Prissy to herself, as the clock struck twelve, "so I'll set the table now, dish up the dinner, and leave it where it will keep warm until he gets here. Then I'll slip away home. I'd like to see his face when he steps in. I suppose he'll think one of the Jenner girls across the street has cooked his dinner."

Prissy soon had the table set, and she was just peppering the turnips when a gruff voice behind her said:

"Well, well, what does this mean?"

Prissy whirled around as if she had been shot, and there stood Uncle Richard in the woodshed door!

Poor Prissy! She could not have looked or felt more guilty if Uncle Richard had caught her robbing his desk. She did not drop the turnips for a wonder; but she was too confused to set them down, so she stood there holding them, her face crimson, her heart thumping, and a horrible choking in her throat.

"I—I—came up to cook your dinner for you, Uncle Richard," she stammered. "I heard you say—in the store—that Mrs. Janeway had gone home and that you had nobody to cook your New Year's dinner for you. So I thought I'd come and do it, but I meant to slip away before you came home."

Poor Prissy felt that she would never get to the end of her explanation. Would Uncle Richard be angry? Would he order her from the house?

"It was very kind of you," said Uncle Richard drily. "It's a wonder your father let you come."

"Father was not home, but I am sure he would not have prevented me if he had been. Father has no hard feelings against you, Uncle Richard."

"Humph!" said Uncle Richard. "Well, since you've cooked the dinner you must stop and help me eat it. It smells good, I must say. Mrs. Janeway always burns pork when she roasts it. Sit down, Prissy. I'm hungry."

They sat down. Prissy felt quite giddy and breathless, and could hardly eat for excitement; but Uncle Richard had evidently brought home a good appetite from Navarre, and he did full justice to his New Year's dinner. He talked to Prissy too, quite kindly and politely, and when the meal was over he said slowly:

"I'm much obliged to you, Prissy, and I don't mind owning to you that I'm sorry for my share in the quarrel, and have wanted for a long time to be friends with your father again, but I was too ashamed and proud to make the first advance. You can tell him so for me, if you like. And if he's willing to let bygones be bygones, tell him I'd like him to come up here with you tonight when he gets home and spend the evening with me."

"Oh, he will come, I know!" cried Prissy joyfully. "He has felt so badly about not being friendly with you, Uncle Richard. I'm as glad as can be."

Prissy ran impulsively around the table and kissed Uncle Richard. He looked up at his tall, girlish niece with a smile of pleasure.

"You're a good girl, Prissy, and a kind-hearted one too, or you'd never have come up here to cook a dinner for a crabbed old uncle who deserved to eat cold dinners for his stubbornness. It made me cross today when folks wished me a happy New Year. It seemed like mockery when I hadn't a soul belonging to me to make it happy. But it has brought me happiness already, and I believe it will be a happy year all the way through."

"Indeed it will!" laughed Prissy. "I'm so happy now I could sing. I believe it was an inspiration—my idea of coming up here to cook your dinner for you."

"You must promise to come and cook my New Year's dinner for me every New Year we live near enough together," said Uncle Richard.

And Prissy promised.

'Twas the Night Before Christmas
A Visit from St. Nicholas

By Clement Clarke Moore

'Twas the night before Christmas, when all through the house
Not a creature was stirring, not even a mouse.
The stockings were hung by the chimney with care,
In hopes that St Nicholas soon would be there.

The children were nestled all snug in their beds,
While visions of sugar-plums danced in their heads.
And mamma in her 'kerchief, and I in my cap,
Had just settled our brains for a long winter's nap.

When out on the lawn there arose such a clatter,
I sprang from the bed to see what was the matter.
Away to the window I flew like a flash,
Tore open the shutters and threw up the sash.

The moon on the breast of the new-fallen snow
Gave the lustre of mid-day to objects below.
When, what to my wondering eyes should appear,
But a miniature sleigh, and eight tiny reindeer.

With a little old driver, so lively and quick,
I knew in a moment it must be St Nick.
More rapid than eagles his coursers they came,
And he whistled, and shouted, and called them by name!

"Now Dasher! now, Dancer! now, Prancer and Vixen!
On, Comet! On, Cupid! on, on Donner and Blitzen!
To the top of the porch! to the top of the wall!

Now dash away! Dash away! Dash away all!"

As dry leaves that before the wild hurricane fly,
When they meet with an obstacle, mount to the sky.
So up to the house-top the coursers they flew,
With the sleigh full of Toys, and St Nicholas too.

And then, in a twinkling, I heard on the roof
The prancing and pawing of each little hoof.
As I drew in my head, and was turning around,
Down the chimney St Nicholas came with a bound.

He was dressed all in fur, from his head to his foot,
And his clothes were all tarnished with ashes and soot.
A bundle of Toys he had flung on his back,
And he looked like a peddler, just opening his pack.

His eyes-how they twinkled! his dimples how merry!
His cheeks were like roses, his nose like a cherry!
His droll little mouth was drawn up like a bow,
And the beard of his chin was as white as the snow.

The stump of a pipe he held tight in his teeth,
And the smoke it encircled his head like a wreath.
He had a broad face and a little round belly,
That shook when he laughed, like a bowlful of jelly!

He was chubby and plump, a right jolly old elf,
And I laughed when I saw him, in spite of myself!
A wink of his eye and a twist of his head,
Soon gave me to know I had nothing to dread.

He spoke not a word, but went straight to his work,
And filled all the stockings, then turned with a jerk.
And laying his finger aside of his nose,
And giving a nod, up the chimney he rose!

He sprang to his sleigh, to his team gave a whistle,
And away they all flew like the down of a thistle.
But I heard him exclaim, 'ere he drove out of sight,
"Happy Christmas to all, and to all a good-night!"

THE END

A Christmas Sermon

By Robert Louis Stevenson

By the time this paper appears, I shall have been talking for twelve months;[1] and it is thought I should take my leave in a formal and seasonable manner. Valedictory eloquence is rare, and death-bed sayings have not often hit the mark of the occasion. Charles Second, wit and sceptic, a man whose life had been one long lesson in human incredulity, an easy-going comrade, a manoeuvring king--remembered and embodied all his wit and scepticism along with more than his usual good humour in the famous "I am afraid, gentlemen, I am an unconscionable time a-dying."

I

An unconscionable time a-dying--there is the picture ("I am afraid, gentlemen,") of your life and of mine. The sands run out, and the hours are "numbered and imputed," and the days go by; and when the last of these finds us, we have been a long time dying, and what else? The very length is something, if we reach that hour of separation undishonoured; and to have lived at all is doubtless (in the soldierly expression) to have served. There is a tale in Tacitus of how the veterans mutinied in the German wilderness; of how they mobbed Germanicus, clamouring to go home; and of how, seizing their general's hand, these old, war-worn exiles passed his finger along their toothless gums. _Sunt lacrymae rerum_: this was the most eloquent of the songs of Simeon. And when a man has lived to a fair age, he bears his marks of service. He may have never been remarked upon the breach at the head of the army; at least he shall have lost his teeth on the camp bread.

The idealism of serious people in this age of ours is of a noble character. It never seems to them that they have served enough; they have a fine impatience of their virtues. It were perhaps more modest to be singly thankful that we are no worse. It is not only our enemies, those desperate characters--it is we ourselves who know not what we do;--thence springs the glimmering hope that perhaps we do better than we think: that to scramble through this random business with hands reasonably clean, to have played the part of a man or woman with some reasonable fulness, to have often resisted the diabolic, and at the end to be still resisting it, is for the poor human soldier to have done right well. To ask to see some fruit of our endeavour is but a transcendental way of serving for reward; and what we take to be contempt of self is only greed of hire.

And again if we require so much of ourselves, shall we not require much of others? If we do not genially judge our own deficiencies, is it not to be feared we shall be even stern to the trespasses of others? And he who (looking back upon his own life) can see no more than that he has been unconscionably long a-dying, will he not be tempted to think his neighbour unconscionably long of getting hanged? It is probable that nearly all who think of conduct at all, think of it too much; it is certain we all think too much of sin. We are not damned for doing wrong, but for not doing right; Christ would never hear of negative morality; _thou shalt_ was ever his word, with which he superseded _thou shalt not_. To make our idea of morality centre on forbidden acts is to defile the imagination and to introduce into our judgments of our fellow-men a secret element of gusto. If a thing is wrong for us, we should not dwell upon the thought of it; or we shall soon dwell upon it with inverted pleasure. If we cannot drive it from our minds--one thing of two: either our creed is in the wrong and we must more indulgently remodel it; or else, if our morality be in the right, we are criminal lunatics and should place our persons in restraint. A mark of such unwholesomely divided minds is the passion for interference with others: the Fox without the Tail was of this breed, but had (if his biographer is to be trusted) a certain antique civility now out of date. A man may have a flaw, a weakness, that unfits him for the duties of life, that spoils his temper, that threatens his integrity, or that betrays him

188

into cruelty. It has to be conquered; but it must never be suffered to engross his thoughts. The true duties lie all upon the farther side, and must be attended to with a whole mind so soon as this preliminary clearing of the decks has been effected. In order that he may be kind and honest, it may be needful he should become a total abstainer; let him become so then, and the next day let him forget the circumstance. Trying to be kind and honest will require all his thoughts; a mortified appetite is never a wise companion; in so far as he has had to mortify an appetite, he will still be the worse man; and of such an one a great deal of cheerfulness will be required in judging life, and a great deal of humility in judging others.

It may be argued again that dissatisfaction with our life's endeavour springs in some degree from dulness. We require higher tasks, because we do not recognise the height of those we have. Trying to be kind and honest seems an affair too simple and too inconsequential for gentlemen of our heroic mould; we had rather set ourselves to something bold, arduous, and conclusive; we had rather found a schism or suppress a heresy, cut off a hand or mortify an appetite. But the task before us, which is to co-endure with our existence, is rather one of microscopic fineness, and the heroism required is that of patience. There is no cutting of the Gordian knots of life; each must be smilingly unravelled.

To be honest, to be kind--to earn a little and to spend a little less, to make upon the whole a family happier for his presence, to renounce when that shall be necessary and not be embittered, to keep a few friends but these without capitulation--above all, on the same grim condition, to keep friends with himself--here is a task for all that a man has of fortitude and delicacy. He has an ambitious soul who would ask more; he has a hopeful spirit who should look in such an enterprise to be successful. There is indeed one element in human destiny that not blindness itself can controvert: whatever else we are intended to do, we are not intended to succeed; failure is the fate allotted. It is so in every art and study; it is so above all in the continent art of living well. Here is a pleasant thought for the year's end or for the end of life: Only self-deception will be satisfied, and there need be no despair for the despairer.

II

But Christmas is not only the mile-mark of another year, moving us to thoughts of self-examination: it is a season, from all its associations, whether domestic or religious, suggesting thoughts of joy. A man dissatisfied with his endeavours is a man tempted to sadness. And in the midst of the winter, when his life runs lowest and he is reminded of the empty chairs of his beloved, it is well he should be condemned to this fashion of the smiling face. Noble disappointment, noble self-denial are not to be admired, not even to be pardoned, if they bring bitterness. It is one thing to enter the kingdom of heaven maim; another to maim yourself and stay without. And the kingdom of heaven is of the childlike, of those who are easy to please, who love and who give pleasure. Mighty men of their hands, the smiters and the builders and the judges, have lived long and done sternly and yet preserved this lovely character; and among our carpet interests and twopenny concerns, the shame were indelible if _we_ should lose it. Gentleness and cheerfulness, these come before all morality; they are the perfect duties. And it is the trouble with moral men that they have neither one nor other. It was the moral man, the Pharisee, whom Christ could not away with. If your morals make you dreary, depend upon it they are wrong. I do not say "give them up," for they may be all you have; but conceal them like a vice, lest they should spoil the lives of better and simpler people.

A strange temptation attends upon man: to keep his eye on pleasures, even when he will not share in them; to aim all his morals against them. This very year a lady (singular iconoclast!) proclaimed a crusade against dolls; and the racy sermon against lust is a feature of the age. I venture to call such moralists insincere. At any excess or perversion of a natural appetite, their lyre sounds of itself with relishing denunciations; but for all displays of the truly diabolic--envy, malice, the mean lie, the mean silence, the calumnious truth, the backbiter, the petty tyrant, the peevish poisoner of family life--their standard is quite different. These are wrong, they will admit, yet somehow not so wrong; there is no zeal in their assault on them, no secret element of gusto warms up the sermon; it is for things not wrong in themselves that they reserve the choicest of their indignation. A man may naturally disclaim all moral kinship with the Reverend Mr. Zola or the hobgoblin old lady of the dolls; for these are gross and naked instances. And yet in each of us some similar element resides. The sight of a pleasure in which we cannot or else will not share moves us to a particular impatience. It may be because we are envious, or because we are sad, or because we dislike noise and romping--being so refined, or because--being so philosophic--we have an overweighing sense of life's gravity: at least, as we go on in years, we are all tempted to frown upon our neighbour's pleasures. People are nowadays so fond of resisting temptations; here is one to be resisted. They are fond of self-denial; here is a propensity that cannot be too peremptorily denied. There is an idea abroad among moral people that they should make their neighbours good. One person I have to make good: myself. But my duty to my neighbour is much more nearly expressed by saying that I have to make him happy--if I may.

III

Happiness and goodness, according to canting moralists, stand in the relation of effect and cause. There was never anything less proved or less probable: our happiness is never in our own hands; we inherit our constitution; we stand buffet among friends and enemies; we may be so built as to feel a sneer or an aspersion with unusual keenness, and so circumstanced as to be unusually exposed to them; we may have nerves very sensitive to pain, and be afflicted with a disease very painful. Virtue will not help us, and it is not meant to help us. It is not even its own reward, except for the self-centred and--I had almost said--the unamiable. No man can pacify his conscience; if quiet be what he want, he shall do better to let that organ perish from disuse. And to avoid the penalties of the law, and the minor _capitis diminutio_ of social ostracism, is an affair of wisdom--of cunning, if you will--and not of virtue.

In his own life, then, a man is not to expect happiness, only to profit by it gladly when it shall arise; he is on duty here; he knows not how or why, and does not need to know; he knows not for what hire, and must not ask. Somehow or other, though he does not know what goodness is, he must try to be good; somehow or other, though he cannot tell what will do it, he must try to give happiness to others. And no doubt there comes in here a frequent clash of duties. How far is he to make his neighbour happy? How far must he respect that smiling face, so easy to cloud, so hard to brighten again? And how far, on the other side, is he bound to be his brother's keeper and the prophet of his own morality? How far must he resent evil?

The difficulty is that we have little guidance; Christ's sayings on the point being hard to reconcile with each other, and (the most of them) hard to accept. But the truth of his teaching would seem to be this: in our own person and fortune, we should be ready to accept and to pardon all; it is _our_ cheek we are to turn, _r_ coat that we are to give away to the man who has taken _our_ cloak. But when another's face is buffeted, perhaps a little of the lion will become us best. That we are to suffer others to be injured, and stand by, is not conceivable and surely not desirable. Revenge, says Bacon, is a kind of wild justice; its judgments at least are delivered by an insane judge; and in our own quarrel we can see nothing truly and do nothing wisely. But in the quarrel of our neighbour, let us be more bold. One person's happiness is as sacred as another's; when we cannot defend both, let us defend one with a stout heart. It is only in so far as we are doing this, that we have any right to interfere: the defence of B is our only ground of action against A. A has as good a right to go to the devil, as we to go to glory; and neither knows what he does.

The truth is that all these interventions and denunciations and militant mongerings of moral half-truths, though they be sometimes needful, though they are often enjoyable, do yet belong to an inferior grade of duties. Ill-temper and envy and revenge find here an arsenal of pious disguises; this is the playground of inverted lusts. With a little more patience and a little less temper, a gentler and wiser method might be found in almost every case; and the knot that we cut by some fine heady quarrel-scene in private life, or, in public affairs, by some denunciatory act against what we are pleased to call our neighbour's vices, might yet have been unwoven by the hand of sympathy.

IV

To look back upon the past year, and see how little we have striven and to what small purpose: and how often we have been cowardly and hung back, or temerarious and rushed unwisely in; and how every day and all day long we have transgressed the law of kindness;--it may seem a paradox, but in the bitterness of these discoveries, a certain consolation resides. Life is not designed to minister to a man's vanity. He goes upon his long business most of the time with a hanging head, and all the time like a blind child. Full of rewards and pleasures as it is--so that to see the day break or the moon rise, or to meet a friend, or to hear the dinner-call when he is hungry, fills him with surprising joys--this world is yet for him no abiding city. Friendships fall through, health fails, weariness assails him; year after year, he must thumb the hardly varying record of his own weakness and folly. It is a friendly process of detachment. When the time comes that he should go, there need be few illusions left about himself. Here lies one who meant well, tried a little, failed much:--surely that may be his epitaph, of which he need not be ashamed. Nor will he complain at the summons which calls a defeated soldier from the field: defeated, ay, if he were Paul or Marcus Aurelius!--but if there is still one inch of fight in his old spirit, undishonoured. The faith which sustained him in his life-long blindness and life-long disappointment will scarce even be required in this last formality of laying down his arms. Give him a march with his old bones; there, out of the glorious sun-coloured earth, out of the day and the dust and the ecstasy--there goes another Faithful Failure!

From a recent book of verse, where there is more than one such beautiful and manly poem, I take this memorial piece: it says better than I can, what I love to think; let it be our parting word.

"A late lark twitters from the quiet skies; And from the west, Where the sun, his day's work ended, Lingers as in content, There falls on the old, gray city An influence luminous and serene, A shining peace.

"The smoke ascends In a rosy-and-golden haze. The spires Shine, and are changed. In the valley Shadows rise. The lark sings on. The sun, Closing his benediction, Sinks, and the darkening air Thrills with a sense of the triumphing night-- Night, with her train of stars And her great gift of sleep.

"So be my passing! My task accomplished and the long day done, My wages taken, and in my heart Some late lark singing, Let me be gathered to the quiet west, The sundown splendid and serene, Death."[2]

[Footnote 2: From _A Book of Verses_ by William Ernest Henley. D. Nutt, 1888.]

Christmas; or, The Good Fairy

By Harriet Beecher Stowe

"O, dear! Christmas is coming in a fortnight, and I have got to think up presents for every body!" said young Ellen Stuart, as she leaned languidly back in her chair. "Dear me, it's so tedious! Every body has got every thing that can be thought of."

"O, no," said her confidential adviser, Miss Lester, in a soothing tone. "You have means of buying every thing you can fancy; and when every shop and store is glittering with all manner of splendors, you cannot surely be at a loss."

"Well, now, just listen. To begin with, there's mamma. What can I get for her? I have thought of ever so many things. She has three card cases, four gold thimbles, two or three gold chains, two writing desks of different patterns; and then as to rings, brooches, boxes, and all other things, I should think she might be sick of the sight of them. I am sure I am," said she, languidly gazing on her white and jewelled fingers.

This view of the case seemed rather puzzling to the adviser, and there was silence for a few moments, when Ellen, yawning, resumed:--

"And then there's Cousins Jane and Mary; I suppose they will be coming down on me with a whole load of presents; and Mrs. B. will send me something--she did last year; and then there's Cousins William and Tom--I must get them something; and I would like to do it well enough, if I only knew what to get."

"Well," said Eleanor's aunt, who had been sitting quietly rattling her knitting needles during this speech, "it's a pity that you had not such a subject to practise on as I was when I was a girl. Presents did not fly about in those days as they do now. I remember, when I was ten years old, my father gave me a most marvellously ugly sugar dog for a

Christmas gift, and I was perfectly delighted with it, the very idea of a present was so new to us."

"Dear aunt, how delighted I should be if I had any such fresh, unsophisticated body to get presents for! But to get and get for people that have more than they know what to do with now; to add pictures, books, and gilding when the centre tables are loaded with them now, and rings and jewels when they are a perfect drug! I wish myself that I were not sick, and sated, and tired with having every thing in the world given me."

"Well, Eleanor," said her aunt, "if you really do want unsophisticated subjects to practise on, I can put you in the way of it. I can show you more than one family to whom you might seem to be a very good fairy, and where such gifts as you could give with all ease would seem like a magic dream."

"Why, that would really be worth while, aunt."

"Look over in that back alley," said her aunt. "You see those buildings?"

"That miserable row of shanties? Yes."

"Well, I have several acquaintances there who have never been tired of Christmas gifts, or gifts of any other kind. I assure you, you could make quite a sensation over there."

"Well, who is there? Let us know."

"Do you remember Owen, that used to make your shoes?"

"Yes, I remember something about him."

"Well, he has fallen into a consumption, and cannot work any more; and he, and his wife, and three little children live in one of the rooms."

"How do they get along?"

"His wife takes in sewing sometimes, and sometimes goes out washing. Poor Owen! I was over there yesterday; he looks thin and wasted, and his wife was saying that he was parched with constant fever, and had very little appetite. She had, with great self-denial, and by restricting herself almost of necessary food, got him two or three oranges; and the poor fellow seemed so eager after them!"

"Poor fellow!" said Eleanor, involuntarily.

"Now," said her aunt, "suppose Owen's wife should get up on Christmas morning and find at the door a couple of dozen of oranges, and some of those nice white grapes, such as you had at your party last week; don't you think it would make a sensation?"

"Why, yes, I think very likely it might; but who else, aunt? You spoke of a great many."

"Well, on the lower floor there is a neat little room, that is always kept perfectly trim and tidy; it belongs to a young couple who have nothing beyond the husband's day wages to live on. They are, nevertheless, as cheerful and chipper as a couple of wrens; and she is up and down half a dozen times a day, to help poor Mrs. Owen. She has a baby of her own, about five months old, and of course does all the cooking, washing, and ironing for herself and husband; and yet, when Mrs. Owen goes out to wash, she takes her baby, and keeps it whole days for her."

"I'm sure she deserves that the good fairies should smile on her," said Eleanor; "one baby exhausts my stock of virtues very rapidly."

"But you ought to see her baby," said Aunt E.; "so plump, so rosy, and good-natured, and always clean as a lily. This baby is a sort of household shrine; nothing is too sacred or too good for it; and I believe the little thrifty woman feels only one temptation to be extravagant, and that is to get some ornaments to adorn this little divinity."

"Why, did she ever tell you so?"

"No; but one day, when I was coming down stairs, the door of their room was partly open, and I saw a pedler there with open box. John, the husband, was standing with a little purple cap on his hand, which he was regarding with mystified, admiring air, as if he didn't quite comprehend it, and trim little Mary gazing at it with longing eyes.

"'I think we might get it,' said John.

"'O, no,' said she, regretfully; 'yet I wish we could, it's so pretty!'"

"Say no more, aunt. I see the good fairy must pop a cap into the window on Christmas morning. Indeed, it shall be done. How they will wonder where it came from, and talk about it for months to come!"

"Well, then," continued her aunt, "in the next street to ours there is a miserable building, that looks as if it were just going to topple over; and away up in the third story, in a little room just under the eaves, live two poor, lonely old women. They are both nearly on to ninety. I was in there day before yesterday. One of them is constantly confined to her bed with rheumatism; the other, weak and feeble, with failing sight and trembling hands, totters about, her only helper; and they are entirely dependent on charity."

"Can't they do any thing? Can't they knit?" said Eleanor.

"You are young and strong, Eleanor, and have quick eyes and nimble fingers; how long would it take you to knit a pair of stockings?"

"I?" said Eleanor. "What an idea! I never tried, but I think I could get a pair done in a week, perhaps."

"And if somebody gave you twenty-five cents for them, and out of this you had to get food, and pay room rent, and buy coal for your fire, and oil for your lamp----"

"Stop, aunt, for pity's sake!"

"Well, I will stop; but they can't: they must pay so much every month for that miserable shell they live in, or be turned into the street. The meal and flour that some kind person sends goes off for them just as it does for others, and they must get more or starve; and coal is now scarce and high priced."

"O aunt, I'm quite convinced, I'm sure; don't run me down and annihilate me with all these terrible realities. What shall I do to play good fairy to these poor old women?"

"If you will give me full power, Eleanor, I will put up a basket to be sent to them that will give them something to remember all winter."

"O, certainly I will. Let me see if I can't think of something myself."

"Well, Eleanor, suppose, then, some fifty or sixty years hence, if you were old, and your father, and mother, and aunts, and uncles, now so thick around you, lay cold and silent in so many graves--you have somehow got away off to a strange city, where you were never known--you live in a miserable garret, where snow blows at night through the cracks, and the fire is very apt to go out in the old cracked stove--you sit crouching over the dying embers the evening before Christmas--nobody to speak to you, nobody to care for you, except another poor old soul who lies moaning in the bed. Now, what would you like to have sent you?"

"O aunt, what a dismal picture!"

"And yet, Ella, all poor, forsaken old women are made of young girls, who expected it in their youth as little as you do, perhaps."

"Say no more, aunt. I'll buy--let me see--a comfortable warm shawl for each of these poor women; and I'll send them--let me see--O, some tea--nothing goes down with old women like tea; and I'll make John wheel some coal over to them; and, aunt, it would not be a very bad thought to send them a new stove. I remember, the other day, when mamma was pricing stoves, I saw some such nice ones for two or three dollars."

"For a new hand, Ella, you work up the idea very well," said her aunt.

"But how much ought I to give, for any one case, to these women, say?"

"How much did you give last year for any single Christmas present?"

"Why, six or seven dollars for some; those elegant souvenirs were seven dollars; that ring I gave Mrs. B. was twenty."

"And do you suppose Mrs. B. was any happier for it?"

"No, really, I don't think she cared much about it; but I had to give her something, because she had sent me something the year before, and I did not want to send a paltry present to one in her circumstances."

"Then, Ella, give the same to any poor, distressed, suffering creature who really needs it, and see in how many forms of good such a sum will appear. That one hard, cold, glittering ring, that now cheers nobody, and means nothing, that you give because you must, and she takes because she must, might, if broken up into smaller sums, send real warm and heartfelt gladness through many a cold and cheerless dwelling, through many an aching heart."

"You are getting to be an orator, aunt; but don't you approve of Christmas presents, among friends and equals?"

"Yes, indeed," said her aunt, fondly stroking her head. "I have had some Christmas presents that did me a world of good--a little book mark, for instance, that a certain niece of mine worked for me, with wonderful secrecy, three years ago, when she was not a young lady with a purse full of money--that book mark was a true Christmas present; and my young couple across the way are plotting a profound surprise to each other on Christmas morning. John has contrived, by an hour of extra work every night, to lay by enough to get Mary a new calico dress; and she, poor soul, has bargained away the only thing in the jewelry line she ever possessed, to be laid out on a new hat for him.

"I know, too, a washerwoman who has a poor, lame boy--a patient, gentle little fellow--who has lain quietly for weeks and months in his little crib, and his mother is going to give him a splendid Christmas present."

"What is it, pray?"

"A whole orange! Don't laugh. She will pay ten whole cents for it; for it shall be none of your common oranges, but a picked one of the very best going! She has put by the money, a cent at a time, for a whole month; and nobody knows which will be happiest in it, Willie or his mother. These are such Christmas presents as I like to think of--gifts coming from love, and tending to produce love; these are the appropriate gifts of the day."

"But don't you think that it's right for those who have money to give expensive presents, supposing always, as you say, they are given from real affection?"

"Sometimes, undoubtedly. The Savior did not condemn her who broke an alabaster box of ointment--very precious--simply as a proof of love, even although the suggestion was made, 'This might have been sold for three hundred pence, and given to the poor.' I have thought he would regard with sympathy the fond efforts which human love sometimes makes to express itself by gifts, the rarest and most costly. How I rejoiced with all my heart, when Charles Elton gave his poor mother that splendid Chinese shawl and gold watch! because I knew they came from the very fulness of his heart to a mother that he could not do too much for--a mother that has done and suffered every thing for him. In some such cases, when resources are ample, a costly gift seems to have a graceful appropriateness; but I cannot approve of it if it exhausts all the means of doing for the poor; it is better, then, to give a simple offering, and to do something for those who really need it."

Eleanor looked thoughtful; her aunt laid down her knitting, and said, in a tone of gentle seriousness, "Whose birth does Christmas commemorate, Ella?"

"Our Savior's, certainly, aunt."

"Yes," said her aunt. "And when and how was he born? In a stable! laid in a manger; thus born, that in all ages he might be known as the brother and friend of the poor. And surely, it seems but appropriate to commemorate his birthday by an especial remembrance of the lowly, the poor, the outcast, and distressed; and if Christ should come back to our city on a Christmas day, where should we think it most appropriate to his character to find him? Would he be carrying splendid gifts to splendid dwellings, or would he be gliding about in the cheerless haunts of the desolate, the poor, the forsaken, and the sorrowful?"

And here the conversation ended.

* * * * *

"What sort of Christmas presents is Ella buying?" said Cousin Tom, as the waiter handed in a portentous-looking package, which had been just rung in at the door.

"Let's open it," said saucy Will. "Upon my word, two great gray blanket shawls! These must be for you and me, Tom! And what's this? A great bolt of cotton flannel and gray yarn stockings!"

The door bell rang again, and the waiter brought in another bulky parcel, and deposited it on the marble-topped centre table.

"What's here?" said Will, cutting the cord. "Whew! a perfect nest of packages! oolong tea! oranges! grapes! white sugar! Bless me, Ella must be going to housekeeping!"

"Or going crazy!" said Tom; "and on my word," said he, looking out of the window, "there's a drayman ringing at our door, with a stove, with a teakettle set in the top of it!"

202

"Ella's cook stove, of course," said Will; and just at this moment the young lady entered, with her purse hanging gracefully over her hand.

"Now, boys, you are too bad!" she exclaimed, as each of the mischievous youngsters were gravely marching up and down, attired in a gray shawl.

"Didn't you get them for us? We thought you did," said both.

"Ella, I want some of that cotton flannel, to make me a pair of pantaloons," said Tom.

"I say, Ella," said Will, "when are you going to housekeeping? Your cooking stove is standing down in the street; 'pon my word, John is loading some coal on the dray with it."

"Ella, isn't that going to be sent to my office?" said Tom; "do you know I do so languish for a new stove with a teakettle in the top, to heat a fellow's shaving water!"

Just then, another ring at the door, and the grinning waiter handed in a small brown paper parcel for Miss Ella. Tom made a dive at it, and staving off the brown paper, developed a jaunty little purple velvet cap, with silver tassels.

"My smoking cap, as I live!" said he; "only I shall have to wear it on my thumb, instead of my head--too small entirely," said he, shaking his head gravely.

"Come, you saucy boys," said Aunt E., entering briskly, "what are you teasing Ella for?"

"Why, do see this lot of things, aunt! What in the world is Ella going to do with them?"

"O, I know!"

"You know! Then I can guess, aunt, it is some of your charitable works. You are going to make a juvenile Lady Bountiful of El, eh?"

Ella, who had colored to the roots of her hair at the expose of her very unfashionable Christmas preparations, now took heart, and bestowed a very gentle and salutary little cuff on the saucy head that still wore the purple cap, and then hastened to gather up her various purchases.

"Laugh away," said she, gayly; "and a good many others will laugh, too, over these things. I got them to make people laugh--people that are not in the habit of laughing!"

"Well, well, I see into it," said Will; "and I tell you I think right well of the idea, too. There are worlds of money wasted, at this time of the year, in getting things that nobody wants, and nobody cares for after they are got; and I am glad, for my part, that you are going to get up a variety in this line; in fact, I should like to give you one of these stray leaves to help on," said he, dropping a ten dollar note into her paper. "I like to encourage girls to think of something besides breastpins and sugar candy."

But our story spins on too long. If any body wants to see the results of Ella's first attempts at good fairyism, they can call at the doors of two or three old buildings on Christmas morning, and they shall hear all about it.

The Elves and the Shoemaker

By The Brothers Grimm

There was once a shoemaker, who worked very hard and was very honest: but still he could not earn enough to live upon; and at last all he had in the world was gone, save just leather enough to make one pair of shoes.

Then he cut his leather out, all ready to make up the next day, meaning to rise early in the morning to his work. His conscience was clear and his heart light amidst all his troubles; so he went peaceably to bed, left all his cares to Heaven, and soon fell asleep. In the morning after he had said his prayers, he sat himself down to his work; when, to his great wonder, there stood the shoes all ready made, upon the table. The good man knew not what to say or think at such an odd thing happening. He looked at the workmanship; there was not one false stitch in the whole job; all was so neat and true, that it was quite a masterpiece.

The same day a customer came in, and the shoes suited him so well that he willingly paid a price higher than usual for them; and the poor shoemaker, with the money, bought leather enough to make two pairs more. In the evening he cut out the work, and went to bed early, that he might get up and begin betimes next day; but he was saved all the trouble, for when he got up in the morning the work was done ready to his hand. Soon in came buyers, who paid him handsomely for his goods, so that he bought leather enough for four pair more. He cut out the work again overnight and found it done in the morning, as before; and so it went on for some time: what was got ready in the evening was always done by daybreak, and the good man soon became thriving and well off again.

One evening, about Christmas-time, as he and his wife were

sitting over the fire chatting together, he said to her, 'I should like to sit up and watch tonight, that we may see who it is that comes and does my work for me.' The wife liked the thought; so they left a light burning, and hid themselves in a corner of the room, behind a curtain that was hung up there, and watched what would happen.

As soon as it was midnight, there came in two little naked dwarfs; and they sat themselves upon the shoemaker's bench, took up all the work that was cut out, and began to ply with their little fingers, stitching and rapping and tapping away at such a rate, that the shoemaker was all wonder, and could not take his eyes off them. And on they went, till the job was quite done, and the shoes stood ready for use upon the table. This was long before daybreak; and then they bustled away as quick as lightning.

The next day the wife said to the shoemaker. 'These little wights have made us rich, and we ought to be thankful to them, and do them a good turn if we can. I am quite sorry to see them run about as they do; and indeed it is not very decent, for they have nothing upon their backs to keep off the cold. I'll tell you what, I will make each of them a shirt, and a coat and waistcoat, and a pair of pantaloons into the bargain; and do you make each of them a little pair of shoes.'

The thought pleased the good cobbler very much; and one evening, when all the things were ready, they laid them on the table, instead of the work that they used to cut out, and then went and hid themselves, to watch what the little elves would do.

About midnight in they came, dancing and skipping, hopped round the room, and then went to sit down to their work as usual; but when they saw the clothes lying for them, they laughed and chuckled, and seemed mightily delighted.

Then they dressed themselves in the twinkling of an eye, and danced and capered and sprang about, as merry as could be; till at last they danced out at the door, and away over the green.

The good couple saw them no more; but everything went well with them from that time forward, as long as they lived.

Papa Panov's Special Christmas

By Leo Tolstoy

It was Christmas Eve and although it was still afternoon, lights had begun to appear in the shops and houses of the little Russian village, for the short winter day was nearly over. Excited children scurried indoors and now only muffled sounds of chatter and laughter escaped from closed shutters.

Old Papa Panov, the village shoemaker, stepped outside his shop to take one last look around. The sounds of happiness, the bright lights and the faint but delicious smells of Christmas cooking reminded him of past Christmas times when his wife had still been alive and his own children little. Now they had gone. His usually cheerful face, with the little laughter wrinkles behind the round steel spectacles, looked sad now. But he went back indoors with a firm step, put up the shutters and set a pot of coffee to heat on the charcoal stove. Then, with a sigh, he settled in his big armchair.

Papa Panov did not often read, but tonight he pulled down the big old family Bible and, slowly tracing the lines with one forefinger, he read again the Christmas story. He read how Mary and Joseph, tired by their journey to Bethlehem, found no room for them at the inn, so that Mary's little baby was born in the cowshed.

"Oh, dear, oh, dear!" exclaimed Papa Panov, "if only they had come here! I would have given them my bed and I could have covered the baby with my patchwork quilt to keep him warm."

He read on about the wise men who had come to see the baby Jesus, bringing him splendid gifts. Papa Panov's face fell. "I have no gift that I could give him," he thought sadly.

Then his face brightened. He put down the Bible, got up and

stretched his long arms to the shelf high up in his little room. He took down a small, dusty box and opened it. Inside was a perfect pair of tiny leather shoes. Papa Panov smiled with satisfaction. Yes, they were as good as he had remembered -- the best shoes he had ever made. "I should give him those," he decided, as he gently put them away and sat down again.

He was feeling tired now, and the further he read the sleepier he became. The print began to dance before his eyes so that he closed them, just for a minute. In no time at all Papa Panov was fast asleep.

And as he slept he dreamed. He dreamed that someone was in his room and he knew at once, as one does in dreams, who the person was. It was Jesus.

"You have been wishing that you could see me, Papa Panov." he said kindly, "then look for me tomorrow. It will be Christmas Day and I will visit you. But look carefully, for I shall not tell you who I am."

When at last Papa Panov awoke, the bells were ringing out and a thin light was filtering through the shutters. "Bless my soul!" said Papa Panov. "It's Christmas Day!"

He stood up and stretched himself for he was rather stiff. Then his face filled with happiness as he remembered his dream. This would be a very special Christmas after all, for Jesus was coming to visit him. How would he look? Would he be a little baby, as at that first Christmas? Would he be a grown man, a carpenter -- or the great King that he is, God's Son? He must watch carefully the whole day through so that he recognized him however he came.

Papa Panov put on a special pot of coffee for his Christmas breakfast, took down the shutters and looked out of the window. The street was deserted, no one was stirring yet. No one except the road sweeper. He looked as miserable and dirty as ever, and well he might! Whoever wanted to work on Christmas Day -- and in the raw cold and bitter freezing mist of such a morning?

Papa Panov opened the shop door, letting in a thin stream of cold air. "Come in!" he shouted across the street cheerily. "Come in and have some hot coffee to keep out the cold!"

The sweeper looked up, scarcely able to believe his ears. He was only too glad to put down his broom and come into the warm room. His old clothes steamed gently in the heat of the stove and he clasped both red hands round the comforting warm mug as he drank.

Papa Panov watched him with satisfaction, but every now and them his eyes strayed to the window. It would never do to miss his special visitor.

"Expecting someone?" the sweeper asked at last. So Papa Panov told him about his dream.

"Well, I hope he comes," the sweeper said, "you've given me a bit of Christmas cheer I never expected to have. I'd say you deserve to have your dream come true." And he actually smiled.

When he had gone, Papa Panov put on cabbage soup for his dinner, then went to the door again, scanning the street. He saw no one. But he was mistaken. Someone was coming.

The girl walked so slowly and quietly, hugging the walls of shops and houses, that it was a while before he noticed her. She looked very tired and she was carrying something. As she drew nearer he could see that it was a baby, wrapped in a thin shawl. There was such sadness in her face and in the pinched little face of the baby, that Papa Panov's heart went out to them.

"Won't you come in," he called, stepping outside to meet them. "You both need a warm seat by the fire and a rest."

The young mother let him shepherd her indoors and to the comfort of the armchair. She gave a big sigh of relief.

"I'll warm some milk for the baby," Papa Panov said, "I've had children of my own -- I can feed her for you." He took the milk from the stove and carefully fed the baby from a spoon, warming her tiny feet by the stove at the same time.

"She needs shoes," the cobbler said.

But the girl replied, "I can't afford shoes, I've got no husband to bring home money. I'm on my way to the next village to get work."

A sudden thought flashed through Papa Panov's mind. He remembered the little shoes he had looked at last night. But he had been keeping those for Jesus. He looked again at the cold little feet and made up his mind.

"Try these on her," he said, handing the baby and the shoes to the mother. The beautiful little shoes were a perfect fit. The girl smiled happily and the baby gurgled with pleasure.

"You have been so kind to us," the girl said, when she got up with her baby to go. "May all your Christmas wishes come true!"

But Papa Panov was beginning to wonder if his very special Christmas wish would come true. Perhaps he had missed his visitor? He looked anxiously up and down the street. There were plenty of people about but they were all faces that he recognized. There were neighbors going to call on their families. They nodded and smiled and wished him Happy Christmas! Or beggars -- and Papa Panov hurried indoors to fetch them hot soup and a generous hunk of bread, hurrying out again in case he missed the Important Stranger.

All too soon the winter dusk fell. When Papa Panov next went to the door and strained his eyes, he could no longer make out the passers-by. Most were home and indoors by now anyway. He walked slowly back into his room at last, put up the shutters, and sat down wearily in his armchair.

So it had been just a dream after all. Jesus had not come.

Then all at once he knew that he was no longer alone in the room.

This was not dream for he was wide awake. At first he seemed to see before his eyes the long stream of people who had come to him that day. He saw again the old road sweeper, the young mother and her baby and the beggars he had fed. As they passed, each whispered, "Didn't you see me, Papa Panov?"

"Who are you?" he called out, bewildered.

Then another voice answered him. It was the voice from his dream -- the voice of Jesus.

"I was hungry and you fed me," he said. "I was naked and you clothed me. I was cold and you warmed me. I came to you today in everyone of those you helped and welcomed."

Then all was quiet and still. Only the sound of the big clock ticking. A great peace and happiness seemed to fill the room, overflowing Papa Panov's heart until he wanted to burst out singing and laughing and dancing with joy.

"So he did come after all!" was all that he said.

Keeping Christmas

By Henry van Dyke

ROMANS, xiv, 6: He that regardeth the day, regardeth it unto the Lord.

It is a good thing to observe Christmas day. The mere marking of times and seasons, when men agree to stop work and make merry together, is a wise and wholesome custom. It helps one to feel the supremacy of the common life over the individual life. It reminds a man to set his own little watch, now and then, by the great clock of humanity which runs on sun time.

But there is a better thing than the observance of Christmas day, and that is, keeping Christmas.

Are you willing to forget what you have done for other people, and to remember what other people have done for you; to ignore what the world owes you, and to think what you owe the world; to put your rights in the background, and your duties in the middle distance, and your chances to do a little more than your duty in the foreground; to see that your fellow-men are just as real as you are, and try to look behind their faces to their hearts, hungry for joy; to own that probably the only good reason for your existence is not what you are going to get out of life, but what you are going to give to life; to close your book of complaints against the management of the universe, and look around you for a place where you can sow a few seeds of happiness--are you willing to do these things even for a day? Then you can keep Christmas.

Are you willing to stoop down and consider the needs and the desires of little children; to remember the weakness and loneliness of people who are growing old; to stop asking how much your friends love you, and ask yourself whether you love them enough; to bear in mind the things that other people have to bear on their hearts; to try to understand what those who live in the same house with you really want, without waiting for them to tell you; to trim your lamp so that it will give more light and less smoke, and to carry it in front so that your shadow will fall behind you; to make a grave for your ugly thoughts, and a garden for your kindly feelings, with the gate open--are you willing to do these things even for a day? Then you can keep Christmas.

Are you willing to believe that love is the strongest thing in the world--stronger than hate, stronger than evil, stronger than death--and that the blessed life which began in Bethlehem nineteen hundred years ago is the image and brightness of the Eternal Love? Then you can keep Christmas.

And if you keep it for a day, why not always?

But you can never keep it alone.

The Other Wise Man

By Henry van Dyke

You know the story of the Three Wise Men of the East, and how they travelled from far away to offer their gifts at the manger-cradle in Bethlehem. But have you ever heard the story of the Other Wise Man, who also saw the star in its rising, and set out to follow it, yet did not arrive with his brethren in the presence of the young child Jesus? Of the great desire of this fourth pilgrim, and how it was denied, yet accomplished in the denial; of his many wanderings and the probations of his soul; of the long way of his seeking and the strange way of his finding the One whom he sought--I would tell the tale as I have heard fragments of it in the Hall of Dreams, in the palace of the Heart of Man.

I

In the days when Augustus Caesar was master of many kings and Herod reigned in Jerusalem, there lived in the city of Ecbatana, among the mountains of Persia, a certain man named Artaban. His house stood close to the outermost of the walls which encircled the royal treasury. From his roof he could look over the seven-fold battlements of black and white and crimson and blue and red and silver and gold, to the hill where the summer palace of the Parthian emperors glittered like a jewel in a crown.

Around the dwelling of Artaban spread a fair garden, a tangle of flowers and fruit-trees, watered by a score of streams descending from the slopes of Mount Orontes, and made musical by innumerable birds. But all colour was lost in the soft and odorous darkness of the late September night, and all sounds were hushed in the deep charm of its silence, save the plashing of the water, like a voice half-sobbing and half-laughing under the shadows. High above the trees a dim glow of light shone through the curtained arches of the upper chamber, where the master of the house was holding council with his friends.

He stood by the doorway to greet his guests--a tall, dark man of about forty years, with brilliant eyes set near together under his broad brow, and firm lines graven around his fine, thin lips; the brow of a dreamer and the mouth of a soldier, a man of sensitive feeling but inflexible will--one of those who, in whatever age they may live, are born for inward conflict and a life of quest.

His robe was of pure white wool, thrown over a tunic of silk; and a white, pointed cap, with long lapels at the sides, rested on his flowing black hair. It was the dress of the ancient priesthood of the Magi, called the fire-worshippers.

"Welcome!" he said, in his low, pleasant voice, as one after another entered the room--"welcome, Abdus; peace be with you, Rhodaspes and Tigranes, and with you my father, Abgarus. You are all welcome. This house grows bright with the joy of your presence."

There were nine of the men, differing widely in age, but alike in the richness of their dress of many-coloured silks, and in the massive golden collars around their necks, marking them as Parthian nobles, and in the winged circles of gold resting upon their breasts, the sign of the followers of Zoroaster.

They took their places around a small black altar at the end of the room, where a tiny flame was burning. Artaban, standing beside it, and waving a barsom of thin tamarisk branches above the fire, fed it with dry sticks of pine and fragrant oils. Then he began the ancient chant of the Yasna, and the voices of his companions joined in the hymn to Ahura-Mazda:

> We worship the Spirit Divine,
>   all wisdom and goodness possessing,
> Surrounded by Holy Immortals,
>   the givers of bounty and blessing;
> We joy in the work of His hands,

216

His truth and His power confessing.

We praise all the things that are pure,
    for these are His only Creation
The thoughts that are true, and the words
    and the deeds that have won approbation;
These are supported by Him,
    and for these we make adoration.
Hear us, O Mazda! Thou livest
    in truth and in heavenly gladness;
Cleanse us from falsehood, and keep us
    from evil and bondage to badness,
Pour out the light and the joy of Thy life
    on our darkness and sadness.

Shine on our gardens and fields,
    shine on our working and waving;
Shine on the whole race of man,
    believing and unbelieving;
Shine on us now through the night,
Shine on us now in Thy might,
The flame of our holy love
    and the song of our worship receiving.

The fire rose with the chant, throbbing as if the flame responded to the music, until it cast a bright illumination through the whole apartment, revealing its simplicity and splendour.

The floor was laid with tiles of dark blue veined with white; pilasters of twisted silver stood out against the blue walls; the clear-story of round-arched windows above them was hung with azure silk; the vaulted ceiling was a pavement of blue stones, like the body of heaven in its clearness, sown with silver stars. From the four corners of the roof hung four golden magic-wheels, called the tongues of the gods. At the eastern end, behind the altar, there were two dark-red pillars of porphyry; above them a lintel of the same stone, on which was carved the figure of a winged archer, with his arrow set to the string and his bow drawn.

The doorway between the pillars, which opened upon the terrace of the roof, was covered with a heavy curtain of the colour of a ripe pomegranate, embroidered with innumerable golden rays shooting upward from the floor. In effect the room was like a quiet, starry night, all azure and silver, flushed in the cast with rosy promise of the dawn. It was, as the house of a man should be, an expression of the character and spirit of the master.

He turned to his friends when the song was ended, and invited them to be seated on the divan at the western end of the room.

"You have come to-night," said he, looking around the circle, "at my call, as the faithful scholars of Zoroaster, to renew your worship and rekindle your faith in the God of Purity, even as this fire has been rekindled on the altar. We worship not the fire, but Him of whom it is the chosen symbol, because it is the purest of all created things. It speaks to us of one who is Light and Truth. Is it not so, my father?"

"It is well said, my son," answered the venerable Abgarus. "The enlightened are never idolaters. They lift the veil of form and go in to the shrine of reality, and new light and truth are coming to them continually through the old symbols." "Hear me, then, my father and my friends," said Artaban, "while I tell you of the new light and truth that have come to me through the most ancient of all signs. We have searched the secrets of Nature together, and studied the healing virtues of water and fire and the plants. We have read also the books of prophecy in which the future is dimly foretold in words that are hard to understand. But the highest of all learning is the knowledge of the stars. To trace their course is to untangle the threads of the mystery of life from the beginning to the end. If we could follow them perfectly, nothing would be hidden from us. But is not our knowledge of them still incomplete? Are there not many stars still beyond our horizon--lights that are known only to the dwellers in the far south-land, among the spice-trees of Punt and the gold mines of Ophir?"

There was a murmur of assent among the listeners.

"The stars," said Tigranes, "are the thoughts of the Eternal. They are numberless. But the thoughts of man can be counted, like the years of his life. The wisdom of the Magi is the greatest of all wisdoms on earth, because it knows its own ignorance. And that is the secret of power. We keep men always looking and waiting for a new sunrise. But we ourselves understand that the darkness is equal to the light, and that the conflict between them will never be ended."

"That does not satisfy me," answered Artaban, "for, if the waiting must be endless, if there could be no fulfilment of it, then it would not be wisdom to look and wait. We should become like those new teachers of the Greeks, who say that there is no truth, and that the only wise men are those who spend their lives in discovering and exposing the lies that have been believed in the world. But the new sunrise will certainly appear in the appointed time. Do not our own books tell us that this will come to pass, and that men will see the brightness of a great light?"

"That is true," said the voice of Abgarus; "every faithful disciple of Zoroaster knows the prophecy of the Avesta, and carries the word in his heart. `In that day Sosiosh the Victorious shall arise out of the number of the prophets in the east country. Around him shall shine a mighty brightness, and he shall make life everlasting, incorruptible, and immortal, and the dead shall rise again.'"

"This is a dark saying," said Tigranes, "and it may be that we shall never understand it. It is better to consider the things that are near at hand, and to increase the influence of the Magi in their own country, rather than to look for one who may be a stranger, and to whom we must resign our power."

The others seemed to approve these words. There was a silent feeling of agreement manifest among them; their looks responded with that indefinable expression which always follows when a speaker has uttered the thought that has been slumbering in the hearts of his listeners. But Artaban turned to Abgarus with a glow on his face, and said:

"My father, I have kept this prophecy in the secret place of my soul. Religion without a great hope would be like an altar without a living fire. And now the flame has burned more brightly, and by the light of it I have read other words which also have come from the fountain of Truth, and speak yet more clearly of the rising of the Victorious One in his brightness."

He drew from the breast of his tunic two small rolls of fine parchment, with writing upon them, and unfolded them carefully upon his knee.

"In the years that are lost in the past, long before our fathers came into the land of Babylon, there were wise men in Chaldea, from whom the first of the Magi learned the secret of the heavens. And of these Balaam the son of Beor was one of the mightiest. Hear the words of his prophecy: 'There shall come a star out of Jacob, and a sceptre shall arise out of Israel.'"

The lips of Tigranes drew downward with contempt, as he said:

"Judah was a captive by the waters of Babylon, and the sons of Jacob were in bondage to our kings. The tribes of Israel are scattered through the mountains like lost sheep, and from the remnant that dwells in Judea under the yoke of Rome neither star nor sceptre shall arise."

"And yet," answered Artaban, "it was the Hebrew Daniel, the mighty searcher of dreams, the counsellor of kings, the wise Belteshazzar, who was most honoured and beloved of our great King Cyrus. A prophet of sure things and a reader of the thoughts of the Eternal, Daniel proved himself to our people. And these are the words that he wrote." (Artaban read from the second roll:) " 'Know, therefore, and understand that from the going forth of the commandment to restore Jerusalem, unto the Anointed One, the Prince, the time shall be seven and threescore and two weeks.' "

"But, my son," said Abgarus, doubtfully, "these are mystical numbers. Who can interpret them, or who can find the key that shall unlock their meaning?"

Artaban answered: "It has been shown to me and to my three companions among the Magi--Caspar, Melchior, and Balthazar. We have searched the ancient tablets of Chaldea and computed the time. It falls in this year. We have studied the sky, and in the spring of the year we saw two of the greatest planets draw near together in the sign of the Fish, which is the house of the Hebrews. We also saw a new star there, which shone for one night and then vanished. Now again the two great planets are meeting. This night is their conjunction. My three brothers are watching by the ancient Temple of the Seven Spheres, at Borsippa, in Babylonia, and I am watching here. If the star shines again, they will wait ten days for me at the temple, and then we will set out together for Jerusalem, to see and worship the promised one who shall be born King of Israel. I believe the sign will come. I have made ready for the journey. I have sold my possessions, and bought these three jewels--a sapphire, a ruby, and a pearl--to carry them as tribute to the King. And I ask you to go with me on the pilgrimage, that we may have joy together in finding the Prince who is worthy to be served."

While he was speaking he thrust his hand into the inmost fold of his, girdle and drew out three great gems--one blue as a fragment of the night sky, one redder than a ray of sunrise, and one as pure as the peak of a snow-mountain at twilight--and laid them on the outspread scrolls before him.

But his friends looked on with strange and alien eyes. A veil of doubt

221

and mistrust came over their faces, like a fog creeping up from the marshes to hide the hills. They glanced at each other with looks of wonder and pity, as those who have listened to incredible sayings, the story of a wild vision, or the proposal of an impossible enterprise.

At last Tigranes said: "Artaban, this is a vain dream. It comes from too much looking upon the stars and the cherishing of lofty thoughts. It would be wiser to spend the time in gathering money for the new fire-temple at Chala. No king will ever rise from the broken race of Israel, and no end will ever come to the eternal strife of light and darkness. He who looks for it is a chaser of shadows. Farewell."

And another said: "Artaban, I have no knowledge of these things, and my office as guardian of the royal treasure binds me here. The quest is not for me. But if thou must follow it, fare thee well."

And another said: "In my house there sleeps a new bride, and I cannot leave her nor take her with me on this strange journey. This quest is not for me. But may thy steps be prospered wherever thou goest. So, farewell."

And another said: "I am ill and unfit for hardship, but there is a man among my servants whom I will send with thee when thou goest, to bring me word how thou farest."

So, one by one, they left the house of Artaban. But Abgarus, the oldest and the one who loved him the best, lingered after the others had gone, and said, gravely: "My son, it may be that the light of truth is in this sign that has appeared in the skies, and then it will surely lead to the Prince and the mighty brightness. Or it may be that it is only a shadow of the light, as Tigranes has said, and then he who follows it will have a long pilgrimage and a fruitless search. But it is better to follow even the shadow of the best than to remain content with the worst. And those who would see wonderful things must often be ready to travel alone. I am too old for this journey, but my heart shall be a companion of thy pilgrimage day and night, and I shall know the end of thy quest. Go in peace."

Then Abgarus went out of the azure chamber with its silver stars, and Artaban was left in solitude.

He gathered up the jewels and replaced them in his girdle. For a long time he stood and watched the flame that flickered and sank upon the altar. Then he crossed the hall, lifted the heavy curtain, and passed out between the pillars of porphyry to the terrace on the roof.

The shiver that runs through the earth ere she rouses from her night-sleep had already begun, and the cool wind that heralds the daybreak was drawing downward from the lofty snow-traced ravines of Mount Orontes. Birds, half-awakened, crept and chirped among the rustling leaves, and the smell of ripened grapes came in brief wafts from the arbours.

Far over the eastern plain a white mist stretched like a lake. But where the distant peaks of Zagros serrated the western horizon the sky was clear. Jupiter and Saturn rolled together like drops of lambent flame about to blend in one.

As Artaban watched them, a steel-blue spark was born out of the darkness beneath, rounding itself with purple splendours to a crimson sphere, and spiring upward through rays of saffron and orange into a point of white radiance. Tiny and infinitely remote, yet perfect in every part, it pulsated in the enormous vault as if the three jewels in the Magian's girdle had mingled and been transformed into a living heart of light.

He bowed his head. He covered his brow with his hands.

"It is the sign," he said. "The King is coming, and I will go to meet him."

II

All night long, Vasda, the swiftest of Artaban's horses, had been

223

waiting, saddled and bridled, in her stall, pawing the ground impatiently, and shaking her bit as if she shared the eagerness of her master's purpose, though she knew not its meaning.

Before the birds had fully roused to their strong, high, joyful chant of morning song, before the white mist had begun to lift lazily from the plain, the Other Wise Man was in the saddle, riding swiftly along the high-road, which skirted the base of Mount Orontes, westward.

How close, how intimate is the comradeship between a man and his favourite horse on a long journey. It is a silent, comprehensive friendship, an intercourse beyond the need of words.

They drink at the same way-side springs, and sleep under the same guardian stars. They are conscious together of the subduing spell of nightfall and the quickening joy of daybreak. The master shares his evening meal with his hungry companion, and feels the soft, moist lips caressing the palm of his hand as they close over the morsel of bread. In the gray dawn he is roused from his bivouac by the gentle stir of a warm, sweet breath over his sleeping face, and looks up into the eyes of his faithful fellow-traveller, ready and waiting for the toil of the day. Surely, unless he is a pagan and an unbeliever, by whatever name he calls upon his God, he will thank Him for this voiceless sympathy, this dumb affection, and his morning prayer will embrace a double blessing--God bless us both, the horse and the rider, and keep our feet from falling and our souls from death!

Then, through the keen morning air, the swift hoofs beat their tattoo along the road, keeping time to the pulsing of two hearts that are moved with the same eager desire--to conquer space, to devour the distance, to attain the goal of the journey.

Artaban must indeed ride wisely and well if he would keep the appointed hour with the other Magi; for the route was a hundred and fifty parasangs, and fifteen was the utmost that he could travel in a day. But he knew Vasda's strength, and pushed forward without anxiety, making the fixed distance every day, though he must travel late into the night, and in the morning long before sunrise.

He passed along the brown slopes of Mount Orontes, furrowed by the rocky courses of a hundred torrents.

He crossed the level plains of the Nisaeans, where the famous herds of horses, feeding in the wide pastures, tossed their heads at Vasda's approach, and galloped away with a thunder of many hoofs, and flocks of wild birds rose suddenly from the swampy meadows, wheeling in great circles with a shining flutter of innumerable wings and shrill cries of surprise.

He traversed the fertile fields of Concabar, where the dust from the threshing-floors filled the air with a golden mist, half hiding the huge temple of Astarte with its four hundred pillars.

At Baghistan, among the rich gardens watered by fountains from the rock, he looked up at the mountain thrusting its immense rugged brow out over the road, and saw the figure of King Darius trampling upon his fallen foes, and the proud list of his wars and conquests graven high upon the face of the eternal cliff.

Over many a cold and desolate pass, crawling painfully across the wind-swept shoulders of the hills; down many a black mountain-gorge, where the river roared and raced before him like a savage guide; across many a smiling vale, with terraces of yellow limestone full of vines and fruit-trees; through the oak-groves of Carine and the dark Gates of Zagros, walled in by precipices; into the ancient city of Chala, where the people of Samaria had been kept in captivity long ago; and out again by the mighty portal, riven through the encircling hills, where he saw the image of the High Priest of the Magi sculptured on the wall of rock, with hand uplifted as if to bless the centuries of pilgrims; past the entrance of the narrow defile, filled from end to end with orchards of peaches and figs, through which the river Gyndes foamed down to meet him; over the broad rice-fields, where the autumnal vapours spread their deathly mists; following along the course of the river, under tremulous shadows of poplar and tamarind, among the lower hills; and out upon the flat plain, where the road ran straight as an arrow through the stubble-fields and parched meadows; past the city of Ctesiphon, where the Parthian emperors reigned, and the vast metropolis of Seleucia which Alexander built; across the swirling floods of Tigris and the many channels of Euphrates, flowing yellow through the corn-lands--Artaban pressed onward until he arrived, at nightfall on the tenth day, beneath the shattered walls of populous Babylon.

Vasda was almost spent, and Artaban would gladly have turned into the city to find rest and refreshment for himself and for her. But he knew that it was three hours' journey yet to the Temple of the Seven Spheres, and he must reach the place by midnight if he would find his comrades waiting. So he did not halt, but rode steadily across the stubble-fields.

A grove of date-palms made an island of gloom in the pale yellow sea. As she passed into the shadow Vasda slackened her pace, and began to pick her way more carefully.

Near the farther end of the darkness an access of caution seemed to fall upon her. She scented some danger or difficulty; it was not in her heart to fly from it--only to be prepared for it, and to meet it wisely, as a good horse should do. The grove was close and silent as the tomb; not a leaf rustled, not a bird sang.

She felt her steps before her delicately, carrying her head low, and sighing now and then with apprehension. At last she gave a quick breath of anxiety and dismay, and stood stock-still, quivering in every muscle, before a dark object in the shadow of the last palm-tree.

Artaban dismounted. The dim starlight revealed the form of a man lying across the road. His humble dress and the outline of his haggard face showed that he was probably one of the Hebrews who still dwelt in great numbers around the city. His pallid skin, dry and yellow as parchment, bore the mark of the deadly fever which ravaged the marsh-

226

lands in autumn. The chill of death was in his lean hand, and, as Artaban released it, the arm fell back inertly upon the motionless breast.

He turned away with a thought of pity, leaving the body to that strange burial which the Magians deemed most fitting--the funeral of the desert, from which the kites and vultures rise on dark wings, and the beasts of prey slink furtively away. When they are gone there is only a heap of white bones on the sand.

But, as he turned, a long, faint, ghostly sigh came from the man's lips. The bony fingers gripped the hem of the Magian's robe and held him fast.

Artaban's heart leaped to his throat, not with fear, but with a dumb resentment at the importunity of this blind delay.

How could he stay here in the darkness to minister to a dying stranger? What claim had this unknown fragment of human life upon his compassion or his service? If he lingered but for an hour he could hardly reach Borsippa at the appointed time. His companions would think he had given up the journey. They would go without him. He would lose his quest.

But if he went on now, the man would surely die. If Artaban

stayed, life might be restored. His spirit throbbed and fluttered with the urgency of the crisis. Should he risk the great reward of his faith for the sake of a single deed of charity? Should he turn aside, if only for a moment, from the following of the star, to give a cup of cold water to a poor, perishing Hebrew?

"God of truth and purity," he prayed, "direct me in the holy path, the way of wisdom which Thou only knowest."

Then he turned back to the sick man. Loosening the grasp of his hand, he carried him to a little mound at the foot of the palm-tree.

He unbound the thick folds of the turban and opened the garment above the sunken breast. He brought water from one of the small canals near by, and moistened the sufferer's brow and mouth. He mingled a draught of one of those simple but potent remedies which he carried always in his girdle--for the Magians were physicians as well as astrologers--and poured it slowly between the colourless lips. Hour after hour he laboured as only a skilful healer of disease can do. At last the man's strength returned; he sat up and looked about him.

"Who art thou?" he said, in the rude dialect of the country, "and why hast thou sought me here to bring back my life?"

"I am Artaban the Magian, of the city of Ecbatana, and I am going to Jerusalem in search of one who is to be born King of the Jews, a great Prince and Deliverer of all men. I dare not delay any longer upon my journey, for the caravan that has waited for me may depart without me. But see, here is all that I have left of bread and wine, and here is a potion of healing herbs. When thy strength is restored thou canst find the dwellings of the Hebrews among the houses of Babylon."

The Jew raised his trembling hand solemnly to heaven.

"Now may the God of Abraham and Isaac and Jacob bless and prosper the journey of the merciful, and bring him in peace to his desired haven. Stay! I have nothing to give thee in return--only this: that I can tell thee where the Messiah must be sought. For our prophets have said that he should be born not in Jerusalem, but in Bethlehem of Judah. May the Lord bring thee in safety to that place, because thou hast had pity upon the sick."

It was already long past midnight. Artaban rode in haste, and Vasda, restored by the brief rest, ran eagerly through the silent plain and swam the channels of the river. She put forth the remnant of her strength, and fled over the ground like a gazelle.

But the first beam of the rising sun sent a long shadow before her as she entered upon the final stadium of the journey, and the eyes of

Artaban, anxiously scanning the great mound of Nimrod and the Temple of the Seven Spheres, could discern no trace of his friends.

The many-coloured terraces of black and orange and red and yellow and green and blue and white, shattered by the convulsions of nature, and crumbling under the repeated blows of human violence, still glittered like a ruined rainbow in the morning light.

Artaban rode swiftly around the hill. He dismounted and climbed to the highest terrace, looking out toward the west.

The huge desolation of the marshes stretched away to the horizon and the border of the desert. Bitterns stood by the stagnant pools and jackals skulked through the low bushes; but there was no sign of the caravan of the Wise Men, far or near.

At the edge of the terrace he saw a little cairn of broken bricks, and under them a piece of papyrus. He caught it up and read: "We have waited past the midnight, and can delay no longer. We go to find the King. Follow us across the desert."

Artaban sat down upon the ground and covered his head in despair.

"How can I cross the desert," said he, "with no food and with a spent horse? I must return to Babylon, sell my sapphire, and buy a train of camels, and provision for the journey. I may never overtake my friends. Only God the merciful knows whether I shall not lose the sight of the King because I tarried to show mercy."

III

There was a silence in the Hall of Dreams, where I was listening to the story of the Other Wise Man. Through this silence I saw, but very dimly, his figure passing over the dreary undulations of the desert, high upon the back of his camel, rocking steadily onward like a ship over the waves.

The land of death spread its cruel net around him. The stony waste

229

bore no fruit but briers and thorns. The dark ledges of rock thrust themselves above the surface here and there, like the bones of perished monsters. Arid and inhospitable mountain-ranges rose before him, furrowed with dry channels of ancient torrents, white and ghastly as scars on the face of nature. Shifting hills of treacherous sand were heaped like tombs along the horizon. By day, the fierce heat pressed its intolerable burden on the quivering air. No living creature moved on the dumb, swooning earth, but tiny jerboas scuttling through the parched bushes, or lizards vanishing in the clefts of the rock. By night the jackals prowled and barked in the distance, and the lion made the black ravines echo with his hollow roaring, while a bitter, blighting chill followed the fever of the day. Through heat and cold, the Magian moved steadily onward.

Then I saw the gardens and orchards of Damascus, watered by the streams of Abana and Pharpar, with their sloping swards inlaid with bloom, and their thickets of myrrh and roses. I saw the long, snowy ridge of Hermon, and the dark groves of cedars, and the valley of the Jordan, and the blue waters of the Lake of Galilee, and the fertile plain of Esdraelon, and the hills of Ephraim, and the highlands of Judah. Through all these I followed the figure of Artaban moving steadily onward, until he arrived at Bethlehem. And it was the third day after the three Wise Men had come to that place and had found Mary and Joseph, with the young child, Jesus, and had laid their gifts of gold and frankincense and myrrh at his feet.

Then the Other Wise Man drew near, weary, but full of hope, bearing his ruby and his pearl to offer to the King. "For now at last," he said, "I shall surely find him, though I be alone, and later than my brethren. This is the place of which the Hebrew exile told me that the prophets had spoken, and here I shall behold the rising of the great light. But I must inquire about the visit of my brethren, and to what house the star directed them, and to whom they presented their tribute."

The streets of the village seemed to be deserted, and Artaban wondered whether the men had all gone up to the hill-pastures to bring down their sheep. From the open door of a cottage he heard the sound of a woman's voice singing softly. He entered and found a young mother hushing her baby to rest. She told him of the strangers from the far East who had appeared in the village three days ago, and how they said that a star had guided them to the place where Joseph of Nazareth was lodging with his wife and her new-born child, and how they had paid reverence to the child and given him many rich gifts.

"But the travellers disappeared again," she continued, "as suddenly as they had come. We were afraid at the strangeness of their visit. We could not understand it. The man of Nazareth took the child and his mother, and fled away that same night secretly, and it was whispered that they were going to Egypt. Ever since, there has been a spell upon the village; something evil hangs over it. They say that the Roman soldiers are coming from Jerusalem to force a new tax from us, and the men have driven the flocks and herds far back among the hills, and hidden themselves to escape it."

Artaban listened to her gentle, timid speech, and the child in her arms looked up in his face and smiled, stretching out its rosy hands to grasp at the winged circle of gold on his breast. His heart warmed to the touch. It seemed like a greeting of love and trust to one who had journeyed long in loneliness and perplexity, fighting with his own doubts and fears, and following a light that was veiled in clouds.

"Why might not this child have been the promised Prince?" he asked within himself, as he touched its soft cheek. "Kings have been born ere now in lowlier houses than this, and the favourite of the stars may rise even from a cottage. But it has not seemed good to the God of wisdom to reward my search so soon and so easily. The one whom I seek has gone before me; and now I must follow the King to Egypt."

The young mother laid the baby in its cradle, and rose to minister to the wants of the strange guest that fate had brought into her house. She

231

set food before him, the plain fare of peasants, but willingly offered, and therefore full of refreshment for the soul as well as for the body. Artaban accepted it gratefully; and, as he ate, the child fell into a happy slumber, and murmured sweetly in its dreams, and a great peace filled the room.

But suddenly there came the noise of a wild confusion in the streets of the village, a shrieking and wailing of women's voices, a clangour of brazen trumpets and a clashing of swords, and a desperate cry: "The soldiers! the soldiers of Herod! They are killing our children."

The young mother's face grew white with terror. She clasped her child to her bosom, and crouched motionless in the darkest corner of the room, covering him with the folds of her robe, lest he should wake and cry.

But Artaban went quickly and stood in the doorway of the house. His broad shoulders filled the portal from side to side, and the peak of his white cap all but touched the lintel.

The soldiers came hurrying down the street with bloody hands and dripping swords. At the sight of the stranger in his imposing dress they hesitated with surprise. The captain of the band approached the threshold to thrust him aside. But Artaban did not stir. His face was as calm as though he were watching the stars, and in his eyes there burned that steady radiance before which even the half-tamed hunting leopard shrinks, and the bloodhound pauses in his leap. He held the soldier silently for an instant, and then said in a low voice:

"I am all alone in this place, and I am waiting to give this jewel to the prudent captain who will leave me in peace."

He showed the ruby, glistening in the hollow of his hand like a great drop of blood.

The captain was amazed at the splendour of the gem. The pupils of his eyes expanded with desire, and the hard lines of greed wrinkled

232

around his lips. He stretched out his hand and took the ruby.

"March on!" he cried to his men, "there is no child here. The house is empty."

The clamor and the clang of arms passed down the street as the headlong fury of the chase sweeps by the secret covert where the trembling deer is hidden. Artaban re-entered the cottage. He turned his face to the east and prayed:

"God of truth, forgive my sin! I have said the thing that is not, to save the life of a child. And two of my gifts are gone. I have spent for man that which was meant for God. Shall I ever be worthy to see the face of the King?"

But the voice of the woman, weeping for joy in the shadow behind him, said very gently:

"Because thou hast saved the life of my little one, may the Lord bless thee and keep thee; the Lord make His face to shine upon thee and be gracious unto thee; the Lord lift up His countenance upon thee and give thee peace."

IV

Again there was a silence in the Hall of Dreams, deeper and more mysterious than the first interval, and I understood that the years of Artaban were flowing very swiftly under the stillness, and I caught only a glimpse, here and there, of the river of his life shining through the mist that concealed its course.

I saw him moving among the throngs of men in populous Egypt, seeking everywhere for traces of the household that had come down from Bethlehem, and finding them under the spreading sycamore-trees of Heliopolis, and beneath the walls of the Roman fortress of New Babylon beside the Nile--traces so faint and dim that they vanished before him continually, as footprints on the wet river-sand glisten for a moment with moisture and then disappear.

I saw him again at the foot of the pyramids, which lifted their sharp points into the intense saffron glow of the sunset sky, changeless monuments of the perishable glory and the imperishable hope of man. He looked up into the face of the crouching Sphinx and vainly tried to read the meaning of the calm eyes and smiling mouth. Was it, indeed, the mockery of all effort and all aspiration, as Tigranes had said--the cruel jest of a riddle that has no answer, a search that never can succeed? Or was there a touch of pity and encouragement in that inscrutable smile--a promise that even the defeated should attain a victory, and the disappointed should discover a prize, and the ignorant should be made wise, and the blind should see, and the wandering should come into the haven at last?

I saw him again in an obscure house of Alexandria, taking counsel with a Hebrew rabbi. The venerable man, bending over the rolls of parchment on which the prophecies of Israel were written, read aloud the pathetic words which foretold the sufferings of the promised Messiah--the despised and rejected of men, the man of sorrows and acquainted with grief.

"And remember, my son," said he, fixing his eyes upon the face of Artaban, "the King whom thou seekest is not to be found in a palace, nor among the rich and powerful. If the light of the world and the glory of Israel had been appointed to come with the greatness of earthly splendour, it must have appeared long ago. For no son of Abraham will ever again rival the power which Joseph had in the palaces of Egypt, or the magnificence of Solomon throned between the lions in Jerusalem. But the light for which the world is waiting is a new light, the glory that shall rise out of patient and triumphant suffering. And the kingdom which is to be established forever is a new kingdom, the royalty of unconquerable love.

"I do not know how this shall come to pass, nor how the turbulent kings and peoples of earth shall be brought to acknowledge the Messiah and pay homage to him. But this I know. Those who seek him will do well to look among the poor and the lowly, the sorrowful and the oppressed."

So I saw the Other Wise Man again and again, travelling from place to place, and searching among the people of the dispersion, with whom the little family from Bethlehem might, perhaps, have found a refuge. He passed through countries where famine lay heavy upon the land, and the poor were crying for bread. He made his dwelling in plague-stricken cities where the sick were languishing in the bitter companionship of helpless misery. He visited the oppressed and the afflicted in the gloom of subterranean prisons, and the crowded wretchedness of slave-markets, and the weary toil of galley-ships. In all this populous and intricate world of anguish, though he found none to worship, he found many to help. He fed the hungry, and clothed the naked, and healed the sick, and comforted the captive; and his years passed more swiftly than the weaver's shuttle that flashes back and forth through the loom while the web grows and the pattern is completed.

It seemed almost as if he had forgotten his quest. But once I saw him for a moment as he stood alone at sunrise, waiting at the gate of a Roman prison. He had taken from a secret resting-place in his bosom the pearl, the last of his jewels. As he looked at it, a mellower lustre, a soft and iridescent light, full of shifting gleams of azure and rose, trembled upon its surface. It seemed to have absorbed some reflection of the lost sapphire and ruby. So the secret purpose of a noble life draws into itself the memories of past joy and past sorrow. All that has helped it, all that has hindered it, is transfused by a subtle magic into its very essence. It becomes more luminous and precious the longer it is carried close to the warmth of the beating heart.

Then, at last, while I was thinking of this pearl, and of its meaning, I heard the end of the story of the Other Wise Man.

V

Three-and-thirty years of the life of Artaban had passed away, and he was still a pilgrim and a seeker after light. His hair, once darker than the cliffs of Zagros, was now white as the wintry snow that covered them. His eyes, that once flashed like flames of fire, were dull as embers smouldering among the ashes.

Worn and weary and ready to die, but still looking for the King, he had come for the last time to Jerusalem. He had often visited the holy city before, and had searched all its lanes and crowded bevels and black prisons without finding any trace of the family of Nazarenes who had fled from Bethlehem long ago. But now it seemed as if he must make one more effort, and something whispered in his heart that, at last, he might succeed.

It was the season of the Passover. The city was thronged with strangers. The children of Israel, scattered in far lands, had returned to the Temple for the great feast, and there had been a confusion of tongues in the narrow streets for many days.

But on this day a singular agitation was visible in the multitude. The sky was veiled with a portentous gloom. Currents of excitement seemed to flash through the crowd. A secret tide was sweeping them all one way. The clatter of sandals and the soft, thick sound of thousands of bare feet shuffling over the stones, flowed unceasingly along the street that leads to the Damascus gate.

Artaban joined a group of people from his own country, Parthian Jews who had come up to keep the Passover, and inquired of them the cause of the tumult, and where they were going.

"We are going," they answered, "to the place called Golgotha, outside the city walls, where there is to be an execution. Have you not heard what has happened? Two famous robbers are to be crucified, and with them another, called Jesus of Nazareth, a man who has done many wonderful works among the people, so that they love him greatly. But the priests and elders have said that he must die, because he gave himself out to be the Son of God. And Pilate has sent him to the cross because he said that he was the `King of the Jews.'

How strangely these familiar words fell upon the tired heart of Artaban! They had led him for a lifetime over land and sea. And now they came to him mysteriously, like a message of despair. The King had arisen, but he had been denied and cast out. He was about to perish. Perhaps he was already dying. Could it be the same who had been born in Bethlehem thirty-three years ago, at whose birth the star had appeared in heaven, and of whose coming the prophets had spoken?

Artaban's heart beat unsteadily with that troubled, doubtful apprehension which is the excitement of old age. But he said within himself: "The ways of God are stranger than the thoughts of men, and it may be that I shall find the King, at last, in the hands of his enemies, and shall come in time to offer my pearl for his ransom before he dies."

So the old man followed the multitude with slow and painful steps toward the Damascus gate of the city. Just beyond the entrance of the guardhouse a troop of Macedonian soldiers came down the street, dragging a young girl with torn dress and dishevelled hair. As the Magian paused to look at her with compassion, she broke suddenly from the hands of her tormentors, and threw herself at his feet, clasping him around the knees. She had seen his white cap and the winged circle on his breast.

"Have pity on me," she cried, "and save me, for the sake of the God of Purity! I also am a daughter of the true religion which is taught by the Magi. My father was a merchant of Parthia, but he is dead, and I am seized for his debts to be sold as a slave. Save me from worse than death!"

Artaban trembled.

It was the old conflict in his soul, which had come to him in the palm-grove of Babylon and in the cottage at Bethlehem--the conflict between the expectation of faith and the impulse of love. Twice the gift which he had consecrated to the worship of religion had been drawn to the service of humanity. This was the third trial, the ultimate probation, the final and irrevocable choice.

Was it his great opportunity, or his last temptation? He could not tell. One thing only was clear in the darkness of his mind--it was inevitable. And does not the inevitable come from God?

One thing only was sure to his divided heart--to rescue this helpless girl would be a true deed of love. And is not love the light of the soul?

He took the pearl from his bosom. Never had it seemed so luminous, so radiant, so full of tender, living lustre. He laid it in the hand of the slave.

"This is thy ransom, daughter! It is the last of my treasures which I kept for the King."

While he spoke, the darkness of the sky deepened, and shuddering tremors ran through the earth heaving convulsively like the breast of one who struggles with mighty grief.

The walls of the houses rocked to and fro. Stones were loosened and crashed into the street. Dust clouds filled the air. The soldiers fled in terror, reeling like drunken men. But Artaban and the girl whom he had ransomed crouched helpless beneath the wall of the Praetorium.

What had he to fear? What had he to hope? He had given away the last remnant of his tribute for the King. He had parted with the last hope of finding him. The quest was over, and it had failed. But, even in that thought, accepted and embraced, there was peace. It was not resignation. It was not submission. It was something more profound and searching. He knew that all was well, because he had done the best that he could from day to day. He had been true to the light that had been given to him. He had looked for more. And if he had not found it, if a failure was all that came out of his life, doubtless that was the best that was possible. He had not seen the revelation of "life everlasting, incorruptible and immortal." But he knew that even if he could live his earthly life over again, it could not be otherwise than it had been.

One more lingering pulsation of the earthquake quivered through the ground. A heavy tile, shaken from the roof, fell and struck the old man on the temple. He lay breathless and pale, with his gray head resting on the young girl's shoulder, and the blood trickling from the wound. As she bent over him, fearing that he was dead, there came a voice through the twilight, very small and still, like music sounding from a distance, in which the notes are clear but the words are lost. The girl turned to see if some one had spoken from the window above them, but she saw no one.

Then the old man's lips began to move, as if in answer, and she heard him say in the Parthian tongue:

"Not so, my Lord! For when saw I thee an hungered and fed thee? Or thirsty, and gave thee drink? When saw I thee a stranger, and took thee in? Or naked, and clothed thee? When saw I thee sick or in prison, and came unto thee? Three-and-- thirty years have I looked for thee; but I have never seen thy face, nor ministered to thee, my King."

He ceased, and the sweet voice came again. And again the maid heard it, very faint and far away. But now it seemed as though she understood the words:

"Verily I say unto thee, Inasmuch as thou hast done it unto one of the least of these my brethren, thou hast done it unto me."

A calm radiance of wonder and joy lighted the pale face of Artaban like the first ray of dawn, on a snowy mountain-peak. A long breath of relief exhaled gently from his lips.

His journey was ended. His treasures were accepted. The Other Wise Man had found the King.

Christmas in Seventeen Seventy-Six

By Anne Hollingsworth Wharton

"On Christmas day in Seventy-six,
   Our gallant troops with bayonets fixed,
   To Trenton marched away."

Children, have any of you ever thought of what little people like you were doing in this country more than a hundred years ago, when the cruel tide of war swept over its bosom? From many homes the fathers were absent, fighting bravely for the liberty which we now enjoy, while the mothers no less valiantly struggled against hardships and discomforts in order to keep a home for their children, whom you only know as your great-grandfathers and great-grandmothers, dignified gentlemen and beautiful ladies, whose painted portraits hang upon the walls in some of your homes. Merry, romping children they were in those far-off times, yet their bright faces must have looked grave sometimes, when they heard the grown people talk of the great things that were happening around them. Some of these little people never forgot the wonderful events of which they heard, and afterward related them to their children and grandchildren, which accounts for some of the interesting stories which you may still hear, if you are good children.

The Christmas story that I have to tell you is about a boy and girl who lived in Bordentown, New Jersey. The father of these children was a soldier in General Washington's army, which was encamped a few miles north of Trenton, on the Pennsylvania side of the Delaware River. Bordentown, as you can see by looking on your map, if you have not hidden them all away for the holidays, is about seven miles south of Trenton, where fifteen hundred Hessians and a troop of British light horse were holding the town. Thus you see that the British, in force, were between Washington's army and Bordentown, besides which there were some British and Hessian troops in the very town. All this seriously interfered with Captain Tracy's going home to eat his Christmas dinner with his wife and children. Kitty and Harry Tracy, who had not lived long enough to see many wars, could not imagine such a thing as Christmas without their father, and had busied themselves for weeks in making everything ready to have a merry time with him. Kitty, who loved to play quite as much as any frolicsome Kitty of to-day, had spent all her spare time in knitting a pair of thick woollen stockings, which seems a wonderful feat for a little girl only eight years old to perform! Can you not see her sitting by the great chimney-place, filled with its roaring, crackling logs, in her quaint, short-waisted dress, knitting away steadily, and puckering up her rosy, dimpled face over the strange twists and turns of that old stocking? I can see her, and I can also hear her sweet voice as she chatters away to her mother about "how 'sprised papa will be to find that his little girl can knit like a grown-up woman," while Harry spreads out on the hearth a goodly store of shellbarks that he has gathered and is keeping for his share of the 'sprise.

"What if he shouldn't come?" asks Harry, suddenly.

"Oh, he'll come! Papa never stays away on Christmas," says Kitty, looking up into her mother's face for an echo to her words. Instead she sees something very like tears in her mother's eyes.

"Oh, mamma, don't you think he'll come?"

"He will come if he possibly can," says Mrs. Tracy; "and if he cannot, we will keep Christmas whenever dear papa does come home."

"It won't be half so nice," said Kitty, "nothing's so nice as REALLY Christmas, and how's Kriss Kringle going to know about it if we change the day?"

"We'll let him come just the same, and if he brings anything for papa we can put it away for him."

This plan, still, seemed a poor one to Miss Kitty, who went to her bed

242

in a sober mood that night, and was heard telling her dear dollie, Martha Washington, that "wars were mis'able, and that when she married she should have a man who kept a candy-shop for a husband, and not a soldier—no, Martha, not even if he's as nice as papa!" As Martha made no objection to this little arrangement, being an obedient child, they were both soon fast asleep. The days of that cold winter of 1776 wore on; so cold it was that the sufferings of the soldiers were great, their bleeding feet often leaving marks on the pure white snow over which they marched. As Christmas drew near there was a feeling among the patriots that some blow was about to be struck; but what it was, and from whence they knew not; and, better than all, the British had no idea that any strong blow could come from Washington's army, weak and out of heart, as they thought, after being chased through Jersey by Cornwallis.

Mrs. Tracy looked anxiously each day for news of the husband and father only a few miles away, yet so separated by the river and the enemy's troops that they seemed like a hundred. Christmas Eve came, but brought with it few rejoicings. The hearts of the people were too sad to be taken up with merrymaking, although the Hessian soldiers in the town, good-natured Germans, who only fought the Americans because they were paid for it, gave themselves up to the feasting and revelry.

"Shall we hang up our stockings?" asked Kitty, in rather a doleful voice.

"Yes," said her mother, "Santa Claus won't forget you, I am sure, although he has been kept pretty busy looking after the soldiers this winter."

"Which side is he on?" asked Harry.

"The right side, of course," said Mrs. Tracy, which was the most sensible answer she could possibly have given. So:

"The stockings were hung by the chimney with care, In hopes that St.

Nicholas soon would be there."

Two little rosy faces lay fast asleep upon the pillow when the good old soul came dashing over the roof about one o'clock, and after filling each stocking with red apples, and leaving a cornucopia of sugar-plums for each child, he turned for a moment to look at the sleeping faces, for St. Nicholas has a tender spot in his great big heart for a soldier's children. Then, remembering many other small folks waiting for him all over the land, he sprang up the chimney and was away in a trice.

Santa Claus, in the form of Mrs. Tracy's farmer brother, brought her a splendid turkey; but because the Hessians were uncommonly fond of turkey, it came hidden under a load of wood. Harry was very fond of turkey, too, as well as of all other good things; but when his mother said, "It's such a fine bird, it seems too bad to eat it without father," Harry cried out, "Yes, keep it for papa!" and Kitty, joining in the chorus, the vote was unanimous, and the turkey was hung away to await the return of the good soldier, although it seemed strange, as Kitty told Martha Washington, "to have no papa and no turkey on Christmas Day."

The day passed and night came, cold with a steady fall of rain and sleet. Kitty prayed that her "dear papa might not be out in the storm, and that he might come home and wear his beautiful blue stockings"; "And eat his turkey," said Harry's sleepy voice; after which they were soon in the land of dreams. Toward morning the good people in Bordentown were suddenly aroused by firing in the distance, which became more and more distinct as the day wore on. There was great excitement in the town; men and women gathered together in little groups in the streets to wonder what it was all about, and neighbours came dropping into Mrs. Tracy's parlour, all day long, one after the other, to say what they thought of the firing. In the evening there came a body of Hessians flying into the town, to say that General Washington had surprised the British at Trenton, early that morning, and completely routed them, which so frightened the Hessians in Bordentown that they left without the slightest ceremony.

It was a joyful hour to the good town people when the red-jackets turned their backs on them, thinking every moment that the patriot army would be after them. Indeed, it seemed as if wonders would never cease that day, for while rejoicings were still loud, over the departure of the enemy, there came a knock at Mrs. Tracy's door, and while she was wondering whether she dared open it, it was pushed ajar, and a tall soldier entered. What a scream of delight greeted that soldier, and how Kitty and Harry danced about him and clung to his knees, while Mrs. Tracy drew him toward the warm blaze, and helped him off with his damp cloak!

Cold and tired Captain Tracy was, after a night's march in the streets and a day's fighting; but he was not too weary to smile at the dear faces around him, or to pat Kitty's head when she brought his warm stockings and would put them on the tired feet, herself.

Suddenly there was a sharp, quick bark outside the door. "What's that?" cried Harry.

"Oh, I forgot. Open the door. Here, Fido, Fido!"

Into the room there sprang a beautiful little King Charles spaniel, white, with tan spots, and ears of the longest, softest, and silkiest.

"What a little dear!" exclaimed Kitty; "where did it come from?"

"From the battle of Trenton," said her father. "His poor master was shot. After the red-coats had turned their backs, and I was hurrying along one of the streets where the fight had been the fiercest, I heard a low groan, and, turning, saw a British officer lying among a number of slain. I raised his head; he begged for some water, which I brought him, and bending down my ear I heard him whisper, 'Dying—last battle— say a prayer.' He tried to follow me in the words of a prayer, and then, taking my hand, laid it on something soft and warm, nestling close up to his breast—it was this little dog. The gentleman—for he was a real gentleman—gasped out, 'Take care of my poor Fido; good-night,' and was gone. It was as much as I could do to get the little creature away from his dead master; he clung to him as if he loved him better than life. You'll take care of him, won't you, children? I brought him home to you, for a Christmas present."

"Pretty little Fido," said Kitty, taking the soft, curly creature in her arms; "I think it's the best present in the world, and to-morrow is to be real Christmas, because you are home, papa."

"And we'll eat the turkey," said Harry, "and shellbarks, lots of them, that I saved for you. What a good time we'll have! And oh, papa, don't go to war any more, but stay at home, with mother and Kitty and Fido and me."

"What would become of our country if we should all do that, my little man? It was a good day's work that we did this Christmas, getting the army all across the river so quickly and quietly that we surprised the enemy, and gained a victory, with the loss of few men."

Thus it was that some of the good people of 1776 spent their Christmas, that their children and grandchildren might spend many of them as citizens of a free nation.